No Limits

No Limits

Jenna McCormick

APHRODISIA

KENSINGTON PUBLISHING CORP.

www.kensingtonbooks.com

APHRODISIA BOOKS are published by

Kensington Publishing Corp.
119 West 40th Street
New York, NY 10018

ISBN-13: 978-0-7582-7285-0
ISBN-10: 0-7582-7285-5

First Kensington Trade Paperback Printing: January 2012

10 9 8 7 6 5 4 3 2 1

Printed in the United States of America

*For the guy with the leather jacket:
Because you told me I needed to know
the rules before I could break 'em. Thanks.*

Acknowledgments

Several people helped transform this idea from the crazy mess in my head into the book it is today:

The hardworking staff at Kensington who helped show a newbie the ropes, especially Martin Biro and my editor, Audrey LaFehr. Thank you so much!

My agent, Jessica Faust, who tweeted the need for an erotic romance. Timing is everything!

My faithful posse of friends and divas who beta read *and* keep me sane. Gail Hart, Liane Gentry Skye, Robin Wright, Candi Wall, Courtney Sheets, and Kaylea Cross. And my fabulously wonderful critique partner, who fields at least ten e-mails a day from me, Saranna DeWylde. I probably would have deleted this sucker without your input. Big hugs and bigger drinks all around.

And to my supportive husband, who said "okay" when I told him I wanted to write dirty books. Thanks, sexy man.

1

"Gen, what should we order tonight?"

Genevieve Luzon twisted her hair and fastened it up with a starburst-shaped clip so it spilled like a dark fountain around the back of her head. Not exactly a sexy look, but tonight was all about creature comforts and self-indulgence. Her friend Gia had just gotten back from her latest training exercise, and they both needed to unwind with a good old-fashioned girls' night in.

Nodding at her reflection, she called to her friend, "Whatever you want, Gia. Pizza would be stellar." *Then again* . . . She lifted her baggy T-shirt and frowned down at the bulge last night's cheesecake had put there. Maybe she ought to skip dinner and take a few laps around the Central Park holographic track instead.

"Ah, who am I kidding?" Disgusted with her lack of willpower, Gen dropped her shirt and slid her feet into cobalt-blue sparkly slippers. She scuffed down the hall to where Gia clicked the vid phone off.

Gia's blond brows drew together. "Is that what you're wearing?"

"What, do you think I'll offend the pizza delivery guy? You've been flying training missions out along the rim too long. This is New New York, hon. I'm sure he's seen worse than my plaid pajama pants. I'll toss him an extra dozen credits and he won't even remember."

"No way." Gia poured the sparkling red wine into a glass and handed it to Gen. "This one is on me."

Gen accepted the glass and smiled at her friend. "That's really sweet of you, but I can pay my own way. So I got fired today. It's not like I'm destitute or anything." *Just too close for comfort.* Pushing the unwelcome thought aside, she offered another bright smile. "What's on the schedule for this evening's entertainment?"

Gia's eyes sparkled mischievously as she took a drink. "It's a surprise. First, though, I have got some oh-so-shocking news. You remember Alison Cartwright?"

Gen tapped her chin. At least there was only one to tap. Maybe she could have pizza after all. "From high school? Quiet girl with bad teeth and a gland problem?"

"Exactly. Well, I bumped into her at the flying coffee cart at the corner of Lexington and Fifth, and oh my fracking God, Gen, has she ever changed. Take a look at her card." Gia rummaged around in her purse and then held up a metal business chip. The 3-D holograph that popped up showed a scantily clad blond bombshell with bedroom eyes and a to-die-for curvy body encased in a formfitting sheath one shade darker than her golden skin tone.

"Wow. If I were a guy, I'd totally pop a woody right now." Gen read the printing that flowed across Alison's impressive C-cups, hoisted high by an antigrav corset. "Illustra? Are you fracking shitting me?"

Gia shook her head. "I shit you not. It's like a really fractured fairy tale. Ugly duckling blossoms into a fornicating swan."

"I wonder what that would be like?" Gen tilted her head, examining Alison's card. "Do you think she likes being a pleasure companion?"

"She seemed content enough, if a bit short on time." Gia swirled her wine in her glass, studying the contents. "Do you ever think that maybe you would try it?"

Gen choked as the liquid went down her windpipe. "You mean, try a career in the skin trade? Nuh-uh. No way."

"Why not? It's a perfectly acceptable occupation. More lucrative than most, actually."

Gen didn't want to explain her archaic mind-set to her friend, so she quipped, "Think how exhausting it would be to fake all those orgasms."

Gia's eyes narrowed. "Have you ever actually *had* an orgasm?"

"Of course. Every time I eat triple turtle cheesecake with fudge sauce. Speaking of food, did the pizza place say how long it would be?"

Gia opened her mouth but was cut off by the dulcet programmed voice of the intercom. "Pardon me for interrupting, but there is someone at the door for you."

"Dinner is served." Gia hopped off the barstool and scooted to answer the door.

Gen didn't bother to argue over the bill. She'd pay Gia back as soon as she found a new job. Closing her eyes, she allowed herself a moment to wallow in her failure. Damn Mrs. Delevopia for getting on board the wrong off-world shuttle! Was it her fault the stubborn octogenarian refused to wear her reading glasses? But no matter how many times Gen had tried to explain, Mr. Parks had booted her sorry ass to the curb because she'd ruined his reputation. Three years she'd given that place, more time than she'd ever invested in a relationship. Was this the reward for her loyalty and hard work? *If so, somebody goofed.*

"Gen?" Gia called from the entryway. "Could you come here?"

Gen opened her eyes and sighed. "That means I have to get up."

"Trust me, it'll be worth it." Mischief laced her friend's words.

Eh, I need more wine anyway. Gen pushed herself off the couch and shuffled out to the hallway.

"What's so damn important—" Gen stopped talking, her mouth hanging open as she observed the pizza guy. Tall and broad shouldered with his dark hair held back in an elegant ponytail. His cashmere coat and tailored slacks made her acutely aware of her own shabby ensemble. Big hands held a vintage black leather satchel. Pretty fracking high-end for a pizza warmer.

"Gen, this is Franco, your evening's entertainment." Gia bounced on her toes like a giddy schoolgirl, a big grin plastered on her elfin face.

Franco bowed—a courteous old-world gesture that appeared so out of place in Gen's raggedy apartment. He clasped her hand and brought it to his lips. "The pleasure, I assure you, is all mine."

Her heart thumped against her rib cage. Damn, he smelled good, like a combination of a fresh breeze blowing off the ocean and clean mountain air. Firm, masculine lips pulled into a seductive smile, and Gen's mouth went dry. Her skin tingled where he touched her hand. She wanted to say something savvy, but nothing came to mind.

The three of them stood awkwardly in the doorway until Gia announced, "Well, I'm gonna scoot."

"Scoot?" The word hit Gen like a cattle prod, and she pulled her arm back from Franco's mesmerizing hold. "Gia, I need to talk to you a second."

She pushed her friend down the hallway into her sister's bedroom. "What the hell is going on? You just got back. I thought we were going to hang out."

Gia held her hands out and shrugged. "Don't be mad, but I got asked out on a date. I didn't want to just bail on you and thought you could use a pick-me-up. Franco's from Illustra. You said I should order whatever I wanted, and I want you to get laid."

"You got me a man whore?" Gen yelped. Sure, people did it every day, but she had never been comfortable with the idea of paying someone to touch her. "Are you out of your ever-loving mind?"

Gia's gaze softened. "Face facts, sweetie. You've been depressed for a while now, ever since your sister dropped out of school and disappeared. You have no job, no social life, and you hardly ever leave your apartment."

"Not true. I visit my grandparents in Connecticut. Sometimes I'll go to the cabin upstate. And I have you," Gen argued, but she could hear how feeble her protest sounded. "It may not seem like much of a life, but it's still a life."

Gia gave her a quick, sisterly hug. "Of course. But there are some gaps even I can't fill." She chuckled at the double entendre before she asked, "How long since you last had sex?"

Gen bit her lip but admitted the truth. "I don't remember."

"Well, I'd hazard a guess that after tonight, you will have absolutely no trouble remembering." Gia winked and gave her a little wave. "Toodles."

"Wait! I . . ." Gen searched for something to say to combat the growing panic. "I'm not dressed for a man whore."

Gia rolled her eyes. "You're not supposed to dress for a man whore—you're supposed to *un*dress for him. Better yet, let him undress you. With his teeth."

"Is there a problem, ladies?" Franco called from the foyer.

His rich accent was melodic and cultured, and Gen couldn't help but sigh. Maybe this wasn't such a horrible idea.

Gia studied her face with her sharp green gaze. "Look, if you're really uncomfortable with this, we can send him away, get a pizza, and watch an old movie. Is that what you want?"

Gen stared down at her petite friend. Gia was trying to do something nice for her, something to help her break out of the malaise of her current life. She could have just called and canceled, but instead, she came up with plan B—a night with Boy Toy. *It would be rude to return her gift. Especially without trying it on to see if it fits.* "Well, he is pretty hot. And he smells divine."

Gia flashed her even white teeth. "Good, it's settled, then."

They marched back into the living room where Franco had made himself at home. He'd crouched down in front of her glass coffee table and lit a bloodred candle. He must have brought it with him, because candles were ungodly expensive, way out of Gen's tax bracket. The wick ignited, and he set it on a glass dinner plate. Gia donned her coat and then reached out to shake his hand. "Show her a grand time, Franco."

Gen noticed the flat glowing spot embedded right beneath the skin in the back of his hand. It went from a pulsing red to a throbbing green when Gia's thumb landed on it. A biomechanical credit payment strip. With one quick handshake, Gia paid Franco for services he was about to render. The technology was extremely new and expensive. He must be doing all right in his chosen line of work. The thought made her shiver in anticipation.

Gia's steps faded and the door clicked shut behind her. The auto lock would engage until someone on the inside pressed a thumb against the metal plate to open it. They were officially alone in her quiet apartment. She bit her lip and stared at the glowing light of the candle, almost afraid to meet his gaze.

What the hell do you say to the man who's being paid to fuck you?

"Why don't you come a little closer?" Franco shrugged out of his coat and draped it over the back of her squat eggplant-colored couch. He unfastened his belt buckle, and her heart rate kicked up to a frantic pounding. This was happening much too fast, and she still wasn't entirely sure she wanted it to happen at all.

"I've never done this before," she blurted out.

He didn't seem startled by her outburst. A small smile played across his lips. "Do you mean having sex or hiring a male companion for the evening?" Rising up to his full height, which was an impressive several inches taller than her own five-foot-eleven stature, he strode toward her.

Note to self—he probably doesn't want to be called a man whore. "No, I've had sex. Just not with anyone else in a while. But I've never . . ." She trailed off as his scent enveloped her senses, his large frame blocking out the rest of the world as though it had never existed.

He loomed over her but not in a threatening way—more like a conquering warlord about to claim his prize. "Never been pleasured by a professional. A novice, splendid. The very first thing you need to do is activate your health guard. Safety first." His melodic voice crooned in her ear.

Swallowing, she did. Pressing down on the small transmitter on the inside of her elbow, Gen activated her germ shield. There was a soft hum as the invisible shielding snapped into place to prevent fluid transfer.

He nodded in approval and reached behind her to unfasten the clip at the crown of her head. Dark hair fell in a wild, unruly riot down to the middle of her back. His scent engulfed her, and she bit back a moan when he ran his fingers through her hair. "You are lovely."

"I'm in my jammies," she protested.

"Not for long." Eyes fixed on her face, as though reading her mood, he slid his hands down over her back to the gap where her shirt and pants met. Dipping his head, he kissed her neck, just a soft peck at the same moment his fingers touched bare flesh.

Gen let her eyes drift shut, enjoying his practiced touch. He was good, thorough, not rushing the encounter, but not dragging his feet either. His hands stroked over her bare skin in a silken caress, relaxing her body to accept whatever he had in store.

"How do you feel?" His hand stroked up beneath her shirt, cupping her unfettered breasts. Her nipples pebbled at the contact, and her body grew wet and needy.

She sighed out a shaky breath and stared up at him. The fact that a total stranger was touching her so intimately both excited and frightened her. "I'm . . . not really sure."

Dark eyebrows drew together, and he glanced over his shoulder at the candle burning on the coffee table before looking back to her. "Tell me what you want."

How could she tell him when she didn't really know herself? Yes, his touch excited her, and she wanted to be petted and stroked, comforted. But how could she say all these things to a total stranger without dying from embarrassment? The thought of taking off all of her clothes in the well-lit room, having him look at her naked body, unnerved her. But she wanted to peruse his body, to know if he appeared as magnificent without his trendy clothes. "I want to see you, all of you."

He didn't hesitate as he untucked his shirt and started working the buttons, feeding them through the buttonholes with agonizing slowness. She bit her lip, greedy for her first real look at him. Palms itching to smooth their way over those broad shoulders, down the trail of dark hair peeping out at her from between the parting fabric, and then lower to explore his sex.

Yes, that's what she craved, to touch him freely and not worry about what he thought of her.

The last button came undone, and he moved with graceful ease, shrugging it off, tossing it on top of his jacket. His health guard snapped to life, emitting a soft blue glow that was reflected in the windows. In the distance, a noise ordinance horn blatted out a warning, popping her fantasy bubble with the sharp pinprick of reality.

"Uh, we should probably move back to my bedroom." The last thing she needed was a rap on the window from the neighborhood decency patrol telling her to shut her broken blinds.

"If that is your desire." Franco toed off his shoes, then picked up the candle and his bag. Gen started down the hallway but stopped and turned to face him. "What about you?"

He blinked at her. "What do you mean?"

She waved her hands in small helpless circles. "Well, how about what you desire? I think sex is better when there is mutual satisfaction."

A smile broke out across his face. "You are an unusual woman, Genevieve. I assure you, before the night is over, I will have found my own slice of bliss." His words made a sensual promise and she shivered.

Not bothering to turn the light on in her room, lest he see the piles of discarded lingerie and other feminine paraphernalia, she took the candle from his hands and set it down on her nightstand. Something about it mesmerized her, the way the flame danced as though performing just for her, and she forgot about Franco, her nervousness, and the rest of the universe, totally lost in the moment.

Warm hands cupped her breasts from behind, and she sighed, allowing her head to fall back onto his shoulder as he kneaded her aching flesh. Wet slickness pooled between her thighs while he murmured soothing words of praise and soft encouragements. The candle seemed to wink at her, conveying a message that this was exactly where she was supposed to be, and everything would be okay.

His clever fingers unknotted the drawstring on her pajama bottoms with ease, and before her mind could form a protest, he slipped the fabric over her hips until it pooled around her feet.

Pushing gently but insistently on her back, he urged her up onto the bed until she was poised on all fours. "Stay exactly like that." The order held the ring of command, and she shivered again, growing even wetter in anticipation. Her channel ached, greedy for his penetration. The only thought in her head was that it had been too long, and she needed the invasion *now*.

The rustling of fabric and her ragged breaths were the only sounds. She was a light sleeper and had searched for an apartment with an utterly soundproof bedroom to help her rest peacefully at night. Now, the quiet created an isolated little cocoon where anything was possible, where she could be free and greedy in her carnal needs. "What are you doing?"

He tapped her lightly on the ass. "I didn't say you could talk."

Did she like his domineering attitude? Not so much, but it did take the pressure off of her to do anything but follow his lead. "Sorry."

"I'm lubing up. Wetter is better, don't you think?" He traced a finger down the crease of her ass, circling the small opening there for an agonizing moment before continuing down to the folds of her sex. "Are you wet yet, Gen?"

She opened her mouth to answer, but paused when she recalled his reaction to speaking out of turn. Instead she decided to go with a nonverbal reply and rocked her hips back to increase the pressure on her aching clit. The light brush of his fingertips over the swollen bud sent sparks shimmering throughout her body. A groan escaped as he stroked her harder, deeper, almost exactly as she needed.

"Do you want my cock inside you? Or maybe my tongue. Should I lick you until you come all over my face?"

The image his words built up in her mind pushed her right to the edge, where she teetered, waiting for him to do something, *anything*. "Please," she gasped as he captured her clit between two fingers and tugged lightly.

"Please what?" His stroking hand disappeared, and she glanced over her shoulder to see him fondling his thick cock. Again, her inner muscles spasmed, but without direct stimulation, the orgasm slipped away. He bent over her, his dark hair unbound and falling forward as he whispered in her ear, "Tell me what you want, Gen."

She panted, poised on the cliff and more than ready. "Make me come."

Strong hands gripped her hips, and he slid his well-lubed cock inside her. Gen groaned at the contact and bucked back to meet him, taking him even more deeply inside of her. His thickness filled her, but she wanted more, wanted him to take her harder. Faster. Now.

His hold on her pelvis tightened, forbidding her frantic movements. "Easy. I'll get you there. Trust me." His agonizingly slow withdrawal made her sigh, and he stopped while the blunt head was still barely inside her. Another smooth, hard thrust and she cried out, wanting more.

"You are so fucking hot," he rasped on his second retreat. His hand snaked over her hip and down until he could tease her throbbing clit with calloused fingertips. "I want to take you hard."

His words made her clench up, and she groaned a breathless acquiescence. "Do it." Tears of frustration had gathered behind her closed eyelids. She needed more, so much more than this light teasing.

"Push back against the wall," he commanded, urging her

torso lower so he could angle his cock inside her. "And hold on."

Spreading her legs wider to make room for his hips, he slammed his thick shaft into her. This time he didn't hold back.

He touched all the right spots—his fingers worked her clit while the head of his shaft angled against her G-spot. Technically speaking, it was a perfect performance, ten out of ten.

But she couldn't come.

"Are you close?" Franco panted as he surged into her again. "Do you want me to go down on you?"

Their germ shields snapped and sizzled at the onslaught of contact. The sex was amazing; he filled her completely, was almost *too* big. He'd made her wet, made her ache. Was it too much to fracking ask for him to finish the deed?

Instead, she fell back on the habits of her sexual lifetime. She faked orgasm. Her cry of supposed ecstasy sounded hollow and phony to her own ears, but she timed the clenching of her inner muscles perfectly. A teeny part of her hoped he'd see through her ruse and not let her get away with it.

"Oh, hell yeah!" His shout echoed off the walls as he thrust against her again, almost to the point of pain. His sharp, stabbing shoves heralded his own orgasm, and he withdrew while their shields gobbled up the discarded genetic material.

She bit her lip and waited while he caught his breath, unsure of what to say and ashamed at herself for wimping out. Franco had been paid to come here and please her. Was it wrong to demand that he give her body her friend's credits' worth?

Could it *sound* any more pathetic?

Luckily, Franco pulled her from that morose train of thought before the pity party turned ugly. "Damn, you are one hot commodity."

Fake it until you make it, babe. "Um, thank you?"

He chuckled and stroked his hand over her naked back. She wanted to preen under the contact. Gen loved being touched, could never seem to get enough of it. His hand glided along her spine in slow, sweeping motions. "So, are we good?"

She nodded. "Help yourself to the sonic shower."

He leaned down, nuzzled her hair. "You really are sweet, you know that?"

Gen listened as he gathered his clothes and padded into the hall, and heard the deep thrumming as the sonic shower turned on.

She couldn't wait anymore. Sucking on her index and middle finger, she wet them good before manipulating her aching clit. *Yessss . . .*

The candle still flickered from the nightstand. She let herself go, timing the thrust of her fingers into her snug sheath to its sensual movements. Soon she needed both hands—one to work her throbbing bud and the other to pump two fingers inside her channel, even as her hips rose to increase the contact. And still she wished for more. The feel of male hands working her body like an instrument designed for pleasure, touching her, licking her, fucking her. It was always like this, her body needing—no, *demanding*—more, no matter how much it received. Was there no limit to her carnal greed?

The orgasm crashed over her and she sighed in relief. Pulling a blanket up to her neck, she curled into a ball on her side, facing away from the door. Her mind drifted, not thinking of anything in particular. She heard the shower go off. Exhaustion swept over her like a thick fog, muddying her senses. Just before she fell asleep, she swore she felt hands running through her hair and an unfamiliar voice whispering words of praise in her ear.

2

As the sensual woman relaxed into sleep, Rhys could no longer maintain his corporeal form. He fought the candle's pull as long as he could, but without the infusion of her raw emotions, he didn't have enough strength to manifest a body. He came apart, atom by atom, his empathic essence pulled like metal shavings to a magnet. Only great power could free an empath from one of Illustra's specially designed prisons. Power he had almost given up hope of finding.

Until her.

For no logical reason, he had almost refused to harvest her emotions the way he had done for countless others. Even though he was starved for the contact, it had seemed wrong to toy with something so pure and bright. He had, though, tamping down her fear and anxiety and seeking out her buried lusts to help her accept what Franco offered.

But he couldn't bring himself to force climax on her.

Her performance had been tactful, the way she'd dismissed the man so she could take matters into her own hands. Her passion was crimson and untarnished, the most delicious emotion he'd ever encountered, and as she'd reached her satisfaction, he'd broken free. However, it had taken too long for his body to form, and he'd heard Franco moving in the other room. Short on time, he'd bent down and just breathed her in. The magnificent fragrance of woman, heady and oh so arousing.

The dark spill of her hair looked so soft and inviting, and he'd touched it before he'd been aware of the burning compulsion. The silky tangles slid through his fingers, and she murmured something incomprehensible, her eyes still closed. She would help him; he knew it. She needed the sexual satisfaction he longed to give her.

The door down the hall opened just as Rhys planted the seed in her mind, a niggling itch that would grow until she sought him out to scratch it. He settled down to wait.

Franco was gone by the time Gen awoke. No light penetrated the room, which meant he'd taken that awesome candle with him. Too bad. She wondered how many organs she'd have to hock to buy one of those. Such a simple prop, but it had set the tone she so desperately needed last night. Bathed in its flickering illumination, she'd felt sensual, sexually confident for the first time in her life.

"Yeah, that's what you should be worrying about," she muttered, and flung the covers back. Between finding a job and searching for her runaway sister, her day was booked solid. Sexual gratification could wait. *Maybe until my next life.*

Padding down the hall, she snorted in disgust when she saw that Franco had left the toilet seat up. Just in case she'd thought it might have all been a dream. She wondered if he had a wife or girlfriend who waited for him to get off work every night. The thought depressed her, so she shoved it away and hummed a wordless tune while waves of sound energy sloughed all the sweat and grime from her body.

Wrapped in a thick robe, she fussed around in the kitchen,

preparing coffee, toasting a bagel, and cutting up fresh fruit into a small bowl. With breakfast on the table, she pressed her thumb to the plate and a door slid open, revealing the coiled asp in the form of the morning news vid disk.

"Come on, baby, show Mama some love." She popped it into the disk player and settled down to read while she ate.

"Oh, big surprise, another politician with his hand caught up a tranny's skirt." She snorted and scrolled to the classifieds. The 3-D imager projected the list of jobs currently available in New New York. Her heart sank when she realized she wasn't qualified for any of them. Since machines took care of all the rote tasks, the need for unskilled labor was at an all-time low in the city. Even the dog walkers had gone animated because bots were more likely to scoop the poop. *I've been outmoded.*

Needing a little reassurance, she gave the voice command for autodial 1 and disengaged the hologram. At 104 years old, Nana was still unbelievably vain and refused to engage the camera most of the time.

"Hello?" A familiar rumbling baritone picked up.

Even though her name and address showed up as soon as the call connected, Gen was used to her grandfather's archaic greeting. "Hi ya, Gramps."

"Hey, punkin head. How's everything with you?"

For a moment Gen considered lying, not wanting him to worry about her. But in the end, she needed someone to confide in. And Nana didn't believe in keeping secrets, so Gramps would find out anyhow. "Not so good. I lost my job yesterday."

He made a sympathetic sound. "Aw, baby, I'm so sorry to hear that. Which job was this again?"

Had he been anyone else in the same age group, Gen would have worried his mind was going. But her grandfather had a habit of letting details drift in one ear and sail right out the other.

"Off-world vacay coordinator. Remember, I booked that cruise for you and Nana to sail around Saturn's rings for your seventieth anniversary last year?"

"Oh, that's right. Don't worry, though, punkin head, you'll find something even better." There was some shuffling and his voice called out, "Cora, Gen's on the line."

"Nice talking to you, Gramps," Gen muttered at the same time Cora's robust voice called out, "Honestly, Jack, would it kill you to talk for more than a minute?"

"You won't get rid of me that easily, hot stuff," Gramps muttered, and Nana let out a squeak. Gen would bet her best pair of high-heeled boots that he'd pinched her grandmother's ass. *One hundred six and still a randy old goat. They don't make 'em like that anymore.*

"What's wrong, lovey?" Cora asked immediately.

Gen rocked back in the chair, then stood, filled with a restless energy she couldn't ignore. "Nothing and everything."

"Give me a play-by-play," Cora demanded.

So Gen did, leaving out nothing, not even her encounter with a prostitute, though she skirted the details. There was no sense trying to hide anything from Nana. She was a powerful telepath who had been trained as a government weapon from an early age. People didn't mess with Nana if they wanted their higher brain functions to stay in working order.

Cora sighed. "Well, is there anything I can do? Do you need money for the man whore?"

"Nana!" Gen shook her head, then cursed under her breath when she remembered the holo wasn't on. "No, he was a gift from my friend Gia. And as far as gifts go, let's just say once was enough for me."

"That good, huh? Do you want to come home for a spell?"

Though the offer tempted her, Gen couldn't take it. "As nice as that sounds, I need to stay here in case Tanny comes back. And I need to find a job, maybe even a boyfriend."

"Things will work out, lovey. You'll get a new job, meet a handsome man, get married, and *bam!* Alone and unemployed is lost in the current of too busy once more."

Gen sighed as she looked out the window into the bright blue sky. A commuter bus whizzed by, filled with people heading to work. "It's not that simple, Nana. People are no longer wired for the kind of commitment you and Gramps have. Men my age don't want more than a quick nail-and-bail."

"Honey, men of *any* age don't know *what* they want. Look at your grandfather."

Jack muttered noncommittally in the background.

Gen shook her head. "That is so not true, Nana. He wanted you right from the start, before he even met you in person. That hasn't changed."

"But everything else did. Gen, he used to kill people for a living. We both had to decide what we wanted in terms of ourselves and each other, then fight like rabid wolves to get it. Society has bled all the fight out of young people—you don't have to do any of the hard stuff anymore. Hell, you can scare up a date with a quick online order and a thumbprint scan. Fantasy made easy."

Gen thought about her earlier encounter with Franco. "And yet there's still something missing."

"Don't those man whores come with some kind of satisfaction-guaranteed clause?"

Gen squirmed in her seat. "Uh, Nana, I'm really not comfortable—"

But Cora was like a supersonic freight train once she got on a roll. "If that man left you less than one hundred percent satisfied, you ought to march your behind right on down to that brothel and demand an exchange."

"Do I need to hear this?" Gramps called out.

"No, dearest heart. I won't be returning you anytime soon," Cora cooed.

"I gotta go," Gen said, figuring her grandparents needed some alone time.

"Oh, are you still going up north this weekend? If so, remember that you need to turn the hot water heater back on in the cabin."

Gen was about to refuse, when she considered the plus side of getting out of town. Namely she could hide from the to-do list for a little while. "I haven't decided yet."

On the other end of the line, things had progressed without her. "Come here, you sassy vixen."

Cora squeaked and giggled like a teenager, and Gen hung up before her grandparents scarred her for life. Instead of diving back into the classifieds, she surfed the Internet for Illustra's Website and pulled up their guarantee clause. Settling down with another cup of coffee, she began to read.

"Hi, I'm looking for Alison Cartwright?" Gen smiled at the blond receptionist over the glass table. She let her gaze wander around the opulent lobby. Every piece of furniture in the building was either glass or chrome, producing an oddly cold and sterile environment. The walls were coated in dove gray, the carpet a nondescript mauve. Nothing she'd seen so far had alluded to sex or passion.

The blonde gave her a cool, detached smile. "Did you have an appointment with her?"

"No." Gen leaned over the massive desk and whispered low, "I actually wanted to speak to her about something in your company's guarantee clause."

The receptionist's already perfect posture went ramrod stiff. "Did she not satisfy you? Do you want to file a formal complaint?" Her loud voice bounced off the walls like a humiliating echo.

Heat crept up her cheeks as she realized the girl had misunderstood her intent. "No! Nothing like that. Alison is an old friend of mine from high school, and I had a couple of questions for her."

"Oh." The girl sagged as though relieved. "Sorry I reacted like that. We've been having some complaints lately and I thought that you—"

A sharp clap cut the receptionist off midstream. "Julia, enough. Don't babble at the customers. It's gauche."

"Oh, I'm not a customer—that is, I was, but I'm really here because . . ." Gen trailed off as she looked the new woman over head to toe. "Alison?"

Heavily mascaraed lashes blinked in surprise before realization hit. "Genevieve Luzon? Oh my God, I would recognize you anywhere!"

Gen couldn't have said the same. Even after viewing Alison's business card chip, she hadn't been fully aware of the other woman's total transformation. Her smile revealed even white teeth that could star in toothpaste advertisements, and she smelled of Venus Allure Number Five. Dressed in a black business suit tailored to fit her trim new figure, Alison looked everything and nothing like her seductive self from the 3-D image.

"You look fantastic!" Gen said instead.

Alison smiled and smoothed a hand across her suit jacket. "Thanks. What's new with you?"

"My sister ran away from home and I got fired." Gen made a face. "Sorry, I know you didn't really want to know all that."

Alison laughed. "Same old Gen. Listen, I'd love to chat, but I'm a bit busy at the moment. Maybe we could have lunch next week and catch up?"

"Actually, I wanted to talk to you about an encounter I had last night with one of your pleasure companions."

Alison glanced around the lobby quickly, checking to see if anyone had overheard. "Let's take this to my office."

Gen followed Alison up a curving flight of stairs and into an office overlooking the Hudson River. "Wow, business must be lucrative." She winced when she realized how that sounded.

Alison closed the door and laughed. "Believe me, I'd never thought of myself as the type to sleep my way to the top. But Illustra is different from the pleasure agencies of yesteryear. I almost never do active fieldwork anymore."

She waved Gen into a mauve armchair and circled the desk.

"I did a little reading online, but I was wondering if you could give me some more background on Illustra."

Alison smiled. "Sure, a little history, then. As you probably know, scores of corporate pleasure troves emerged when prostitution was legalized in 2059, after the advent of personal health shields. Most of those starter businesses were individuals or small groups specifically geared toward male clientele. Prostitution is, of course, the oldest profession known to humanity, and with the safety screens preventing both transfer of disease and unwanted pregnancy, well, it was really just a matter of time until everyone wanted a piece of the action, so to speak."

Gen nodded. "From what I read, that time period was chaos—people misrepresenting themselves in online databases, moral objections, especially from women's rights groups."

Alison smiled. "Exactly so. What sets Illustra apart is the packaging. We abolished the skeeve associated with prostitution, the old-style whorehouse concept, while still offering a taste of the forbidden. We were the first to make our database women-friendly by acquiring male therapists who then agreed to give out free samples, keeping quality control of our roster. Our commitment to excellence is what sets us apart."

Gen squirmed in her seat. "Yeah, about that. Gia ordered up one of your nighttime escorts for me, and something was missing."

Alison shook a finger in her face. "Well, for starters, you should never let someone else pick out a pleasure companion for you. Women like different things when it comes to sex, different builds on their partners, different physical stimulation. Even the best pleasure professional isn't a one-size-fits-all. But setting that aside, what else didn't please you?"

Gen winced, not wanting to admit her own dumb mistake. "I faked an orgasm."

Alison threw her hands up in exasperation. "Gen, for the love of God, why would you do that?"

"I don't know. It seemed like a good idea at the time. He was doing everything right, technically speaking—"

"No, no, he wasn't if you felt the need to fake it." Alison rose out of her chair and began to pace. "Why women do that is beyond me. It's only teaching men to do all the *wrong* things. We put the men through a rigorous training program to perfect their technique, but if women don't step up and own their own pleasure—" Alison stopped moving and talking simultaneously. Slowly, she turned to face Gen. "I have a proposal for you. Hear me out before you say anything."

Gen nodded and waited.

"Between you, me, and the wall, we've had several complaints from women just like you, ordinary women looking for a quickie. The men are too rough, or not forceful enough, too slow on the uptake, and even"—she rolled her eyes—"on enhancement supplements. We don't own these men, and when they know they are being surveyed, they perform beautifully. What we need to do is catch them with their pants down, so to speak."

"And this has what to do with me?"

Alison flashed her beautiful teeth in a brilliant smile. "I want you to be my secret shopper."

"What?" Gen exploded out of the chair. "You want me to be like a crash-test dummy for your men?"

"It's perfect! We'll set you up like a wealthy customer and send some of the guys we've had complaints about to take care of your needs. You'll take them for a spin and report back to me."

"Um, Alison, one itsy-bitsy problem. I have no idea how to be a prostitute." Wait, was she actually *considering* this?

"Which is why you'll be perfect. They won't expect you to do anything fancy. Just lie there and let them work you into a lather."

"Yeah, but why should I do this?" She hadn't seen Alison in over a decade, and this was one hell of a favor.

"You just told me you lost your job. So I'm offering you another one. Genevieve Luzon, corporate spy." Extracting her personal comm unit, she typed in something, then angled it to sync up with Gen's. The connection went through, and Gen gaped at the huge credit number flashing on her display. Her gaze flew to Alison's, wondering if the other woman was serious.

Alison nodded once, confirming her astronomical offer. "Half up front and half after the job is complete. Listen, think it over and then let me know one way or the other. You might find out things about yourself that you never even knew existed."

3

Nana and Gramps were waiting for Gen when she returned to her apartment. Cora bustled around the galley kitchen, fixing tea from her own hydroponic blend of leaves and herbs that she grew in her greenhouse. She smiled at Gen and waved her to the table.

"How did you know?" Gen cupped her hands around the steaming mug, allowing the heat and aromatic fragrance to seep into the cold places inside of her.

Cora tapped a purple polished fingernail to her temple. "World's most powerful telepath, remember?"

"And so modest too." Gramps kissed the top of Nana's head.

Cora waved him off. "Modesty never once benefited me. I was the shock-and-awe girl, the government's secret weapon." She batted her eyelashes at her husband, and Gen could tell they were communicating mind to mind.

Jack grunted and squared his still-impressive shoulders with military precision. "I'm going to take a walk."

"It's thirty degrees out," Gen remarked.

"Then I won't need a coat." Jack gave her a one-armed hug. "Stand tall, punkin head."

Cora sighed as Jack ambled out. "They just don't make 'em like that anymore."

Gen agreed. No need to say anything out loud, since Cora skimmed her thoughts to pick up on the juicy tidbits. "I see you've taken my advice."

"Yeah, and it landed me a job offer." Somehow she couldn't get excited over the prospect, no matter how ridiculously tempting the salary might be.

Cora tilted her head to the side as if doing so could grant her better reception into Gen's mind. Gen hissed out a breath. "Nana, for God's sake—"

"Shhh," Cora cut her off, concentrating on something only her powerful mind could pick up. Narrowing her eyes, she looked more like a petulant young girl than a 104-year-old telepath. "I'm listening to your subconscious mind, something you ought to do more often."

"Unless it has a way to help me find Tanny or get a real job—"

Again, Cora interrupted her with a quick slashing motion. Gen heaved a great sigh and sipped her drink. The strong woodsy aroma was more like a rich blend of coffee than an herbal tea. Gardening had long been Cora's outlet for her frenetic backlog of energy. How pathetic that Gen wished she had half of her grandmother's zest for life.

Pretty damn sad.

"Actually, it's not," Cora answered her unspoken thought.

"You know I hate it when you do that. Can we have a normal verbal conversation, please?"

Cora shrugged her slim shoulders. "If you would prefer. Now, do you want to talk, or do you want to know what you need to do?"

Gen pushed her chair back and took her empty mug to the

sink. "I know what I need to do. I need to find a new job and wait here for Tanny."

Cora made a rude noise. "Oh, fuck that. You are not your sister's keeper, Genevieve. Your own life is passing you by at an astronomical rate. Honey, you need to get laid."

The spoon Gen had been washing clattered into the sink. "This conversation is disturbing on so many levels!"

"Forget that you're talking with good old Nana for a second and talk to me, woman to woman. You're alone and you're lonely. Believe me, I remember what that feels like. But closing yourself off from the world doesn't keep it at bay. You still have to do the drudgery, the mundane things. Honey, you're taking on all of the challenges and ignoring the rewards that are just waiting out there for you to grab them. Touch, comfort, self-confidence. Look me in the eye and tell me you don't crave more of all three."

Gen squared her shoulders. "So what if I do? What do you suggest?"

"Take Alison up on her offer. Do the secret-shopper gig, find your bliss. All of your problems will still be waiting for you when you come back, I promise. And who knows, maybe you will be in a better place to tackle them?"

Gen bit her lip.

Cora took a step closer and gripped Gen's hand. "Do you remember when you wanted to take antigrav dance lessons? Your mother thought it was indecent, improper. What did I say to her?"

Gen grinned at the memory, one of her favorites from childhood. "'Take that stick out of your ass, Lorna, or I'll beat you over the head with it.'"

"I've always been your advocate, Genevieve, and I will continue to be, even if I have to advocate *against* you. For your own good, lovey."

Gen blew out a breath. "There's so much to do. I need to

pack, call Alison. And what if Tanny calls or comes back here looking for me?" Gen cringed, thinking of her sister showing up at the upstate cabin to find her entertaining a bunch of problematic man whores.

Cora walked into the living room and held up a packed suitcase. "Gramps and I will stay here until you get back. Call Alison from the car. Go on, scoot and get yourself shagged silly."

Rhys let his conscious mind drift so as not to dwell on the discomfort. Even though his body was trapped light-years away, twinges from his physical self produced a phantom pain that resounded in his empathic essence.

How long had it been? With no way to mark the passage of time, he couldn't even begin to guess. He missed the vivid colors of fresh green and growing things, the salty taste of the stew his brothers had eaten nightly, the coarse textures of the robes they wore while in training. Other sensations seemed even dimmer, barely within his grasp. The feel of a woman's soft body beneath him, her sighs of pleasure in his ears, the wetness between her legs.

He thought about the magnificent beauty he had last seen. What he would give to explore her generous curves, to run his hands through her dark hair, to siphon off the pleasure he needed to give her.

The fantasy unfolded in his mind, and he saw her on the bed, face flushed with arousal, lips parted on a gasping breath. He couldn't decide where to touch her, where to taste her first. Her lush pink lips, or the stiffened nipples of a deep wine color? No, first he'd lick her to orgasm, his tongue dragging through the folds of her sex. *That's* what he wanted, what she needed. Her pleasure building as he flicked her clit again and again. He'd help her climb the slope, poise her on the ledge, then use his fingers to fill her sheath and send her flying.

Her colors would explode in a magnificent rainbow, feeding

him until he glutted on her emotions. She'd beg him to fill her then, to slide his cock into her wet, silky depths. Her legs would wrap around his waist as he pumped in and out of her body. He'd kiss her, use his tongue to possess her mouth the same way she possessed his mind.

He'd come in a rush, thrusting into her and she'd cry out, milking every bit of jism his body had to offer. Then replete, he'd rest his head on the full mounds of her breasts and breathe in her contentment, listen to the pounding of her heart.

Rhys sighed as the dream evaporated from his mind like mist. She wasn't coming to him, hadn't gotten the message. Otherwise she would be here by now.

His time would be better served if he just forgot about her, formed a new plan of escape. But he couldn't seem to keep himself from clinging to her image, to all the ways he wanted to touch her, kiss her, use his body to pleasure hers.

"Can you replicate these in a size nine, please?" Gen smiled at the shoe store clerk as he scurried off, eager to make his commission. Gen stared at the new leather spike-heeled boots she'd purchased to give herself the confidence to take this leap. It was either footwear or cheesecake, and since she was scheduled to spend the rest of the weekend naked, the boots won out.

The clerk handed her the newly replicated boots, and she sighed in bliss as she slid her foot home. "Perfect fit."

He held the credit scanner in one hand. "Anything else you would like me to show you today?"

Her gaze slid to the leather duster that matched the boots. Maybe after Alison paid her the second half for a job well done. "I'd better stop there." Pressing her thumb to the plate, she was instantly three hundred credits lighter. No turning back now.

Striding out of the store, she made her way across the street to the Central Park replica. The chill winter wind at New New York's obscenely high altitude made the park less than desirable, unless you wanted complete privacy in the middle of the city.

"Thank you for calling Illustra. This is Staci speaking. How may I direct your pleasure?"

Here goes everything. "This is Genevieve Luzon. I spoke with Alison earlier about arranging for some company this weekend."

"Hold one moment, please, and I will transfer you."

A few soft pings indicated Staci was busy pulling up her phony file. Alison had created an entire fictional backstory for her. Her profile would indicate she was recently widowed and looking for a pick-me-up in the form of a few men who desired her company. She was to use them in whatever way she saw fit.

"This is Alison Cartwright." Her tone was brisk and no-nonsense.

"It's me. Are you sure I need to take them all at once?" Gen couldn't believe those words had just come out of her mouth.

In the tiny viewer, Alison nodded definitively. "If they think you are distracted with one of the others, they are more likely to say or do something to give themselves away."

Gen paced, bent away from a particularly harsh gust of wind. "What exactly am I looking for?"

"Satisfaction. I want you to make note of any conduct unbecoming a professional pleasure companion. Not enough attention to your needs or too much focus on their own. You will have them record your sessions, and then play them back for me so I can judge for myself."

"Isn't that entrapment?"

Alison shook her head. "I'm not going to prosecute them, just fire them if they are taking a walk on the wild side on the corporate dime. Times are tough, and we can't afford to have any excess baggage sponging off the company."

Gen didn't know how she felt about Alison watching her homemade porn, and she really didn't like the idea of getting a decent guy like Franco fired just because they were sexually incompatible. But Alison was right; times *were* tough, and what Illustra was offering her was a lot better than any job she'd ever found on her own.

"I'll send GPS coordinates to the cabin upstate to your comm. Reception can be spotty up there, especially if bad weather rolls in, so if I don't call you back right away, don't freak out."

Alison's smile was pure cat-in-the-cream. "Believe me, Gen. You won't regret this."

4

A few hours later, weighted down with enough stuff for a week in upstate New York, Gen sat watching the world through the transparent force field of mass transit Hudson line 1. The descent down the airway from New New York to the polluted rubble of the original city flew by as the sonic train built up speed to hit Mach 1.

Her family's cabin was located on Lake George, due north of Albany. Mass transit would get her most of the way there at the speed of sound, but she'd need to credit a rental vehicle for the rest of the trip. It was probably for the best that she didn't have time to think, seeing as how panic lurked just beneath the surface.

Gen had to settle for a two-seater rental. The hum of the solar-powered engine reminded her of a gnat buzzing in her ear. She glanced at the slate-colored sky, shivering as thick clouds blocked out the weak sunlight. Not exactly a terrific snow car, and if they had enough precipitation, she'd be stranded.

Well, that's the idea, isn't it? To wallow in hedonistic revelry?

Why couldn't she work up more enthusiasm over the prospect of getting shagged silly? Gen pondered the question as she stocked up on food and other staples at the local store. The aisles had been picked clean—another sure sign that winter weather closed in.

She pulled up the gravel drive, missing the sound of crunching stones under tires. The hover car set down with an easy bump, so different than Nana's big black truck. There had been something so quaint about the sound of gravel under the wheels, as if the give of the driveway had welcomed them, the noise heralding the final moment when the journey ended.

Maybe deciding to bring her pleasure companions here had been a mistake. After all, how could she possibly hope to lose all her inhibitions in her childhood bedroom? But the thought of doing this anywhere else seemed wrong.

Irrational anger bubbled up as she exited the car and hunched against the wind. Why was she already getting herself worked up over her inability to orgasm? Sex was a biological need, an instinctual drive every adult animal obeyed. While love . . . Well outside of her grandparents, Gen had yet to witness one true-to-life example of romantic attachment. *Nana and Gramps are just freaks of nature, that's all.*

Case in point, she had to dig out an actual *key* to enter the house, as Gramps refused to upgrade to a thumbprint reader. The air smelled musty inside, since the cabin had been closed up for quite a while. Braving the cold, she threw open the windows to air the place out.

The cabin had six bedrooms and a spacious main living area. As testament to a technology-free life, the building didn't have any modern appliances. The windows were made of actual glass instead of insulated energy screens. The door sat on hinges and creaked when opened. Heat came from a woodstove and the large river-stone fireplace. Food was stored in an actual refrigerator and prepared on a gas stove. They didn't even have a microwave, for pity's sake, technology so old it outdated Nana!

Despite its rustic nature, this cabin, with its view of the lake and the foothills of the Adirondacks beyond, was Gen's favorite spot in the world. Resting her palm and forehead against the glass, she watched night roll in. A small measure of peace filled her, the first since she'd been fired. The world slowed down here, let her catch her breath, focus on the important stuff. *If I could just figure out what the important stuff is.*

A shiver of anticipation flowed through her. What would this session be like? Would these professionals ease her in, or would they expect to perform the moment they walked through the door? The cold air from the open window made her nipples tighten into rigid peaks that jolted awareness through her. *I am really going to do this!*

Her comm unit chirped, relaying a message. With an automated prompt, she asked for vocal replay only and busied her hands with lighting a fire in the grate.

"Hi, Gen, it's Alison. We've got four pleasure companions lined up, but one, Marshal, can't make it until tomorrow due to a prior commitment. Javier, Steven, and Franco will be there by seven o'clock. They're all good guys, no history of violence or criminal records. But make sure you ask for ID before you let them in, okay? Remember, you are the one holding the reins. They're there for you." Silence reigned, and Gen could imagine Alison sucking in a breath. "I really appreciate this. Call me when you have a little downtime and update me on your progress."

The message ended as Gen struck a match. Javier, Steven, and Franco with a Marshal kicker. She didn't feel brave—more like psychotic for having agreed to this madness. Four men were coming here to fuck her senseless. A slow grin stole across her face. *Secret shopper, my lily-white ass. I'm a slut in training.*

Her heart rate kicked into overdrive as she thought about the logistics of it. If they were all as hot as Franco, maybe she'd be able to come after all.

Glancing at her comm timepiece, she saw she had an hour to get ready for their arrival. Hauling all her stuff out of the car, Gen set up for her stay, planning where she'd do what with whomever had been selected. She'd just hopped out of the shower when a knock sounded on the outer door.

Taking a moment to survey herself in the mirror, Gen studied her violet eyes, apple cheeks, and long, dark wet hair that was only just starting to thread through with gray. Opening the towel, she stared at her full breasts, softly rounded belly, and the dark tangle of curls at the apex of her thighs. *Venus on the half shell, anyone?*

The knock came again, and she dropped the towel and slipped her arms through the sleeves of her silk robe. Her eyes glowed with a primal knowledge, anticipation zinging through her veins like lightning bolts. *Javier, Steven, Franco, and Marshal, you don't know what you're about to get yourselves into.*

"Damn, *chica*, you are totally fuckable." The dark-haired Hispanic man gave Gen a quick up-and-down look and smirked. "This ain't gonna be no hardship."

Gen blinked, not sure she'd heard him right. Had he paid her a compliment? Somehow, being called "totally fuckable" didn't seem to warrant a thank-you. "Won't you please come in?"

Double entendre much, Genevieve?

"Yeah, man, move your hairy ass. It's fracking cold out here." A massive blond shoved the first man out of the way. He didn't even glance at Gen as he stomped his way inside. "Hurry up, Franco. Let's shut the door sometime this century."

Franco scowled at the other two as he entered the cabin, which seemed much smaller than it had before the testosterone level had spiked to cardiac-arrest levels. He turned to face Gen, and his expression thawed. "Nice to see you again so soon, my lovely." In a curiously old-fashioned gesture, he took her hand and bent low to brush his lips over her knuckles. His long dark hair was pulled into a tight braid. She wondered if he suspected that she was more than just a client.

"Jesus, man. Enough with the fracking act already." The blond rubbed his hands vigorously, taking up residence in front of the fireplace.

Franco scowled at the other man's back. "Courtesy, Steven, is a habit, not an act."

Plastering what she hoped looked like a genuine smile on her face, Gen fell back into the role of hostess. "Anyone hungry?"

The blond, Steven, glanced over. "You bet your sweet ass we are. That was one hell of a trip, and I pulled a doubleheader last night. Need to feed the big soldier if you want the little one to stand to." He winked at Javier, who laughed.

Note to self: that was not a very sexy response. Steven seemed to have a bit of an attitude problem. Javier, uncouth though he may be, was at least trying. Franco was as smooth as ever, but something about him unsettled her. Nothing definitive she could report back to Alison. "I can just go and fix—" Gen started toward the kitchen, but Franco stopped her, placing a hand on her arm. His touch was light but somehow menacing at the same time.

"Dinner can wait. You are the client, and we should get started with you. Perhaps you need to warm up a bit. Come sit over by the fire." Franco took her hand in a firm grip and tugged her toward the hearth. Pushing lightly but insistently on her shoulders, he forced her down onto the couch. "Do you require something to drink? I can get you a glass of wine or maybe some hot tea?"

"No thanks." Gen got the feeling he was maneuvering her,

just as he had done the night before. Was his personality really so dominant that he would keep pushing her even when she felt unsure?

Slipping his hand beneath the crook of her knee, he used his thumb to lightly massage the skin there, a few buzzes from their health shields taking care of any unwanted guests at this private moment. Even under his masterful touch, her mind would not stop churning, and she froze up, bombarded with the stark reality.

Franco's mouth replaced his thumb as he kissed the sensitive skin at her knee. He wouldn't get paid if she didn't use him to satisfy herself sexually. She wondered what would happen if she told him to bugger off. Would he continue to push her against her will? Her gaze shifted to where Javier and Steven flanked the fireplace, exchanging significant glances at each other as though she and Franco didn't exist.

She recalled Alison's words about how *she* was supposed to be in control. *Fake it till you make it, babe.* Her mind flitted back to the best part of their earlier encounter, the part she'd missed when it was over. "Do you have that candle with you?"

His tongue darted out, licking a trail along her inner thigh, her germ shield preventing the wet contact. "Liked that, did you?" Lifting his head, he nodded to Javier, who lit the candle someone had perched on the fireplace. She watched the wick catch fire, seeming to spark, and felt a corresponding ignition deep within her belly. Knots of tension unfurled, letting her relax and enjoy his ministrations.

"Good girl," Franco murmured as she sank back into the soft cushions of the couch, ready to let him do whatever he intended. She was just the town bike this time out—everyone got to ride. Not yet, though; she hadn't advanced that far and wanted to work her way up the ladder, not have a line waiting for her services. "Can we have a little privacy, please?"

Doors closed, and she smiled down at Franco. "We're really going to do this again, huh?"

"Tell me what you like, Genevieve." His hands started working on her bathrobe, fumbling with the knot there. Had she really tied it so tightly? Oh well, she didn't feel even remotely interested in helping him. Big, strong man could work this out all by his lonesome.

Feeling coy all of a sudden, she asked, "What's your specialty?"

He glanced up from her ritualistic disrobement. "Domination, of course."

She thought about that for a beat. "Like whips and chains, bondage—that kind of thing?"

Through clenched teeth, he explained, "Those are just props. Domination is all about control."

She fingered his braid, enjoying the silky texture of it. "And you like to be in control. Is that right, Franco?"

"It's my specialty." The frantic tugging increased. "I'm a master in the art of shibari. I have tied up countless bottoms with intricate patterns designed to stimulate as well as immobilize the willing recipient."

A little thrill shot straight to her core. "Tell me more about the . . . stimulation."

"I prefer to show rather than tell." The corner of his mouth kicked up. "Would you like to play at submissive for me, Gen?"

The idea intrigued her. What better way to shop out Franco's abilities than to have him play on his area of expertise? "I'm not into pain."

He smiled. "There are many different levels of shibari. Tease and denial are often used to add a little . . . spice to vanilla sex. First thing, though, you need to pick a safe word."

She felt her eyebrows draw together in confusion. "Safe word?"

He stroked his finger down between her eyebrows in a featherlight touch. "Something you wouldn't ordinarily say, a code that if you speak aloud, I will stop whatever I'm doing immediately."

Her mind went blank. "Um . . . ?"

Franco took pity on her. "How about the name of a place? A city you've never been to."

"New Chicago? I heard that the rebuilding on the hover foundation attached to the old city is almost as good as in New New York." Gen winced as her babble switch flipped to the gibbering setting. She couldn't help it; she always prattled when she felt nervous.

From the look on Franco's face, he considered stuffing a ball gag in her mouth. She wanted to hide, but then she remembered that any negative experience was his fault, not hers. After a lifetime of taking on the blame for everything, she had to school herself to remember that. With another glance at the candle, she squared her shoulders and lifted her chin.

Franco raised an eyebrow. "New Chicago it is."

He reached into his man bag and extracted a length of white rope. "For this session, you will call me *nawashi.*"

"Why?"

"Loosely translated, it means 'master rope artist.' Stand up and disrobe." His tone brooked no argument.

Gen's heart kicked in her chest and her mouth went dry. Slowly, she rose from the couch and worked free the loosened knot on her bathrobe. With an easy shrug, the fabric slipped off her shoulders and pooled at her feet.

Franco surveyed her from head to toe, his expression pleased. "Very good. Do not resist my orders, because you want this even more than I do."

God help her, she did. She wanted to know what that rope felt like across her naked skin. It looked so smooth, and the way he stroked it between his tanned fingers was incredibly arousing. He slid it back and forth in an erotic rhythm, the tight weave not even the least bit frayed. Perhaps she could fully let herself go if she knew the rope would contain her.

He nodded once, as if satisfied. "Spread your legs."

She moved her feet a few inches apart.

"More," he barked, and she jumped to obey.

"Very good." He trailed the rope over her shoulder and down her arm. "Feel the power in the rope. It's dormant now, but touching your body will wake it up until it's a living, breathing thing."

"Like the candle," she whispered, seeking it out again. The flame seemed to wink at her, and for a moment, she saw another face, another man smiling at her, pure light in his eyes.

The vision dispersed when Franco took hold of her left arm and then her right, pulling them behind her until they met at the small of her back. He slid the rope over the sensitive skin of her wrists, wrapping the cord around and teasing back and forth. Every muscle in her body grew taut, clenching.

There was a sharp tugging, and she bit back a moan as he cinched her wrists together. She struggled against it, but the knot held firm, not yielding an inch.

"Do you want more?"

Gen didn't know, but she wasn't about to back out now. Gaze locked on the candle, she nodded.

"Are you wet?"

"Yes." His commanding presence did nothing for her, but the feel of the rope and the flickering candle light had aroused her body. With a start, she realized it was the teasing she enjoyed, the anticipation.

He brushed the ends of the rope over the swells of her ass and her sex clenched. Instead of moving the rope down as she half hoped he would, he doubled the line and wrapped it around her waist, not tightly like a belt but more like an embrace, like a lover circling his arms around her.

Eyelids at half-mast, she watched Franco angle the rope to just above her hips with enough play to move her hands away from her back a few inches. Restrained, yet not entirely immobilized.

Once her binding was in place, he rose to his full height, purposefully trailing the ends of the rope over her pubic hair. His every move held intent, meant to provoke an erotic response, and Gen appreciated his adept skill. The same way she would enjoy a fine work of art displayed in a museum or a night at the symphony. From a distance.

Fingers gliding over the smooth rope as though masturbating it, Franco watched her. "You want to feel the rope caress your sex, don't you?"

She licked her lips and nodded.

Crouching before her, he skillfully measured out the exact amount. Then, eyes fixed on her face, he tied a knot in the length with an abrupt tug. A whimper escaped her and he smiled, obviously pleased by her response.

Slowly, he eased the rope between her legs. The knot brushed against her engorged clit and her channel clenched. Her knees felt rubbery, as though they would give out at any moment. Franco maneuvered the smooth length through the tender folds of her labia, so every part of her could experience the unusual and delicious touch.

The glide of the fibers through her sopping wet sex created a delicious friction. Her lube coated the rope, easing its way. The knot pressed against the bud at the top of her cleft. Her chest rose and fell in time with her rapid breaths, her heartbeat thundering in her ears.

"Do you feel it? The power the rope wields over you? The power I have over you?" As though to illustrate his point, he let go. The rope fell away, dangling down the front of her body uselessly.

She groaned in frustration. "Put it back."

"I beg you to put it back, nawashi," he corrected.

Staring straight into his eyes unflinchingly, Gen said, "New Chicago."

He blinked. "What's wrong? You were enjoying yourself."

Frustration sharpened her tongue. "Yeah, and you keep getting in the way. Just like last time."

His mouth fell open. "What do you mean? You came like a rocket."

"I was faking it."

He reared back and rose to his full height. "What the hell are you talking about? I felt you go off!"

His narrow-eyed glare didn't intimidate her. She thrust her breasts forward, lifted her chin. Even naked with both arms tied behind her back, she could take this guy. "I'm just that damn good."

He ran a shaky hand through his hair. "I don't need this crap. I'm outta here."

The door slammed behind him as he left, leaving her arms bound and her gaze riveted on the candle, which danced merrily as if in celebration.

5

"What the fuck do you mean, Franco quit?" Steven thundered as Javier untied her. "Where the hell is he?"

"He's gone. Took the rental and zipped off." The men exchanged another look of silent communication, and Javier held out his hands, palms up. Her fingers tingled as circulation returned. Gen shrugged back into her robe, stealthily storing the rope in her pocket. One day, after she met the right man, it might come in handy. Javier helped her to her feet, and she made a beeline for the candle. For some bizarre reason, she couldn't bear to let it out of her sight.

"Day-um, that must be some snatch you're packing to make a seasoned pro like Franco hightail it after just one shot." Javier licked his lips. "Is it my turn yet?"

He activated his germ shield and unfastened his pants with a speed that made her dizzy. His erection stood straight out, demanding attention. Gen studied it, biting the inside of her lip to keep from laughing and insulting him. What was it about the sight of a naked man that was so damn funny?

She turned to Steven to get a male reaction to the same stimulus and was surprised to see he'd looked away. A flush of red stained his cheeks, and his shoulders had rounded as though he was bracing for a hit. She glanced back at Javier, who had started stroking his shaft and eyeing the gap in her robe where her cleavage was revealed, then to where Steven's erection tented his sweatpants as he stole little glimpses of Javier's movements.

Gen stroked her finger over the wax base of the candle. "Follow me, gentlemen." Without looking back to see if they followed her, she headed toward one of the spare bedrooms.

"You're going to take both of us on at once?" Steven's voice sounded strained. Gen ignored him as she set the burning candle on the dresser. The loss of warmth ran deeper than just missing the heat it yielded, almost as though it melted something deep inside of her.

Funny, the wax hadn't been displaced at all even though it had been lit over an hour ago. She wondered if it was some experimental kind of illumination, but she felt the heat from the flame.

Dismissing her curiosity, she dug through the boxes of supplies the men had brought with them. One crate had obviously been Franco's, as all sorts of restraints and handcuffs in every color of the rainbow nested inside, a tribute to his profession. Gen set that crate to the side.

The next one held all sorts of creams and lotions, every flavor she'd ever heard of and then some. She glanced at Javier. "What's your preference?"

A huge grin split his face and he winked at her. "Strawberry."

Sorting through the stack, she came up with a bottle of strawberry-flavored warming lubrication and tossed it to him. Snatching it out of midair, he flicked the top up. "Come here so I can lube you up good."

Gen shook her head. "Nuh-uh. Not for me. For him." She pointed at Steven.

Both men's eyes went wide. "What?"

She focused on Steven and gestured over the open crate. "Pick a flavor, any flavor."

His mouth opened and closed a few times before he finally uttered, "Vanilla."

She chucked it at him, then hefted herself up on the dresser next to her candle. "Whenever you're ready."

Steven looked from the bottle in his hand to Javier, then back to her. "Gen, I don't know what you're trying to do here, but we're not—"

She waved her hand in a sharp, slicing motion. "I want to watch. Customer's always right, right? I've seen the way you two look at each other. Now I want the whole show."

There was no further hesitation, and Gen grinned as they came together, arms reaching, bodies caressing. Her instincts had been right. They wanted each other more than either wanted her. They were both handsome men, and watching them was aesthetically pleasing in every sense.

Masculine lips met, tongues twining together. Their skin gleamed golden in the light of the flickering candle and the moonlight spilling in through the east-facing window.

Entranced by the erotic sight, Gen's breath came out in shallow pants. Javier's dark brown hands smoothed down Steven's heavily muscled shoulders, his short nails clutching his lover to him. Inexplicably, her nipples tightened, abrading against the silky fabric of her robe. The reaction eased something she hadn't realized was bound in her chest as tightly as one of Franco's intricate knots.

Her thighs tingled when Steven bent Javier backward, bracing himself in position to trail his lips and tongue down the smooth chest. Worshipping his way down to the jutting erection waiting for his attention. Liquid heat pooled between her thighs, and for a moment she thought she might come from observing the sensual dance.

Yup, that settled it. Two men together were not about the foreplay. She bit her lip as Steven sucked the straining cock into his mouth, his hands molded to the back of the other man's thighs, creeping upward to cup his butt. Gen squirmed on the dresser, tilting her head, greedy to see everything at once. Javier's chest heaving, his dark brown fingers tunneled into Steven's blond hair. He placed his feet flat on the mattress to help him buck his hips toward the sensual onslaught.

Steven pulled back, until just the tip of his tongue laved the slit of Javier's cock head. Moisture beaded there, and he swirled it around with his thumb, his gaze roving up the smaller man's shuddering body.

The look shared between them was so intimate, Gen felt horribly guilty for watching what should be a private moment. Job or not, she wouldn't want her lovemaking put on display. "I'll just leave you two alone . . ."

Steven glanced over his shoulder at her and winked. "You can watch if you want. We're good with that."

"Oh, she wants. Would you look at the pretty blush on her cheeks?" Javier winked at her. "Does watching him suck my cock do it for you?"

She nodded. "It makes no sense to me, but yeah, more than anything has in a long time." She'd sort out the whys later. Now was all about living in the moment.

"Then you're gonna love this." Javier flipped open the top to the strawberry lotion and pulled Steven up to him so their tongues could tangle. His hands glistened as they smoothed over the bulging muscles along Steven's arms, chest, and taut abdomen. The lube shimmered in the light of the flickering candle. Steven moaned as Javier sucked his earlobe into his mouth, whispering words too low for Gen to hear. Javier licked his way down the other man's neck, his dark-skinned hands skimming across every bulge and dip in a sensual caress.

She bit her lip when Javier straddled Steven's chest, mounting the larger man and lying across the top of him so his mouth aligned with Steven's erection. His gaze locked with hers as the tip of his tongue darted out to trace the thick pulsing vein on his lover's shaft. Glistening hands wrapped around him from behind, scooting his hips back until they formed a sparkly sixty-nine position.

Gen had been wrong; they were *all* about the foreplay, teasing each other, working themselves up and then stopping before they reached the point of no return. Like a contest in which one player would up the ante to see who could hold out the longest. Javier caressed Steven's balls, hefting the twin weights while he deep-throated his lover's cock. Steven gasped and retaliated by lubing his fingers and inserting them into Javier's ass. Javier groaned and rolled to the side. Splaying Steven's legs wide, he licked the small bundle of nerves centered on the other man's anus. All while his hand pumped faster on Steven's cock. Their dexterity and flexibility amazed her. Sweat mingled with the gleaming oil as each man strained, loving each other with lips and tongues, their hands and minds all working toward mutual release.

Gen's body clenched up as they found their satisfaction, the amount of pheromones in the room making her dizzy. Steven came all over Javier's chest, while swallowing what his lover's body yielded.

Though she really wanted to keep watching, she popped up off the dresser and gathered her candle and the coconut verbena lotion she'd pilfered. Afterglow was not a moment they ought to be forced to share with a secret shopper.

They didn't look away from each other as she shut the door behind her. With a sigh, she murmured, "And then there was one." She headed to her room, the only one with a private bath. Stopping to check her reflection in the mirror, Gen wondered if it wasn't better to just admit defeat now. She'd craved sex, real, honest, raw, heel-pounding sex. The cherry on top of Alison's sweet offer. But with those guys . . . *Not gonna happen.*

Rhys had never been more aroused in his entire life. Gen wanted him, couldn't bear to be parted from him, or at least from the candle, which essentially was him since his own body lay in stasis on a distant world. The click of the door closed them in together. He sensed no other person in the room, but her emotional frequencies were so bright that any other being would be a pale reflection, a moon to her burning sun.

Though he could feel no direct connection to the candle, he knew she was touching it, and he pressed his empathic essence against the wax wall, trying desperately to touch her back. She could free him, just like she'd done before, give him enough emotional fortification to manifest into corporeal form once again. And once he got there, then what?

One step at a time, Rhys.

Her arousal was a deep pink, and he drank it in greedily, pulling on her mental desire. She was a smoking-hot love goddess, a volcano that needed to erupt. Rhys understood what those other men had missed—Gen wanted to be wanted, to be craved like the delicious morsel she was, yet he had no way to convey his admiration to her.

But he could stoke her fire. Collecting all his pilfered energy, he projected the thought directly into her head. *Go lie on the bed.*

Fabric rustled and bedsprings creaked. A soft thump as she put the burning candle down, and he could imagine how she looked. The warm radiance from the candle's flame would seem to dance over her skin, heating her flesh as it kissed her, caressed her like a lover's touch.

Run your hands over your body.

With a moan, she did and he imagined the feel of her beautiful, full breasts cupped in his hands, the silk of her skin as he trailed his fingers over her luscious curves. Her breaths came out in short, sharp pants, her desire intensifying as her pull on him grew stronger than that of the candle.

More, he urged her, eager to break free, to see the pleasure written across her face when she climaxed. To be the reason she exploded. *Show me where you want me next. Show me how wet you are for me, how ready your body is to be filled.*

A breathy sigh escaped and she answered him out loud. "I wish you would kiss me."

Oh, I want that. You have no idea how much I want to taste every last bit of you, until you beg me to stop.

It wasn't enough, the pull of the candle was still too strong as her desire plateaued. What would send her over the edge? He recalled his fantasy, of what he most wanted to do to her.

Let me lick you, Gen.

"Oh, yes," she gasped, on the verge of going up in flames herself. His prompt sent her higher, and his essence was pulled toward her, the strongest emotional presence available.

Concentrating, Rhys focused his energy into taking humanoid shape once more. To her he would look, sound, and feel absolutely real, but he was a shallow echo of the man he had been, his mind and soul divided from his body.

He gazed down at the erotic banquet on the bed. She was even more incredible than he remembered. The flush of her face—eyes squeezed tightly shut, both hands between her legs, one rubbing steadily on her clit and the other plunging in and out of her wet core. She cried out in frustration, grasping for the release that eluded her.

Rhys refused to make her wait another second. Though he wanted to fall on her like a ravening beast, he sensed that right now, at this moment, she needed tenderness. If he did it right, there would be time for more later. He eased onto the mattress, positioning himself between her spread thighs, careful not to disturb her until he was ready for his first taste.

His tongue darted out to caress the entrance to her body. She stiffened, her eyes still squeezed tightly shut. He pushed deeper, loving the sweet lube that poured from her in a wet rush. He kissed her fingers, which still worked her clit in a frenzy.

Why hadn't she stopped him? Or at least opened her eyes and demanded his identity? The notion that she didn't care rankled, especially after all the time he'd spent envisioning this exact moment. He needed to see her come.

"Look at me, Gen."

Her head thrashed wildly. "No, I can't. I'll lose it . . ."

He licked again, his tongue dragging through her folds slowly, savoring her. "I want to see your eyes, watch your face as I send you over. Please, give me this."

It was the "please" that did it. Her eyelids fluttered up, and she gasped as their gazes locked. Something clicked into place as he stared into the blue-violet depths, innocent and wanton, hot and cold, all delectable woman. His for the taking.

Rhys smiled and licked his lips. Her chest heaved, her straining nipples pointed toward the ceiling. He circled one taut bud, then drew his index finger down her abdomen. The digit was calloused, such a delicious contrast to her smooth skin, and she shivered as he moved it lower, between her legs.

She cried out wordlessly as he tormented her engorged clit. Her fingers threaded through his hair, holding him to her.

"Are you real?" she whispered.

"Thanks to you," he breathed deeply, then dipped back down, suckling her flesh, making her entire body tremble. His fingers thrust inside her at the same moment he tugged her clit with his lips, thrashing the bud with his tongue in a quick trilling motion. She screamed, and cataclysmic release ripped through her like a whirlwind.

On and on it went, with him guiding her body through one orgasm, barely letting her down before boosting her up as another wave crashed through her. He kept his movements sure and confident, reveling in her absolute bliss. After too short a time, she tugged him away, begging, just like he'd wanted. "Please, no more."

He owed her everything. As he moved back, his mind whirled. How could he explain it all to her, make her understand?

A beautiful flush of red stained her cheeks and she bit her lip. "So, I guess you're Marshal."

He didn't want to lie to her. After all, she was his savior, and he needed her strong emotions to help sustain him until he could be reunited with his body. His ephemeral form could only accomplish so much. While his flesh and soul remained separated, the threat of imprisonment in the candle was very real.

Staring into her beautiful violet eyes, he dismissed the tender feelings he longed to nurture and moved ahead with what had to be done.

"Yes, yes, I am."

6

The soft locks of his red-gold hair brushed over her legs as he moved back, putting space between them as though he recognized her need to gather her thoughts. "You are a truly magnificent gift, Gen. Never have I felt desire the way you experience it."

Maybe her brain was addled from the glorious release, but something about his words seemed peculiar. She surveyed him now from a distance and found him just as mouthwateringly incredible. His skin had a honey hue, so unusual with that flame-colored hair. His face was hard, angular, with sharply bladed cheekbones and a cleft in his chin. However, it was his jade-green eyes and the fire burning within that nearly stopped her heart. His was not the face of a man who drifted through life content with the cards he'd been dealt. He possessed drive, purpose. He was hard everywhere, including the enormous erection pointed directly at her. God, how she wanted that inside her, stretching her, giving her another one of those cataclysmic orgasms.

But her embarrassment was stronger than her desire. Jeez,

he'd walked right on in on her masturbating and had helped himself to her goodies. As Nana would say, that makes for a fine how-do-you-do!

She shuddered, really not comfortable thinking about Nana after what they had just been doing.

If she was a more experienced kind of girl, she would grab hold of that stiff cock and return the favor. It wouldn't be a chore. Her tongue darted out as she thought about licking and sucking on him. In fact, she was sort of surprised he hadn't suggested it already. But the small smile playing across firm masculine lips was one of satisfaction, as though he was content to simply look at her. To just be with her.

"Wow, you're . . . very different from the others."

The smile grew as if he liked what she'd said. "How exactly?"

She thought about it for a beat. "I'm not really sure. It's just a feeling, like you actually want to be here with me, instead of have to be here with me as part of your job."

His green eyes glowed in the dim light. "I do want to be here with you, Gen. You have no idea how much."

Her gaze dropped to his erection. "I've got a pretty decent idea."

Easing up over the top of her, he guided her to lie back until his body surrounded hers like a living blanket. He zeroed in on her face. The intense connection she'd experienced when she'd first seen him returned, as if she'd been waiting for him all her life.

His red-gold hair formed a curtain around them as he rested his forehead against hers. "I know how much you want me. I can sense your needs."

She felt her eyebrows draw together. "What do you mean?"

Their skin barely touched, but she felt as though he enveloped her completely. "I'm an empath."

Her lips parted, but she didn't know how to respond to his

statement. An empath? Like a life-sized mood ring? She couldn't think between his overwhelming presence and her body's eager response to it. He stole her breath, scattered her already-frazzled wits.

He took advantage of the situation and swept his tongue into her mouth in a lusty kiss. His mouth tasted of salt and spice and her recent orgasm. Gen shivered as he tangled his tongue with hers in slow strokes, exploring her mouth as if he had all the time in the world. That rock-hard shaft brushed over her belly, and without conscious thought, she lifted her hips, letting her body ask for the fulfillment it desperately craved.

He didn't hesitate to grab his erection and align it with her sex. His eyes remained fixed on her face, and he entered her in one smooth thrust.

Though she had thought her body had been adequately prepared, he stretched her on a rack somewhere between pleasure and pain. Too much, too soon and still not enough. He studied her face for a moment with a quizzical arch to his brow, as though they weren't intimately joined, and then shifted his body up so he didn't fill her quite as fully. Rocking back and forth, he slid in and out of her and pressed the base of his shaft against her clit.

Sensation swamped her. She cried out, digging her nails into his muscular shoulders, losing a piece of herself in his green eyes.

"Gods, Gen," he gasped, leaning into his weight, pressing down harder on that sweet spot. "You amaze me."

He slowly withdrew and rocked forward again, observing her every reaction to his movements. Tension coiled tighter in her core, and she had to squeeze her eyes shut for fear of losing herself completely.

He stilled. "No, sweetness, I need you to look at me. Open your eyes, let me see your pleasure."

"I can't . . ." She shook her head wildly. "It's too much."

The feather-light touch of his lips brushed across her cheek. "Please. Let me see you."

She could no more deny him than she could deny herself. Though her eyelids felt weighted down, she managed to look up at him.

He rewarded her with a glorious smile before rearing back and lifting her legs to his shoulders so he could thrust more deeply inside of her slick passage.

As his cock head stroked her G-spot, she gave in to the tide of release, holding his gaze the entire time.

He stayed within her until the last ripple of pleasure left. Then slowly he withdrew his still-hard shaft from her body. Lying on his side, he faced her as though entranced by the sight of her.

"You didn't come?" she asked as she reached for him, curling her fingers around his erection, glorying in the intimate contact.

"I can't." He bucked into her hold, groaning into her mouth as he kissed her. This was what she wanted. No orchestration or awkward commands, just her enjoying him and him seeming to relish her. He made it so easy, the way she imagined sex with a professional ought to be. His cock was slick with her lube, and she swirled her thumb over the head, delighting in the skin-to-skin contact.

"Wait!" Gen gasped, shoving him away.

He released her at once. "What's the matter?"

"My germ shield wasn't up." Licking her dry lips, she forced her gaze away. "I thought I was alone, so I didn't activate my shield when you . . . when we were . . ."

"When I pleasured you." He didn't appear at all concerned. In fact, a grin tugged at the corners of his mouth, and the fire in his eyes, combined with his huge hard-on told her he would be more than willing to do it all again.

She reached for her robe, clearing her throat even as her pulse pounded. "This is serious, a health code violation."

He moved closer until she could feel the heat off his body. The candle flickered, casting their shadows against the wall. "I won't tell if you won't."

She stared up into his eyes, and the temptation to pretend that what he suggested was completely acceptable nearly overwhelmed her. Pressing her fingertips to the bridge of her nose, she muttered, "It would be irresponsible, especially considering your line of work."

He reached out, tucking a strand of hair behind her ear. "If it pleases you, by all means, use your health guard."

She activated her shield. "What about you?"

His face didn't hold a trace of guile as he said, "I do not have one."

"What?" Gen scooted back, wary. "How is that even possible? Everyone is equipped with a permanent shield at adolescence. You can't enter high school without one."

He held his hands out, palms up. "I'm not a citizen of your world. Besides, it's impossible for me to carry disease or impregnate you in this form."

She shook her head. "I don't understand."

He paused, as though choosing his words carefully. "Right now, my body is an empathic projection. One I want to use to pleasure you endlessly, because your fulfillment makes me stronger, more real."

She sucked in a breath as he drew his thumb along her collarbone, the sensual glide dulled somewhat by her germ shield. Again she was tempted to shut it off, but she didn't know anything about Marshal. He could be lying through his teeth. "I'm not sure I'm up for this."

Those luminous eyes searched hers. "You don't need to pretend with me, Gen. I feel your desire. I can use it, stoke your fire until it burns hot and warms us both."

The way he touched her, she had no doubt he could deliver on his promise.

He sucked on her ear and then breathed, "Do you want to watch them again?"

It took her brain a moment to catch up with her hormones. "You mean Steven and Javier?"

He smiled and the skin around his eyes crinkled, lending him a mischievous air. "You watched them earlier. Seeing the two of them together awoke your passions."

How did he know about that? She narrowed her eyes on him, feeling as though she were missing something. With a wave of his hand, the wall between the rooms became transparent. She straightened up, totally awed by the spectacle of male flesh. Both men were still naked, their skin glistening in the light. Javier stood facing them, his erection jutting proudly. Steven had positioned himself behind his lover and rocked his hips in a slow, rhythmic dance. Gen gasped as he bit the tendons on Javier's neck while caressing his hand over the other man's swollen shaft. It took her a moment to realize what was missing.

"They don't have their germ shields up."

Marshal knelt behind her on the bed, mirroring Steven's pose. His stiff erection prodded the small of her back through the thin fabric of her robe. His hands pulled the material away from her breasts, cupping them and kneading her aching flesh. "They are in love. Technology designed to distance people from one another has no place in true bonds of the heart."

His fingers teased her nipples, and she leaned back into him, watching the erotic show he'd provided while enjoying his languorous touch. Her nails rasped over the fine red-gold hair on his arms, and she swayed slightly, enjoying his ministrations.

"Why does seeing them turn you on? Do you wish to join them?" he whispered in her ear as his fingers trailed down to her sex. His hands ghosted over her flesh, the tiny sparks having nothing to do with germ shields. Spreading her legs to grant him better access, she let him do with her as he would, eager to see and feel what would happen next.

They were beautiful together. Steven's eyes grew heavy-lidded as he urged Javier to bend forward on the bed, his hands caressing the smaller man's spine all the way down to the cleft of his ass. Marshal stroked her clit until she shivered.

Javier turned his head sideways to gaze up at his lover, trust and rapture written clearly across his face.

"No," she breathed. "There's no room for me in that scene. They only have eyes for each other."

Marshal urged her down onto the mattress until she mirrored Javier's receptive pose. Her sex was wetter than she'd ever been. His fingers trailed down the bumps of her spine until he filled her sheath from behind. Stroking the sensitive tissues and making her pant until she was desperate for more.

"Is it the unknown you crave, your desire to do that which you have never done?" To underscore his point, he circled her anus with a fingertip. She wanted to ask how he knew she'd never engaged in anal sex before, but what he was doing felt too sinful to challenge. She had no idea how he continued to keep his wits about him during this sensual interrogation. She could barely recall her own last name.

His hand slid farther down to delve into her saturated folds, and she gasped, reveling in his skillful touch. Rocking her hips back to meet his questing fingers, she shook her head. "That might be part of it, but there's more."

Out of the corner of her eye, she watched Steven stroke his cock. Marshal withdrew from her, and she envisioned him doing the same thing behind her, coating her lube over his un-shielded penis. She bit her lip when she felt the blunt head of his shaft probe the entrance to her body. As if they had choreographed it, Marshal and Steven thrust forward in sync. She and Javier cried out in unison, receptive to what their lovers needed to give.

Lost in the sensation of her flesh joined with his, she watched the erotic show next door, enjoying Marshal's possession. Her germ shield didn't even waver, lending credibility to his story that he had no real, solid genetic material. She would ask him more about it later.

Gen leaned her head on her folded arms and panted, torn between watching Javier and Steven's pleasure and closing her eyes to enjoy the way her body was being thoroughly invaded.

Marshal made the choice for her. "Look at them again. Tell me what it is you want, Gen. What do you desire?" His fingertips swirled over her clit in time to the stirring of his cock in her wet channel.

She turned her head to face the wall, watching as Steven increased his pace, thrusting inside Javier while stroking his lover's cock feverishly. Javier pushed back against the headboard, an eager recipient for everything Steven did. They worked each other, both lost in a shared dream turned reality. She turned away from the spectacle, ready with her answer. "It's the feeling, the emotional connection with another person. The trust is what I want."

His body stopped in mid-thrust, fit snuggly inside her, the head nestled up against her G-spot. "Then trust me. Let me love you the way you need to be loved."

The word *love* made her breath catch in the back of her throat. Was he serious? "I don't know anything about you. Other than you know your way around a woman's body. "

He leaned forward, impaling her fully so he could whisper in her ear, "Not just any woman, Gen. *You*. You are who I need."

Her heart pounded in her chest, eager to accept his offer, no matter how foolish it might seem. Pivoting back to the wall, she watched Steven delve deep inside Javier with sharp lunges. Javier's hand curled over Steven's, and he pumped his shaft until white jets of semen spurted out past their clenched fists. Both wore an expression of utter bliss.

Could she have that too? Was Marshal playing up some fantasy, or was he for real? "I don't know. . . ."

"Do you want to see what I really am, know what I am capable of? I want your permission before I enter your body."

Since she could feel the evidence of him deep inside her, she wasn't sure what he meant, but curiosity and the need to keep him with her as long as she possibly could urged her to nod. "You can do whatever you wish to me."

The vision on the wall died off as her lover turned into a shimmering gold mist and seeped inside her body. The world went dark.

7

Rhys opened his—Gen's—eyes and sat up. The candle still danced merrily, unaware that its captive had possession of a real body for the first time in months. Her consciousness lay dormant, a passenger in the vehicle of her own flesh.

What demon had possessed him to take her over like this? Maybe it was her total abandonment in the throes of ecstasy. He'd reveled in her carnal delight even while he'd envied the joy she experienced. Jealousy was a forbidden emotion to one of his order, a serious violation of their moral code. Those they helped to heal entrusted them with their physical and mental selves, a most sacred honor. The brotherhood would strip him of rank, perhaps even excommunicate him if they discovered he'd used his abilities for sexual gratification. Even if it was not his own.

If that was what they decided, he wouldn't fight their edict. But he had to free them all first.

Before he could do that, he had to get to know Gen's physical form, literally from the inside out. Breathing deep, he tested her lung capacity, listened to the rhythmic *lub-dubbing* of her strong heartbeat.

Shifting his weight, he stretched and rolled to his side. First he focused on large motor functions, stretching limbs and contracting the muscles in her core to sit up. He surveyed the room through her eyes. Though his emotional resonance could perceive a three-dimensional world, the vivid colors and rich textures didn't translate the same as when he took on corporeal form. Commanding his hands to trace over the comforter, he luxuriated in the soft fabric. Her hands were beautiful, with long elegant fingers, the hands of an artist. Reaching around, he traced sensitive fingertips over the skin on her forearm. Smooth, magnificent, and utterly glorious.

He had cohabitated his emotional resonance with willing souls more times than he could count, so being a woman was not exactly a new experience for him. But never before had he craved the emotional depth inside of one of his partners.

Earlier, as he'd pleasured Gen's body, uttered the words he thought she wanted to hear, he'd watched her aura grow brighter, more vibrant until it shot through with purple and gold sparks. He'd tuned in to her frequency, and as with any choice drug, it made him crave more and more until he would risk anything to be closer to its source.

From inside her he could feel again, like a real person. Anger rose as he thought of how he'd been forced to survive, imprisoned on a whim by a greedy company eager to test the emotional controls the empaths could exert. Using them to ease the anxiety of nervous clients was just the beginning. Piecing together bits of conversations he'd heard, Rhys understood that the colony Illustra had enslaved was the tip of the iceberg. The ultimate goal was to control people in power, government officials, military leaders, all directed by caged empaths, who would feast on lust, pride, greed, and rage just to live. The humans they fed from would be imprisoned themselves, subjugated to their own overwhelming desires.

For the sake of his people and hers, Rhys had to proceed with Gen's seduction.

Would she help him? She was such a startling mix of contradictions, bold and recalcitrant, passionate yet thoughtful and a little bit cagey.

"Gen?" He spoke her name aloud, eager to get back to their play. He used her hands to cup her breasts, the tips of which were still pebbled. Lube coated her luscious sex and the insides of her thighs, evidence of her arousal.

Marshal? What's going on? Why can't I see anything? The apprehensive thought resounded in her brain, and he could hear her clearly.

"I wanted to play with you, sweetness. From deep inside you, I can better orchestrate your pleasure." Dipping a hand down into the pocket of her robe, he fingered the rope Franco had used on her earlier. The knot was still pulled taut, and he imagined uncoiling the length and having her straddle it while he worked it over her wet folds, the friction rubbing her to climax.

He felt a tremble of excitement, and her heartbeat kicked into high gear. Gen could still sense what he did with her hands, with her body, and he needed to explore further, deeper, for both of their sakes.

"I don't have enough coordination to do that to you right now, my sweet, but how about a bath?"

He could sense her eagerness. From this close range, she could keep no secrets from him. Even an idle thought would flash from her mind to his. *You promise to stop if I don't like something you're doing?*

"I do," he spoke the words aloud and meant it. Because of his training, he still kept his secrets from her, specifically his true identity. Again uneasiness gripped him, but he pushed it aside and focused on maneuvering her body.

Sliding his feet over the edge of the bed, he leaned forward slowly, so as not to overbalance. He caught sight of her reflection in the glass mounted above the dressing table. A few shuffling steps drew them closer. Rhys took his time, learning the way her form naturally moved. When he reached the dresser, he rested his palms flat on the wood and surveyed Gen's body.

"You are absolute perfection," he breathed, taking in the sway of her generous breasts, the taut nipples that stood to attention from the chill in the room.

Thank you. He sensed her mingled embarrassment and pleasure at his heartfelt compliment. Such fascinating contradictions.

"Don't you see it?" He watched as her eyebrows drew down in the mirror, telegraphing his frustration.

Her embarrassment unfurled, showing him the self-conscious center she kept hidden behind bluster. *It's just a body.*

"No, it's so much more than that. The curves, the dips and hollows, so smooth. Gorgeous, perfect skin, soft hair," Rhys murmured, enjoying the sound of her voice. The pitch grew lower, huskier when heard through her ears. He trailed his fingertips over her gently rounded belly, the flare of her generous hips. "You are the incarnation of what a woman ought to be, what every man desires."

Not all men. Her mind flashed him a picture of Javier and Steven. He smiled in understanding.

"I'll grant you that. Should we go visit them?" He made the offer because he understood how much watching their play had distracted her from her mental composure. Truth be known, he didn't want to share her, even just to watch the others. She was his task and his pleasure all rolled into one.

And as long as he remained inside her, he would be safe from the pull of his wax prison.

No. They have things to work out on their own. I'm happy where I am.

He sagged, surprised at how much that relieved him. "So, bath, then?"

I'd like that.

Using her hands, Marshal explored her body, building arousal in their wake. The warm water felt heavenly, and after all the touching, she couldn't deny her craving for an orgasm or two or a dozen.

Hot water poured from the tap and lapped against her nipples. He'd also discovered the jets built into the oversized spa tub, the forced air maneuvering the water until it eased the knots along her spine.

"I need to get to know you, to better control your movements," he explained as his hands again went to her chest. Marshal had her totally blissed out with the way he touched, pinched, strummed, and stroked. She'd had no idea her breasts were so receptive to that sort of stimulation. Still she felt the need to offer a token protest.

That sounds like a very convenient excuse to me, Marshal, she all but purred.

His hands stilled and she sensed something had unsettled him. He didn't speak, though, and she couldn't read his thoughts the way he did hers.

What? Did I say something wrong?

After shutting the water off, he reclined her body back in the tub, letting the jets pulse against her while he continued to dabble. "I've never felt true arousal from a woman's perspective before. It's . . . unique."

So he didn't want to play question-and-answer. His dismissal hurt, but she shoved it away. He wasn't rejecting her, just the topic of conversation. She decided to retrench.

Now, why don't I believe that?

The organic loofah he washed her with dripped little splashes of water over her puckered nipples. "Believe what you will, Gen. But I'm no ladies' man."

Though she might be a total fool, she believed him. Curiosity goaded her into asking, *So, how is female arousal different?*

As if she'd given him permission, Marshal skimmed her hands down between her legs. "It's more scattered throughout your body, though no less intense. I feel it in your head and belly, as well as in your reproductive organs."

He made it sound so clinical, which was bizarre considering the tender way he stroked her clit, varying pressure and rhythm to see what her body responded to best. "How does this feel to you right now, Gen?"

Awesome, she thought before she could help it.

"Don't hide from it, sweetness. You have nothing to be ashamed of." He stroked harder until her hips rocked up to meet the touch. The finger traced lower, beneath the waterline.

Ripples from movement caused the bathwater to lap against her engorged clit. They gasped as one. He propped her foot up on the cold edge of the tub, spreading her legs wider. Fingers crept down, thrumming her clit wickedly until her hips bucked. He pushed her finger in to swirl in the wetness there.

"Oh, Gen, this need to be filled, it's unbelievable." The fingers plunged deep again, exploring the delicate tissues inside her sex. "How can you stand it? It's not enough and too much all at once."

You get used to it. . . . She groaned when the fingers vanished, only to brush against her lips. *Don't!*

She felt him inhale, though she scented nothing. "The finest bouquet I've ever experienced. I want to taste you again, Gen. For real this time, not through dulled senses."

The concept made her shiver, sharing this level of intimacy with him beyond even her most wild fantasies. But still, a good-girl token protest was in order. *Not with* my *mouth, you don't!*

She felt him raise one of her eyebrows. "Don't tell me you never wondered what your lube tastes like?"

Never. The lie became a line in the proverbial sand. She'd already had a taste of it when he kissed her after licking her to orgasm. But tasting her lube just for the sake of it was well beyond her comfort level. How far was she willing to let him push her, anyway?

Right over the edge, into multiple orgasms.

His smile spread across her face. "I know you want this, but I want to hear you say it."

After a moment of gathering her resolve, she let it all go and took the leap. *Taste me.*

"Yes." The word still echoed off the walls when she felt him take her fingers between her lips. He sucked them deep, his tongue sweeping over the digits in a most erotic way.

Though she didn't taste anything, her body tightened up and every cell went on alert. Marshal groaned, clearly lost in the experience, grazing the pad of her fingers with sharp teeth. When her hands slid back down to rub her clit more aggressively, she couldn't help but ask, *Good?*

"Sublime," he replied, working her body faster. "Like nectar from a flower. Now I want to feel you come."

Arching up, he spread her legs, letting the soles of both her feet rest on the cool porcelain edges of the tub. They let out a gasp as the cold air stroked her wet flesh. More, she needed more, harder, deeper, now. A finger found her clitoris and fondled lightly, teasing the bud out from its hood.

"So greedy and so shy all at once," he murmured as another finger delved between her spread labia to play with the slick folds. "Hungry and yet afraid to be satisfied. Just like you."

Her hips rocked up to meet the fingers, increasing the pressure. Gen shuddered in delight, relishing the languorous way he learned what her body liked, what it craved. Instead of a frantic rush to crest the hill she usually experienced while masturbating, he built the foundation for something much bigger. Every word had been chosen carefully, every touch a new threshold for pleasure, the possibilities limitless. It all added to her pleasure and increased her anticipation for what came next.

Gen couldn't gather her thoughts. She was used to lots of downtime to process every experience, but since agreeing to become a mystery shopper, her life had spun out of control. Too much sensation, not enough understanding, and she felt like she was on a downward spiral into chaos. As though a two-ton anvil hung over her head, waiting to crush her to a bloody, twitching pulp.

Wait, Marshal. Stop for a second so I can think.

Two fingers swirled over her clit once more before delving through her saturated folds and circling the opening to her body. "Is that really what you want? To think?"

Torn between the demands of her mind and body, she hesitated. He took advantage of her indecision and maneuvered her so the pulsating jet of water from the tub was aimed right at her sex.

Her nipples had grown as hard as diamonds. First one finger, then two stretched her snug channel, delving deep, hitting all the pleasure spots while the water thrummed against the sensitive flesh, boosting her desire to a fever pitch.

He groaned in bliss. "I love this, love feeling your response. I'm tempted to leave you so I can plunge my cock inside here, send you flying. It wouldn't take much, would it? But I don't want to miss the feeling. Tell me, Gen, what would you have me do?"

Stay with me. The thought formed before she really considered what she was saying. Having him inside her body, in control of her pleasure, gave her the opportunity to just enjoy. Just like when the rope had contained her, she delighted in the freedom. No worries, just ecstasy.

"I'm going to rub you harder now, fast, until you come. And I want you to think about what else would bring you pleasure. What would you do to my body?"

Tie you up so I can suck your cock. Gen was almost shocked by her own thoughts, but her sex clenched around the invading fingers, telegraphing her true feelings.

"Oh, yeah," he breathed, stroking harder until water sloshed over the sides of the tub. "What else?"

She pictured it in her mind, his hands bound in front of him with that silky length of rope holding his wrists together. That green gaze would fix on her, heating her blood as she sank to her knees, letting soft wisps of breath fall on his huge erection. In her mind's eye, she watched as his big body trembled while her tongue darted out, licking the slit, sucking on the crown. His hips would rock in a silent plea for her to take more, take all of him. She'd tease him first, though, explore his body the way he had done to hers, letting her fingers cup his ass, and explore the crevice as she took him into her mouth. Maybe she would grow bold enough to insert a lubed finger into his anus and pleasure *him* from the inside out. . . .

"Oh, yes, I'd love it," he panted, using another finger to stretch her sheath. "Love for you to penetrate my ass while you sucked my cock. I'd come so hard, Gen—"

The orgasm swept over her body in a tsunami of sensations. Every muscle in her body clenched and released as they rode the fantasy to new heights. Soaring, spiraling out of control and relishing every second of it.

Slowly the storm ebbed, leaving her shipwrecked within her own body. *I had no idea. No clue I was so . . .*

"Sensuous?" Marshal supplied. "Stick with me, and I promise that together we will discover every secret you never knew you had."

8

Rhys silently cursed himself as he maneuvered Gen's body from the tub. He needed to be more careful. Her orgasm had ousted his essence from her, and for a moment he'd floated over the top of her, awed by her incredible body flushed from the heat of her bath and that cataclysmic release.

He'd thought nothing could turn him on more than her contradictory responses. He'd been wrong; that wild imagination of hers had awoken a sleeping giant, the dormant hedonism he'd repressed before going to the abbey for spiritual training.

The brotherhood had believed the time of spiritual enlightenment should be entered cleansed and purified of all the baser needs. Fasting and ritualistic bathing as well as long hours of meditation and prayer led up to the final trial a novice took before becoming a full-fledged member of the order. One was not required to be a virgin, but he was supposed to repress those sexual appetites until after the training period was completed. His had just ended when Illustra arrived.

Though he'd thought about sex almost constantly during his

long confinement, the distance of time and the haze of memory had dulled the remembered pleasure until he'd almost convinced himself that it didn't matter. Being with Gen brought it all roaring back. Instead of just wanting to fuel her desire, he craved her touch, the feel of her hands on his skin, her little pink tongue darting out to lick the slit of his cock head. To feel of the snug walls of her cunt gripping his shaft, milking him until he released his seed into her body.

Sensation from her responsive body had tossed his essence around like foam on the tides of the sparkling sea. He'd felt insignificant and almost ready to drown. Rhys wanted the anchor of his own release to join the symphony of hers.

Perhaps her sexual response was *too* much for him to handle from inside her. His pride balked at the thought, but Rhys had been schooled to recognize the dangers of allowing arrogance to blot out reasonable judgment. Safe in his own body, he would gladly take her on, any role she wanted to play, any way she wished to be caressed or to stroke him. He would jump at the chance.

But now, when his situation teetered on the brink between successfully escaping from his wax prison and abject failure . . . no, he couldn't afford to wallow in sensual delight with her no matter how tempting she might be.

Marshal?

He flinched. Every time she called him by the traitor's name, Rhys felt as though he'd been stuck with a pin. Guilt for lying to her and anger at Marshal's role in his captivity threatened to overwhelm him, but he ruthlessly locked his feelings away. Strong emotion experienced while cohabitating within another's body could skew the way the host perceived her own feelings after his departure. The very last thing he wanted to do was cause Gen harm.

"What is it, sweetness?"

She hesitated a moment, and he sensed the direction of her

thought before it fully formed. *Not to be rude or anything, but are you going to get out of me anytime soon?*

He had to play his hand very carefully, prey on her need to make others more comfortable than she insisted on being. Her altruism was the key to his continued freedom. "Are you not enjoying my company?"

Of course! It's just a little . . . unsettling not having control over my own body.

Rhys understood exactly what she meant. Stalling for time, he retrieved the comb from the dresser and ran it through her damp tresses. After a thorough search through his mental database on human women, he found the spin most likely to work. "I like touching you this way. Pampering your graceful body. It's so different from my own, and I've never had a chance to explore a woman like this. Let me pamper you and treat you like a goddess, fulfill your every need and want. You can sit back and relax, enjoy a vacation while I investigate what makes your body tick."

If you really want to . . . She sounded unsure, but at least she didn't demand he get out of her right away. Humming under his breath, Rhys finished untangling her hair and removing the last few droplets of water from her soft skin. Given his druthers, he would have enjoyed playing her lady's maid. Instead of a towel, he would use his tongue to swipe away the stray beads of moisture on her breasts and belly, reveling in the feel of her fingers in his hair, the heady scent of her arousal as she spread her legs for him. Granting him access to the well of her sweet honey while her lips parted to breathe his name on a sigh . . .

Best not to dwell on what would never be.

"Are you hungry?" he asked instead, heading out of the bathroom toward the exit of her private chamber. "It's morning; perhaps breakfast is in order?"

Wait! Don't go out there yet. You need to dress me first.

He paused with a hand on the knob. "Why?"

Humans think naked flesh is arousing, and the sight of it is taken as an invitation to fornicate. After last night, Steven and Javier wouldn't understand why I decided to parade around in front of them in the raw. Jeez, what planet are you from again?

"What would you like me to dress you in?" He intentionally dodged her question, unsure of how much she knew about the universe beyond her own world. From his studies, most humans were content to live out their lives on their home planet or one of the nearby space stations in their solar system. Exploring the great beyond was a pastime left for a few, well-financed adventurers or for shady businesses with ulterior motives.

Surprise me.

Dressing Gen's body drained Rhys's energy reserves. Donning clothing complicated the hell out of daily life, as one had to put it on *and* take it off. Gen didn't seem at all impressed with his efforts, but of course she couldn't see the magnificent result in the mirror the way he could.

The undergarments alone had taken a quarter of an hour, what with straps and hooks holding various bits of scrap cloth in place.

"What do you call this fabric?" he asked, stroking the smooth texture covering her arms. Where it met bare flesh, it caressed skin like a lover's gentle touch, foreshadowing all possibilities for hedonistic exploit. The cut of the top exposed her lavish breasts, which had been pushed together and propped up to obscene proportions by the undergarment she called a bra. The reflection was mouthwatering but hurt like the very devil.

Silk, and be careful with it—that's my best dress.

"Noted." Taking the candle, Rhys moved carefully to the door, ready to make his first public appearance.

Pay attention to the way you walk. You're moving me like a space freighter pilot after an eighteen-hour run with a load in her drawers.

His hand hovered over the knob. "How do you suggest I remedy this?"

Take smaller steps and roll my hips. If you got 'em, flaunt 'em.

Sweet stars above, there was so much to remember! "Wait, you just said you don't want them to look at you."

It's not for them. It's for me.

"I doubt I'll ever understand the way women think."

In his mind's eye, he saw her grin. *Doesn't mean you should stop trying.*

Her comm device chirped shrilly from the counter. Rhys debated answering the incoming call, but Gen took the decision out of his hands. *I really need to take that.*

A sense of impending doom flowed over him. "You're supposed to be relaxing."

That iron will of hers rose up. *Either answer the call or get out of me so I can do it myself. In fact, this might be job related, so you really should—*

Rhys set down the candle and activated the unit.

"How's it going?" the cool blonde on the other end asked.

Alison, shit! Gen thought at the same time Rhys forced a smile onto her face. "Fine. We're all fine, Alison."

Blonde eyebrows drew together and she narrowed her eyes. "Are you feeling all right, Gen? You look a little pale."

"All the activity, you know? I was just sitting down to breakfast."

This isn't fun anymore. I could lose my job if Alison finds out—

"Anyway, I wanted to let you know that Marshal called, and he'll be there by late morning."

Rhys cursed silently. It was too soon; he hadn't gained her trust yet. He nodded her head woodenly.

Marshal, what the hell is she talking about? Tell her you're already here.

Rhys nodded, his mind already on his next move. "I'll be ready for him."

Deactivating the comm unit, he turned back to Gen's room.

Rhys really hoped Gen would let him run with her body. The idea of sharing her emotional rainbow with another empath, especially one like Marshal, sickened him. Sure she was strong, but could she feed two empaths at one time? Though Gen was no shrinking violet, Marshal would tower over her; he could hurt her beautiful body so easily—break her if the mood struck him.

And it would be Rhys's fault.

What the hell is going on? Her anger was back, building every time she asked the question and Marshal—if that really was his name—didn't answer. Fear made her stomach clench tight, but she didn't know if it was hers or his or some hybrid combination of the two.

Their kinky game had taken a decidedly sharp curve back to reality and she was left without a view or a choice. What the hell had she been thinking, ceding control over her body, and for what? A few fleeting moments of bliss?

I want my body back, now. And some answers, goddamn it! Are you Marshal or not?

"No."

Something shattered inside her soul at the admission.

"Damn it, I need more time," he muttered as though he hadn't heard a word she said. Thought. Whatever. "I refuse to go back!"

Gen paused in mid mental rant and tried another tactic to get his attention. *Back to where?*

The sharp rap of her heels on the wood floor told her he paced the length of the room. He moved like a cornered predator, ready to lash out at any moment. Yet she couldn't forget the gentle way he'd touched her, made love to her, as though her pleasure truly mattered to him.

"It does, Gen." Bedsprings creaked as he sat down. "I need you."

She detected a plea in the words, and that scared her more than anything else so far. *Then get out of me and tell me who you are and what you need. I can't help you if you don't trust me.*

He nodded once. "I'm left with no other choice. If I run with your body, I'll be no better than those who imprisoned me."

Gen wanted to sigh in relief that this nightmare would soon be over. His next words made her pause.

"Understand this, sweetness. Your actions from this moment on affect not just me but my entire race of people. We all need your help."

Before she could ask what he needed help with, he seeped from her every pore, leaving her in command of her body and exhausted as if she'd run a 5K. She braced her palms flat on the bed, swaying, and watched as a shimmering gold cloud took the form of the man who'd mysteriously appeared. He crouched on the floor, his red hair spilling over his golden shoulders, knuckles supporting his weight. Even now she couldn't help but admire his physical perfection. He lifted his chin and stared at her, those green eyes pleading. Despite his recent actions, she wanted to reach out to him, run her hand through his hair to ease his burden. She'd lost her last marble.

Sinking her nails into her palms, she kept her hands where they were, thinking of one of Nana's favorite sayings: *Fool me once, shame on you. Fool me twice, I'm an idiot.* Then again, no one could fool Nana because she could see their every move as soon as the notion flitted across their brains.

"I'm sorry I deceived you," he began, and her shoulders

sagged as her last trace of hope faded away. He wasn't Marshal, and he'd lied to her about his identity and then had sex with her, invaded her body and mind.

Squaring her shoulders, she gazed down at him. "Who are you?"

He met her gaze unflinchingly but retained his supplicant posture, as though prepared for a beating. "My name is Rhys."

Gen held out her hand. "Nice to meet you, Rhys." *Wait for it . . .*

Hesitating, he searched her face before extending his own hand. Once it was clasped firmly in hers, she held tight and leaned in close until only a hairsbreadth separated their noses. "Now tell me, where the *hell* did you come from?"

His gaze shifted to the candle still burning on her nightstand. "In there."

Gen scowled and followed his pointed glance. "The candle?" A shiver racked her that had nothing to do with the cold. She recalled her unusual attachment to it, the way the dancing flame had mesmerized her, relaxed her and brought down her wall of inhibitions one stubborn brick at a time.

As though preparing her to accept him.

"I know you're angry," he said. "I can see it in your aura."

"I don't believe in that New Age garbage." She took her hand back and rose to pace.

He stood, too, towering over her at his full commanding height, though he didn't try to use his size to intimidate her. "Some things are true whether you believe them or not. Right now, your colors are crimson and black, telegraphing the rage you are dealing with."

She stopped and pivoted toward him, jabbing a finger at his chest. "Don't tell me how I feel! It's *rude.*"

Rhys didn't reply and her gaze dropped. His erection still stood at attention, and a small part of her wanted to drop to her knees and take him in her mouth. She wanted to tie his wrists with her rope and play out the fantasy that had sent her flying in the tub. Damn it, what was wrong with her? Sexy time had come to an abrupt halt. The man had been lying to her, using her, and here she just wanted more. His stiff cock seemed to mock her, and she focused her rancor on it. "You've got to be kidding me. Doesn't that thing ever get tired?"

He didn't appear remotely embarrassed. "I want you, want to pleasure you. My empathic resonance is taking on the form most likely to please you."

She'd never heard of a race of empaths who could apparently jump bodies the way she changed clothes. "So this is what you people do? Swap skins for fun?"

He shook his head. "Not all of my people could manage this. Their emotional selves are too incoherent, a mere resonance of their physical body. I have training, though."

Her eyes narrowed. "Like combat training?"

Rhys shook his head again. "Almost the exact opposite. Spiritual training, in discipline and divinity."

"You're a *priest*?" Gen scrambled away from him until her back hit the wall with a dull thump. *Oh, hell, what did I do?*

The way those luminous eyes studied her, she got the impression he was cataloguing her reactions. "The equivalent is more like monk, specializing in theological study and energy manipulation."

"You didn't, um . . . take a vow of chastity or anything, right?" Her tone sounded shrill and laced with desperation. Though most religions were considered barbaric in modern society—an opiate for the unwashed masses—Nana and Gramps had remained devoted Catholics and had raised Gen as such. *Nana will flay the skin from my hide for sullying a monk.*

So, great, not only had she violated the health code, but she had also begged a holy man to fuck her. Though technically he had started them down that path. She groaned, knowing she could never even speak to her grandparents again, because Cora would pick this tasty little nugget out of her brain and then crucify her for it.

But thank the stars above, he shook his head. "No such thing exists in my culture, although we are expected to abstain from all hedonistic pleasures during the period of emotional enlightenment. I had just completed the trials when they arrived." His gaze focused on the far wall, as though reliving the darker moments.

Hesitantly, she moved toward him again. "Who? What are you talking about?"

A muscle jumped in his jaw. "They landed on our moon, capturing every man, woman, and child. No one would fight back, no matter what they did, how they abused us. Pacifists to the bitter end."

"Who did this?" Gen feared she already knew. In her mind, she traced over events and was able to pinpoint exactly when everything had changed. *Damn Gia for talking me into the need for a man whore!*

Rhys held her gaze as he confirmed her fears. "The company you call Illustra."

9

A chill slithered down Gen's spine. "You're telling me I'm working for slave traders? What would they hope to get from something like this?"

He didn't blink, didn't back down, and the yawning chasm in her belly expanded as he said, "Power. Control over people and their feelings."

"To what end? So people would hire more prostitutes, have more sex? That doesn't seem to have much of a payoff."

He glanced at the candle as though the very sight of it made him wary. "Think about the type of people who use Illustra's services."

She fisted her hands on her hips and narrowed her eyes. "You mean people like me? Lonely, borderline desperate people?"

He shook his head. "*Busy* people, people with important jobs or other obligations who don't take the time to grow an organic relationship. Powerful individuals who make decisions for all of humankind. So what do they do to satiate their biological drives? Pay a professional to take care of those inconvenient needs. The prostitute arrives with an empath in tow, equipped with a small device embedded under the skin to shield their emotional resonance the same way your health guard shields your body. The empath has no other choice but to pull on the client because he's starved for emotional connection.

"I was once used to help quell a reporter who had unearthed a blackmail scheme. One of the professionals was sent to him under the guise of a government lobbyist. She seduced him, and when he took her to his apartment, she lit the candle. Because they'd kept me on the shelf too long, I was damn near starved to death, so I yanked on his emotions until he couldn't see straight.

"Meanwhile, she had plenty of time to find all of his evidence and destroy it, with him being none the wiser. By the time he came out of it, she was gone and so was his story."

Gen sat on the edge of the mattress, clutching the bedspread in a white-knuckled grip. It all sounded so seedy and underhanded. Evil. Enslaving an entire race of people to make your own stock go up? Alison wouldn't work for people like that. Wouldn't recruit Gen into an organization like that. Would she? "I can't get my head around this."

He reached out and clasped her hand in his. "How else do you explain how I came to be here? Why would I lie?"

Floored, she sucked in a deep breath. "Rhys, it's not that I don't believe you, but someone would have uncovered this . . . conspiracy before now. Some government task force or newsfeed reporter would have exposed them. There's no way to keep something like this a secret from the general public for long."

She expected more arguments, not the ripple of pleasure that shook her entire body. Having just taken back control, she fought the deluge of sexual need sparking low in her abdomen and spreading like wildfire. Her breasts tingled and her nipples grew hard, pressing against the soft cups of her bra. Rhys hadn't bothered to put underwear on her, and liquid lust pooled at the juncture of her legs. Her channel clenched and released, demanding fulfillment. Now.

Quivering in delight, she moaned and fell back on the bed, a slave to her own overpowering desire. The sheen of sweat on her skin shimmered in the candlelight, but she didn't care, lost in the quest for pleasure. Her fingers dug into the blankets to keep from touching her sex, to assuage the ache, but she didn't know how much longer she could withstand the sensual assault. Would she beg him to touch her, just to make it stop?

Squeezing her thighs together only made the craving stronger until she could think of nothing else. "Rhys, please." Gen wasn't sure what she asked him for, but she had to ask.

Between one heartbeat and the next, the desire evaporated as if it had never been, leaving her shaken and jittery like she'd OD'd on coffee. She sucked in a deep breath and stared up at Rhys, who hadn't moved from his kneeling position by the bed. He shivered as though relishing the last wisps of her response. She felt cheap and dirty because he'd made her feel that way while he remained otherwise indifferent and just sucked up what he needed regardless of what she wanted.

His green eyes bore into her. "Do you understand now, Gen? How emotion can blot out reason and thought? Lust, rage, joy, sorrow, fear—any strong emotion can be manipulated. Usually empaths enjoy one another, finding fulfillment in daily highs and lows. We accept the emotions of those around us and nurture the most positive feelings to bring about a communal sense of balance. Harmony.

"When an empath is starved for sensation, he or she no longer possesses the control to moderate the exchange of feeling. It's like being trapped in a small, dark room with only the occasional glow seeping under the doorway. They keep us safely contained and sensory deprived so when we do sense emotion, we cling to it for dear life. They want to control us all, my people and yours. I have to stop them and I need your help."

And here she'd begun to hope he actually cared about her, or at least had been enjoying her company. It would have been humiliating enough if she'd become infatuated with a man whore who didn't return her feelings, but he'd just been *feeding* off of her, because he could.

Shame burned through her. She'd believed he felt something more, something akin to the connection she had experienced when he made love to her. As if some missing piece had all of a sudden materialized only to be snatched away again. Of course, she couldn't blame him for his use of her, not when he just wanted to be free.

But she could blame him for the lies, the deceit, and his sudden holier-than-thou attitude.

Sliding off the bed, she marched toward him, the fires of hell blazing deep inside her. "Don't you *dare* toy with my emotions to prove a point! It's *rude!*"

His expression turned wary. "I won't do that again if you don't want me to."

"I don't want you to do anything to me, understand? Keep your emotional resonance to yourself."

"Then you won't help me." It wasn't a question.

She still didn't know. "Tell me about Marshal, the real Marshal. Is he an empath too?"

"Yes, he's an empath and a traitor. He was sent to our moon to take out our defense grid from the inside. The shield around the moon was our only protection from hostile forces. The turncoat arrived under the guise of a grieving father who mourned the passing of his child. After discovering our weaknesses, he reported back to Illustra. He sold his own people into bondage, Gen. Marshal has no feelings of his own. He's a cipher, and he'll drain you dry, then leave me to rot, with no remorse."

Gen pinched the bridge of her nose. "I can't deal with this."

He reached forward, as though to touch her hair, but withdrew when she shot him a killing glance. "I need you."

Shaking her head, Gen considered everything. The smart thing to do would be to call Alison and tell her everything Rhys had just said. Maybe he wasn't really empathic, just intuitive. *Then how did he get inside you and play your body like a fracking violin?*

Betrayal and humiliation left icy pits inside her. He'd lied to her, had engaged in sexual congress with her while allowing her to believe he was someone else! Why should she accept his wild tale over the proof of what she'd known her entire life? "You're asking me to trust you, even though you've deceived me since the minute we met. How many shades of stupid do you think I am?"

A muscle jumped in his perfectly chiseled jaw. "I don't think you're stupid. And I wouldn't ask, but believe me when I tell you, Gen, that you *are* my one in a million. No one else has ever been emotionally strong enough to pull me away from the candle before."

"So you need me to what, feed you my feelings? I have a life, Rhys. Responsibilities. I can't simply drop everything and go jaunting off carrying a lit candle around the universe to hunt for your body."

His eyes never wavered as he stared at her face. "And what of my responsibilities? My plans? It was your people who did this to me, to others like me. The least you can do is help me get my life back on track."

Offering him a false smile, she shook her head slowly and leaned toward the nightstand. "No, you're wrong. The least I can do is *this.*" With a puff of air, she blew the candle out.

Rhys disappeared.

*   *   *

"Are you sure you guys have to go so soon?" Gen hugged first Steven and then Javier. Sorry to see the two of them leave. Afterward, she'd be alone at the cabin with only her guilty conscience and troubled thoughts for company. Shoving the worry aside, she murmured, "I have a knack for running off the man whores, don't I? Could give a girl a complex." She winked to lighten her statement.

Javier laughed and squeezed Steven's hand. "Don't take it personally, Gen. We're both tired of the business and all the bullshit that goes with it. If you could see that we'd rather do each other than anyone else, we've definitely stayed at the table too long. Thanks for being cool with us. Besides, Marshal should be here soon, so you'll have someone new to play with."

She just managed to stifle a grimace. "Lucky me."

Steven winked at her. "Give us a call sometime. We'd be happy to put on a show for you whenever you like."

After a final round of good-byes, they climbed into the waiting cab and left. Gen watched as the taillights faded down the steep incline of the drive and cast her gaze out at the lead-colored sky. A storm was brewing. She could feel it in the wrist she'd broken during one particularly difficult antigrav dance recital when her units had failed in mid-pirouette. She'd crashed onto the stage in an ungraceful heap, landing on her wrist. The pain was nothing compared to the scalding humiliation. She shivered in the chill wind and straightened her spine. The past was what it was, and she had bigger problems. Namely, what to do about Rhys.

Returning to the cabin, she cooked herself a decadent breakfast. Belgian waffles topped with real whipped cream and crushed pineapple chunks, bacon, and fresh-squeezed orange juice. Plus coffee.

Should she relight the candle, offer Rhys some food? Could

emotional echoes even eat? His body had felt real to her, the perfection of his golden skin and soft hair. His tongue had been wet when he kissed her, his cock hard as he drove it into her. Her sex clenched at the remembered pleasure, but she stuffed the hormones away. Now was the time for rational thought, not angsty feelings. While she ate, she mulled over everything he'd told her, putting off the conversation she knew approached in tandem with the gathering storm.

Alison would expect an update, her official secret shopper report on Franco, Steven, and Javier. And as an employee of Illustra, wasn't it her job to report Rhys? After all, he had masqueraded as one of their pleasure companions and then spread wild accusations. A good employee would keep her boss up-to-date on such things.

Licking the last of the cream off her fork, Gen pushed back from the table to refill her coffee mug. Problem was she felt like a narc, or the prostitute hall monitor.

Franco really had done his best with her; she just didn't like his master-and-commander attitude. He didn't turn her on, end of story. And Steven and Javier were on their way to start their own little happily-ever-after, well away from Illustra's strict rules.

So that left Rhys. Trudging to her bedroom, she retrieved his candle and her comm unit. Setting the candle on the hearth, she paced the room, staring out the window, seeing nothing of the natural beauty outside. "Dial, Nana."

Cora picked up on the first ring, vid screen blocked, of course. "Genevieve Luzon, don't think I'm so damned old that I can't turn you over my knee and—"

"Sorry, Nana. I didn't mean to worry you."

Cora's tone turned sly. "Who said anything about worry? I want to know how tricks are going. Have you gotten your groove on yet?"

"Um, yeah, about that. The situation is sort of *complicated*."

Gen put extra emphasis on the word, hoping Cora would probe her mind and find out all the gritty details. She really didn't want to say it all out loud over a traceable line. Maybe Rhys did have her believing in some of his conspiracy theories.

Unfortunately, Cora wasn't tuned in to her frequency. "How on earth can sexual relations with professionals be complicated? I thought you were working for Alison, the whole secret-shopper gig. You aren't running around telling all the man whores about that, are you? Because you know when I was an undercover agent..." Nana rambled on, but Gen stopped listening. Usually she loved Cora's wild tales of the bad old days, how she and Gramps had teamed up to fight a secret government task force, but right now she was too preoccupied to hear about how Nana had saved the world. Again.

Damn it, of all times for Cora to be more interested in herself than what was doing with Gen. "I've been learning all sorts of stuff." *Come on, Nana, read between the lines.*

But Cora's mind had wandered too deep into the gutter outside la-la land to pick up on her granddaughter's cues. "What kind of stuff? Oh, do they offer samples? Or maybe a senior citizen discount—"

"Not gonna happen," Jack called from the background.

Gen smacked the heel of her hand to her forehead. Time to change tactics. "Nana, have you heard from Tanny?"

"No, lovey, she hasn't tried to reach out at all. Tanny's decisions are her own, Gen. You need to accept that. She'll come back when she's ready."

Gen glanced back at the candle and thought, *I bet you'd be plenty juiced off of all this misery, Rhys.* "You think I'm wasting my time, leaving the home fires burning for her, don't you?"

Cora's voice softened. "No, baby doll, I'd never think that. I'm just glad you're capable of genuine love. Few people are anymore and it's so important."

"It hurts though, Nana." Gen found herself reaching for

Rhys's candle again. She relit the wick and moved away. Whether this confession came from her need to get the weight of misery off her chest or to feed Rhys, she didn't care. "I don't know if I can do it anymore—keep opening myself up to it when all I get is bitch-slapped for my trouble."

"Believe me, I know, sweetheart. Do you think I wanted to love your grandfather? An assassin sent to kill me? The thing you need to understand about love is it doesn't give you a choice in the matter. Will you ever stop loving Tanny, no matter how much of a little shitbird she is?"

Gen sniffled. "Of course not."

"Do you think I'll ever stop loving you, no matter how much of a little shitbird you are?"

Laughter bubbled up. "I love you, too, Nana."

"Good. Now go on and enjoy yourself. And remember to be safe!"

The door behind her creaked open, and Gen swallowed hard.

"It's a little too late for that, Nana."

10

Gen's first sight of Marshal stole the breath from her lungs. He was as handsome as Rhys, dark where her empath was bright. His hair was long, dark, and thick and would be the envy of any woman worth her estrogen. If she wasn't too busy running her fingers through it. He had sharp slashing eyebrows and eyes that seemed to suck all the light from the room. A long aquiline nose was his most prominent feature, and his lips curved up into a predatory smile. He was tall, just as tall as Rhys's projected self had been, but otherwise there was no way to tell he was part of an alien species.

She shivered and his expression turned apologetic.

"I'm sorry to interrupt, but the cold is cutting through my clothes."

"Who is that?" Cora's voice had picked up a lusty note. "Genevieve, put on the vid. I want to see if the face matches my—"

Without waiting for the rest to be delivered, Gen disconnected. Nana would be livid. No getting around that now, though. Instead, she set her sights on the new man in her life.

"You are a tasty morsel, you know that, Genevieve?"

"Now, how would you know what I taste like, hmmm?" Forcing her shoulders back, Gen lifted her chin, painting a picture of pure defiance. She knew men like Marshal, the kind interested in breaking a spirited filly. At least Rhys had dressed her well. She didn't allow her gaze to rove to the candle. Too much weirdness and not enough time to process, but Gen knew one thing for sure. She didn't trust either man to play straight with her. Rhys had already made it clear that her wishes were secondary to his desires, and Marshal . . .

Marshal looked like trouble incarnate.

"Is that an invitation to find out exactly what you taste like?" That dark gaze probed her face, searching for something.

"I'm going to play it straight with you here, Marshal. I've heard some less-than-complimentary stuff about you. Your reputation, I mean. The past week has sucked rotten produce, and the last twenty-four hours have been beyond odd. I don't want to cook, clean, talk about the state of any society, childhood trauma, psychology, religion, or career goals. I'm not looking for anything but a good old-fashioned fuckfest. You up for the task?"

"Hot *and* forthright. I believe I've met my match." He moved forward, a predator stalking his prey, but though her heart thundered in her rib cage, Gen stood her ground, her body responding with all the blatant signs of arousal.

He stopped when the toe of his leather shitkickers were an inch away from her bare feet. "What's with the candle?"

Gen searched his face. Did he know about Rhys and the other empaths? One eyebrow was raised, and his lips curved up in a cat-that-ate-the-canary smile. "Ambience, I think. Franco lit it, and no one has bothered to blow it out. I kind of like it. Makes me feel . . . hot." She forced her lips into a feline smile. There was no way she could hide her nervousness, but if Marshal was like every other man she'd ever met, he'd attribute her case of the jitters to his proximity.

"So where do you want to start?" Marshal may have been the source of all evil, but he smelled terrific, like the cold winter wind with a touch of male spice.

She scowled up at him, annoyed that she was with yet another man who hadn't taken charge of the sexual situation to her liking. Maybe it was time to assert herself. "Aren't you supposed to be the expert?"

One finger reached out and snagged a strand of her hair. "I am going to show you the most pleasure it is possible for a body to accept, then push you even beyond those limits. It might save us both time and energy if you helped in the process."

She activated her health guard. There was a faint hiss as it gobbled up all traces of foreign genetic material on her person. "Safety first."

His lips twitched and he shook his head. "I need a shower before anything else, to warm up a little bit. Stage a fantasy for us—I'll be out in five." She watched him walk down the hall. The moment the bathroom door clicked shut, anger flared up inside her.

Was it her destiny to be manipulated, controlled, pushed around by everyone, including strange men she'd just met? If so, it was about time she snared fate by the short and curlies so they could have a powwow. *No more, do you hear me? I am snagging the reins and riding this bitch.*

After picking up the candle, she placed it on the mantel where the glow from the firelight would hopefully mask Rhys's dancing light. She marched into the room where all the crates of supplies had been left and popped open the first one. Franco had derived some sense of control from dominating his bed partners, even if it was only skin-deep. If she couldn't have what she really wanted, maybe she needed to set the bar a little lower. Here she had a man who desired her body and might be an emotional black hole. Well, she would feed him big steaming fistfuls of the rage buried deep within her until he begged for mercy. Yeah, she had plenty of fuel for his and Rhys's fire both.

Her fingers brushed across a velvet box. Curious, she lifted the lid and peered in at the thin metallic bands. She let out a low whistle at the quality of the tech and design. "Damn, Franco, you didn't skimp." Antigrav strips. She could totally get into that.

Digging farther into the box, she hit pay dirt. She could only imagine the look on Marshal's face when she said she wanted to use this on him. On them. Or maybe she'd just be a turbo bitch and not tell him until they reached the point of no return. The toy was still in its casing, obviously new. She wondered why Franco even had a magic wand—it wasn't exactly something a guy would need since the Y chromosome equaled outdoor plumbing.

She ripped open the packaging and read the small instruction sheet. The toy had three settings: beginner, intermediate, and advanced. Averaging her experience with Marshal's, she selected the intermediate setting. The power pack lit up as fully charged, which according to the sheet translated to "hours of sensual delight."

"Find something you like?" Marshal asked from the doorway. She gave him a slow once-over, starting at his feet and slowly moving up his trim legs and taut thighs to the undersized towel that barely covered his hips. His flat abdomen sported an eight-pack of lean muscle, and his chest was totally devoid of hair. *Probably been lasered off.* His arms were corded with muscle; his hands were big and rough-looking.

His wet hair dripped water onto his tanned forehead, those light-consuming eyes fixed on her. "Like what you see?"

Her eyes narrowed. She did and he knew it. Licking her lips, she envisioned what waited beneath the towel. An image of

Rhys surfaced, him caressing her sex with his hardened shaft, his green gaze locked on her face, but she ruthlessly shoved it away.

"Since there's no one else here, let's do this in the great room. By the fire."

He nodded and she watched him walk away, making sure he didn't notice her picking up the cache of goodies. Her dress had deep pockets, and when not activated, the magic wand was only about three inches long. Excitement rushed through her as she followed him out into the great room.

Marshal took the towel off and turned to face her. "Time to let it all hang out."

"Do you want me?" Gen asked, her gaze glued to his straining erection.

He activated his own germ shield before taking his cock in one hand, fisting the swollen head. "What do you think?"

She assessed him from head to toe, a slow sweeping caress that lingered on his shaft. "I think you're into head games."

"All parts of the body are meant to be played with." He chucked his chin in her direction. "Let's see those pretty tits."

Setting down her wares, Gen trailed her fingers up to her collarbone and ran them back down to hover over the top button. "Slow down there, big boy. You want boons, you gotta earn them."

His lips twitched. "Oh, so that's how you want it to be. Power games. I feel ya."

"Not yet, but you will, if you do exactly what I tell you." She bent down and flipped open the box with the antigrav strips. Proffering four of the smaller ones to him, she backed off before he could grab her. "Know how to work these?"

He raised an eyebrow. "You sure you want to go vertical the first time?"

She thought of what was coming. "You bet. Gear up and then we play."

Gen watched Marshal's movements as he bent to fasten the straps. His body aroused her, especially the thought of owning him the way she was going to. *No more Ms. Nice Gal.*

Marshal activated the strips, which changed his center of gravity. He floated in the air above her, and Gen walked beneath him, trailing her fingertips along his torso but dodging his erection. He had to crave her touch there before she would give it to him.

He shivered under her caress as her germ shield sparked against his. "Now do I get to see your tits?"

Slowly, Gen unbuttoned her dress, exposing the flesh beneath. A case of nerves struck, not because she gave a flying fuck what this flying fuck thought of her body, but because it somehow felt disloyal to Rhys to share herself with another.

Oh, get over yourself, Gen. He wants you to do this, would have done it for you, probably without your consent, if he could have. Because he didn't care about her.

Hurt and anger roiled in her stomach, and Marshal closed his eyes. "You're killing me here, baby."

"Don't call me baby," she snapped.

Those pitiless eyes cracked open and fixed on her. "What are you going to do about it, baby?"

She didn't react right away, letting her hand take its time until she cupped his stones. With one sharp fingernail, she applied even more pressure, not enough to break the skin, but he hissed and tried to jerk out of her grasp. "What did I just say?"

"Don't call you baby," he grunted.

She released him and studied his swollen shaft. A drop of moisture beaded at the head. Whether it was her act or her emotions, Marshal was enjoying the sparring.

A rush of power filled her, and she glanced at the flickering candle. It might have been her imagination, but she thought she heard Rhys say, *What's not to enjoy?*

Stepping out from underneath Marshal, Gen scooped up a bottle of sandalwood-scented oil. "Lube up."

The reality of germ shields blocking fluid transfer required an external lube to ease any sort of penetration and prevent chafing. Marshal swayed in the air and popped the seal on the bottle. Pouring a dollop of liquid onto one hand, he began to coat his hard-on.

Gen tsked at him. That would not cut the mustard. "More, damn it. I want you dripping with it."

Groaning, he did as she commanded, moving his hands over his inner thighs, around his sac, and back behind it. She moved forward again and blew her hot breath against his glistening skin. He jerked at the light contact, and she took his lubed-up hand, germ shield crackling, and rubbed it into the crease of his ass. "Pour it everywhere."

He kept going, applying more of the transparent liquid onto his body, and kept his gaze fixed on her.

She unsealed her own bottle and unfastened the front clasp of her bra. Parting the fabric, she poured a generous splash of the lube onto her breasts and massaged it into her straining nipples before trailing her hand down across her belly. This particular bottle had a warming ingredient, which along with the fire, helped dispel the chill from Marshal's soulless stare.

"Show me that pussy, already," the impatient bastard panted.

Gen glowered at him. "Shut up." Yeah she could do this with her clothes mostly on—he didn't deserve to look at her body.

Taking her time, she slid the antigrav strips over her arms and legs. When the last one cinched lightly around her thigh, she activated them and floated up. She stared him down when they were at eye level, but his gaze fell to her breasts.

"What are you doing?" he asked when she swam through the air, executing a neat somersault in midair and coming up behind him. Nana had been right—those antigrav dance lessons did pay off.

"Getting ready to fuck you." Again, she let her fingers play lightly over the skin on his shoulders and back. However, when he tried to turn around, she sank her nails into his hips. "Be a good boy and lie still."

"You sure you're new to this?" Marshal panted when she slid a finger into the crack of his ass. "You've got moves like a seasoned pro."

"Flattery will get you nowhere." Her finger breached his anus and his body bowed. She smiled as she took the wand out of her pocket. At the last second, she added a little more lube to the end of the toy before pushing it up inside him.

"What the—" His words cut off as she activated the phallus that extended six inches into his channel. She flicked another switch and the toy started to vibrate, the protruding end rubbing through the material of her panties until it moved against her clit.

Pleasure spiked through her. Enraptured, she watched his big body heave as the wand retracted and then thrust forward once more. Sweat beaded on his skin. Their shields crackled as she pressed her slick breasts against his back, working the toy around her throbbing bud as it fucked him.

"How does that feel?"

He responded in incoherent babbles, his body shaking. Reaching around to his front, she gripped his shaft, thumbing the slit. "Do you want to come?"

He nodded and she pressed down harder on her end of the wand, changing the angle slightly as it expanded inside of him again, thrusting just like she had a cock of her own to ram up in him. "Beg me."

"Please," he panted. "Please, I'll do anything."

The rush of power those words gave her was indescribable.

She stared at the candlelight as she worked Marshal's cock, thinking of Rhys and how he told her you don't have to hurt someone to beat them.

Marshal's entire body tensed and he groaned in release. Gen felt the shield surrounding her hand spark as it consumed his seed before the genetic material could touch her skin. He shuddered and then went completely limp in her arms.

"Marshal?"

No answer. His chest wasn't expanding the way it ought to be. With trembling fingers, she felt for a pulse. Nothing.

Oh, shit, did I kill him?

She's magnificent. Though Rhys wouldn't tell her directly, he heard everything she said, felt everything she did to Marshal, playing her part to perfection. He sensed her anger—it washed over him in huge red waves, engulfing his reserves like a cup overflowing. Marshal would be strong after this encounter, feeding off her emotions, too, but Rhys held the element of surprise.

The control she took over Marshal was awe-inspiring. Rhys lost himself listening to her commands, the whisky tone that invited no questions. More than once, he'd had to stop himself from charging out to protect her. Gen had not seen the devastation Marshal had wrought—had not witnessed the bleak faces of blameless people as they were forced onto an alien vessel where they would be made into slaves.

Remembering those faces along with his trust in Gen's innate moral compass was all that kept him sane as he listened to her intimacy with the traitor.

Because he'd been waiting for it, Rhys sensed the exact moment Marshal's spirit abandoned his body, the bliss from whatever Gen had done too much to endure in corporeal form any longer. *That's my girl.*

Taking one more hit off of Gen, whose fear had overcome

the sexual heat, he gathered his strength and launched himself from the candle, picturing her, imagining the look on her face when she realized what had happened.

Though Rhys couldn't see, he sent out emotional antennae, which bounced off of living entities, detecting the feelings of others. Marshal's essence resembled thick, black smog hanging in the air, suspended over his body. Whatever Gen had done had truly brought him pleasure, for he made no move to descend, to reclaim control over his body. That hesitation would be his downfall.

Stealth and speed, in addition to Marshal's blissed-out state, allowed Rhys to sneak into the unoccupied body. Slithering in through the occipital lobe, he quickly went through the major systems of Marshal's form, not trying to control it, only to keep it alive, making his heart pump blood, lungs suck in air, brain rest in a dormant but not dead state. As he traveled, he fortified the body's natural defenses, just as he'd been taught to do when he was first learning how to project his essence. An empath who traveled out of his corporeal form did not want to leave his flesh unprotected. The body and spirit could be divided, just as lovers could be separated by time and circumstance, but one could not live without the other forever.

He finished just in time. Marshal's essence attempted to drift back inside but couldn't settle anywhere, his presence now a foreign invader to his own form. The darkness swirled, weakening already—he really had screwed around too long out in the ether. From any other being, Rhys would have sensed desperation and determination, but Marshal truly was the living dead. He felt the blackness move away—he must have sensed the candle that emitted an artificial frequency that attracted empaths like a magnet to steel.

At the last moment, before the flame engulfed it, the malignant cloud changed course, perhaps recognizing the trap that waited in the candle, and focused on the only other sustainable environment in the room . . . Gen.

No! Rhys's panic made him sloppy, and he missed the cerebral cortex on his first pass. For the second time that day, he struggled to open the eyelids of the body he had invaded. After the battle he'd just had, he could have easily slept for a week, but not until he felt sure Gen was safe.

"Marshal?" he heard her ask, though she still appeared fuzzy to him.

"No," he rasped, unable to control this body yet. "Gen. He's coming for you. If he gets inside, your soul will be trapped and he'll feed off of you until you die. Run, now."

She hesitated. "Will you be all right?"

He felt her concern, breathed it in like a drug addict desperate for a hit. "Yes, now go."

Her warmth and light departed, leaving him free to concentrate on forcing Marshal where he needed to go—into the candle. *Just stay away until I come for you, Gen.* He understood there was no way she could hear him, but he still thought the words, hoping she would receive his silent plea. Taking over Marshal's body would be a bitter victory if he lost Gen in the process.

In his incorporeal form, Marshal had no way of keeping up with Gen's body when she left the house. He wasn't trained for this as Rhys had been; he had no way of knowing such a thing was even possible. For a moment, Rhys felt a surge of pity for his enemy, who flailed about, seeking anything other than the justice awaiting him. *And that's what separates the two of us, Marshal. I have the ability to feel remorse, where you just feed from it.*

The noxious cloud hung suspended over the flame, and Rhys froze as another possibility occurred to him. Marshal might let his essence fade rather than be imprisoned in the candle, left at the mercy of others.

If that happened, his body would die, leaving Rhys power-less once more. As he watched Marshal, he thought about all of the times he'd considered letting his own essence disperse, end his misery. He had loved ones to protect, though, his brother-hood to free, and now Gen to look out for. Rhys refused to be so selfish. No, he would not choose to walk the shadowed path, but watching Marshal consider ending his own existence, he understood the why behind such a notion.

Finally, Marshal's blackness sought out the candle, follow-ing the burning wick to the wax that never melted. He must have decided to bide his time, gather his strength, and wait for Rhys to make a mistake. *It's exactly what I would do in his place.*

Unable to relax just yet, Rhys assessed his new physical form once more. He needed to put out the flame before Gen re-turned—he couldn't risk Marshal going after her again. With-out her in the room, Rhys was losing energy, wanting to sleep. *One thing at a time here.*

Once he was sure the life processes would remain intact, he focused on coordinating his large motor skills, ignoring all the unusual sensations that threatened to overwhelm him. *Process later, act now.* Arms and legs flopped about like a newborn foal that couldn't gain purchase, and the bizarre uncontrolled feel-ing registered when he couldn't push off the ground. Because he floated in midair.

It seemed a lifetime since zero-G training, but Rhys remem-bered enough to flip himself toward the nearest wall. The pads of his bare feet touched the smooth surface, and he pushed off in the direction of the blurry glow he assumed was the fire-place.

His hands just scraped over the stone mantel when he heard the front door open.

11

"Rhys?" Gen peeked around the door and scanned the cabin. Was she doing the typical idiotic horror movie broad shtick, getting in the hero's way at a critical moment? Probably. But who said he got to be the hero of this piece anyhow? He was the fracking body snatcher!

How had he taken over Marshal? Even though he had done almost the same thing to her hours earlier, she thought Marshal would have erected some kind of defense against the invasion since he was an empath.

Unless Rhys was lying and *he* was the rogue imprisoned for the betterment of society . . .

Gen shook her head, unwilling to consider the possibility. Rhys had shown her good faith by pleasuring her body instead of harming it. He could have maintained control, but he had let go when she'd started to panic. His actions enlightened her to the ugly reality she didn't want to accept—Rhys was the good guy.

Which meant Illustra had imprisoned him against his will. Used his ability to line their pockets.

Now that she felt sure of him, she almost wished she didn't. Because with understanding came the urge to do something. But how the hell could she help him when she couldn't even get her own shit together? All of a sudden, she doubted Alison and Illustra and her own naïve universal view.

Yet she didn't doubt that Rhys was looking out for her. When Marshal had regained consciousness, she hadn't known what to expect, but seeing Rhys's green gaze blazing out of his face, her heart had skipped a beat. And when he'd warned her that Marshal was coming to invade her body and eat her soul, she'd believed him and had beat feet to the rental car.

Where she'd felt like a chickenshit. What, should she lurk in the bushes while one man––being, whatever—died?

She didn't doubt for an instant it was Rhys floating around inside Marshal's body with a white knuckled grip on the stone mantel. His arms shook, and tremors racked his entire body as he coughed, trying to blow out the candle's flame.

Recalling how shaky he'd been in her body, Gen took charge and darted over to the fireplace. Ignoring Rhys's feeble protests, she picked up the metallic snuffer and put the flame out. "He's in there, right?"

Rhys's head flopped forward like a puppet with its strings severed. "Yes. You should have waited for me to come for you."

"You were taking too long there, light of my life." She cringed at the intimate phrasing. What was *wrong* with her, flirting with a body-snatching liar? Taking him by the arm, she guided him over to the couch. She made sure to align him with the plush cushions before deactivating his antigrav strips. He flopped down onto his back with a dull thud. "Are you all right?"

"I will be." A weak smile tilted his lips. "What did you do with this body, sweet Genevieve? It feels a little . . . raw."

She stood back and fisted her hands on her hips. "Really? You're gonna bitch about my methods?"

His eyelids fluttered, but he shook his head. "Not criticism." He sounded absolutely drained. "Admiration. You are a goddess among mortals."

Pleasure licked deep inside her at his excessive compliment. To give herself a little distance, Gen circled around the back of the couch and fetched a blanket from the hope chest under the window. Spreading it out over his naked body, she studied the changes from a few minutes ago and wondered why, when she'd been intimate with both Marshal and Rhys, the man before her seemed like a total stranger, one she felt comfortable with on a level that transcended physical relations. This kind of thing could drive a girl nuts.

His breathing grew deeper, more rhythmic. "Stay with me."

Her lips parted. How exactly did he mean that? Until he woke up? For the duration of his mission? Until the end of time? And why did her heart flutter like she'd been slamming coffee all night at the thought? *Paging Dr. Freud, we have a rabid case of Stockholm syndrome skull-fucking me here.*

Rhys had a body now, an identity that he could use to screw his way to the top, if such was his goal. Gen was free to go about her life, find a real job, anything she desired. Yet as his soft snore filled the room, all she wanted was to stay here and puzzle him out. Understand who he was and why, even after his lies, she felt drawn to him.

Forcing herself not to hover like a lunatic watching him sleep, Gen scurried around putting away the props from the role-playing. Though she'd never admit it out loud, it had been so damned erotic she'd almost begged Marshal to fuck her. Who would have guessed her to be a closet dominatrix? Although the boot fetish was probably a big fat clue that she was a closet dominatrix.

Now Marshal was Rhys, who had already spent time with

her, discovering her hot spots, feeding her compliments. Of course, once he woke up, Rhys would probably only want her help driving him to the spaceport where he could hitch a ride to whatever solar system he came from.

That was the crux of it, wasn't it? She bit her lip, staring down into his face. His lie, no matter how justified, hurt. But not as much as the knowledge that he didn't care about her. Rhys was an empath, a pacifist; he didn't want to see her or anyone get hurt. It was her own tender heart that had hoped maybe she had finally found *the* one. . . .

She'd watch him walk away and then settle back into her apartment, back to pretending she had a life, whittling her time away waiting for Mr. Right.

The sound of her buzzing comm link broke her from her brooding. The screen stayed blank, so it wasn't one of her pre-programmed contacts. Glancing to where Rhys lay snoring, she decided to take the call. "Genevieve Luzon."

"Gen? How's it going?" Alison's perfectly polished image wavered to life.

Gen adjusted her gaping bodice, not even bothering to consider the state of her hair. She probably looked like she'd been ridden hard and put away wet. "Fine and dandy."

Alison nodded once. "Do you have time now to fill me in?"

Gen glanced over her shoulder to where Rhys slept, utterly defenseless. Did Alison know about the empaths? Worrying her lower lip, Gen considered whether she should put her trust in her old friend. In the end, she decided it was more Rhys's decision than hers. "We're in between sessions right now. Can I give you a call a little later?"

Alison's eyes narrowed to suspicious slits. "Is everything all right, Gen?"

"Why wouldn't it be? I've got a whole host of men willing to fuck me until I turn blue." Gen had to school her features. *Emphasis on* host.

Alison's smile looked a little plastic. "There's a first time for everything. Call me later."

"Cuntrag," Gen muttered. Though Alison may have been trained in how to be a smooth operator, she had less tact than Nana after a bender. And that's saying something.

"I have a sister," Rhys murmured.

Gen jumped at the sound of his voice. "You scared me." She moved back over to the couch and crouched down to look at him. "What brought that nugget to the forefront of your thoughts?"

"I want you to understand why I'm so determined to free my people. The thought of Sela enslaved and suffering like this tears me apart. I'm sorry I lied to you, sorry for using you. Though my actions seem cruel, I really had no other choice."

She licked her lips. "You could have asked me for help right away. I'm a soft touch, a pushover."

He shook his head and winced when the movement seemed to jar him. "I couldn't risk you saying no. You *did* say no. Even though you helped me unintentionally."

Shifting into a more comfortable position, Gen perched on the end of the couch so they could continue their dialogue. "How did I help, exactly?"

Rhys drew in a deep breath. "My people believe when your body reaches the pinnacle of sexual relief, your consciousness leaves your physical self. All the natural defenses are down and the soul is left wide open. Because I was aware of what you were doing and Marshal was not, I struck in that moment. Our emotional resonances traded places, and I shut him out. In our recorded history, it's never been successfully done before. I was wrong not to place my faith in you from the very beginning. You've proven yourself to be a formidable ally. I bet you can change the orbits of entire solar systems if you put your mind to it."

Those green eyes sucked her in like a vortex, making her

forget that he was in a different body. Her heart pounded in her chest, and she had to struggle to breathe. Names meant nothing and appearances even less, the connection between them too strong to ignore, too demanding to be denied.

"Genevieve," he whispered.

Leaning down, she closed the distance and brushed his lips with hers. His scent enveloped her, that cold and wood smoke combination along with potent male spices. The press of his mouth moved with hers as though he sought a deeper contact. He let her direct the kiss and keep the pressure light. The gentle melding of mouths moved her more than the entire sexual encounter with Marshal. Then she'd felt only her own power, reveled in her femininity. It had been basic supply and demand; she had what he wanted, and she'd leveraged her value to him in order to fulfill her own needs. Raw, primal, and utterly basic. No hearts involved.

This was smaller, sharper, an acute pleasure that transcended flesh. A taste of what had been missing all her life. Except when she was with Rhys.

Pulling back, she stared into his face. His eyelids stayed closed, dark lashes casting shadows under his eyes. A small smile played across those firm masculine lips.

Her breath escaped in a whoosh. "You're doing it again, aren't you?"

His eyes opened as his brows drew together. "Doing what?"

Her shoulders sagged and she rose up from the couch, needing to put some distance between them. "What it is that you do—pull my strings. Your emotional puppet-master tricks." A cold metal weight took up residence in her gut. She could never trust what she felt around him, because she'd never know if the feelings were genuinely her own. She couldn't trust him, couldn't trust herself. . . .

This relationship had *toxic* written all over it.

"Gen." Rhys tossed the blanket back, and she quickly

averted her gaze to the view of the half-frozen lake out the window. Fat dopey flakes fell from the sky and began to blanket the frozen ground. She needed to get rid of him before they were snowed in here together, or she'd lose herself in the constant quest for what only he had been able to give her—a sense of her own value.

"Get dressed. Take Marshal's car and leave." She wrapped her arms around herself and kept her posture ramrod stiff. The sooner he left, the sooner she could forget about him and move on with her own life.

His hand gripped her upper arm, and he spun her to face him. "I don't know what you think I did, but I can feel your anger rolling off of you in giant red waves. Believe me, I have no desire to pull your emotional strings. And I'm not going anywhere without you."

His expression softened. "I still need you, Gen. Still need your emotional input to maintain my strength."

She ground her molars together. "This isn't fair."

"Life seldom is, my sweet." He released her and ran a hand through his hair. "Gen, it's not just my selfish need to keep you by my side. Sooner or later, Illustra will discover that you helped set me free. I know what they are doing, and now you do too. They'll come for you. Torture you until you reveal my plans. And once you do, they'll kill you and anyone close to you. I refuse to let that happen."

She laughed humorlessly. "So, what you're saying is, in for a penny, in for a pound?"

He nodded once. "Is being with me so difficult?"

Frustration boiled over. "I don't even know who you are, Rhys!"

He took her hand and brought it to his lips, and her germ shield crackled at the contact. "Then allow me to show you. Once I do and I'm sure of your safety, you can walk away if that's what you want."

Could she do it? Stay with him, growing even more attached to him for the duration of his mission? The longer they were together, the harder it would be to say good-bye. But what if he's right? Was she willing to risk Tanny, Gramps, and Nana? In that light, she really didn't have a choice. "I'll go pack my bag."

Rhys remained in the great room listening as the door to her bedroom slammed shut. Wrapped in the blanket she'd so thoughtfully covered him with, he stared out at the winter wonderland, totally at a loss. That kiss, that sweet touch of her lips to his was the first he'd experienced in months, perhaps even years. And Gen had enjoyed it just as much, her feelings coating them both in a puffy pink euphoria.

He wanted more, wanted to kick open her door, strip the dress from her luscious body, and set to exploring every inch of her. The cold from the floorboards seeped into the soles of his bare feet. Warmth from the crackling fire coated his left side. Sensation, so long denied him, rushed back at an overwhelming clip, like he'd been trapped on a one-dimensional plane and suddenly thrust into a three-dimensional world.

Reaching down, he stroked the half-hardened shaft between his legs, remembering all the things he'd done with Gen. His mouth went dry when he thought of really tasting the honey between her legs, delving his tongue deep inside her core and then laving those glistening folds. Seed pearled at the tip, and he groaned as he swirled it around his cock head.

"Are you ready to . . . ?"

He glanced over his shoulder, one hand still working his shaft. Gen dropped the suitcase she'd been holding and watched his movements, her eyes wide as he masturbated to fantasies of pleasuring her body.

"I'm ready for something." He didn't slow his movements as he recalled the fantasy she'd had while he'd been within her.

Meeting her gaze, he saw the shared remembrance there as she thought about it too. Her nipples stiffened, pressing against the thin fabric of her dress, and a flush of desire crept up her cheeks.

Torn with indecision, he didn't know whether he ought to lift her skirt, move aside her complicated undergarments, and feast on her sex or ask her to take him into her mouth. Words had not served him well with her so far, and the ache in his balls grew with every heartbeat. The blanket fell to the floor as he strode to her, set on his path.

"What . . . ?" Gen stepped away from him until her back hit the wall separating the great room and the kitchen. He pinned her there with one hand on either side of her body.

"Say no if you don't want this." Determined to allow her plenty of time, he lifted her hands to his lips, caressing her knuckles with a soft kiss before placing a hand on each of his shoulders. Nuzzling his way down her body, he rubbed his face against the soft fabric, luxuriating in the rasp of his whiskers against the silk. Her breasts rose and fell in quick movements and her arousal deepened. He received more and more feedback from her responsive body, but now it only twined around his own desire to touch and lick and love her.

Parting the front of her dress, he suckled her breast right through the thin cup of her bra. She gasped and threw her head back, rocking her pelvis against his aching cock. The bud stiffened under his relentless lashes, and he snapped the plastic clasp so there would be nothing between his tongue and her flesh.

"Germ shield," she panted, staring down at him.

Rhys let out a breath. "Fine, but only because I'm wearing Marshal's form. The stars alone know where it's been. But I vow to you, Gen, when I get back to my own body, there will be nothing between us when I love you."

She pressed against that small square on her inner arm, and

her health guard snapped into place. He moved back, fighting a grimace at the snap and sizzle, but she held his face. "What about yours?"

He shook his head. "No, I need to feel you, to taste you. Don't ask me to deprive my senses anymore. I refuse to endure it."

She didn't say anything, just stared down into his eyes. He thought he saw acquiescence there. Slowly, he bent his head back to her breasts.

Tugging the other nipple lightly with his teeth, he caressed it with his tongue even as his hands stayed busy unwrapping the rest of her body, careful not to damage her favorite dress. The prize beneath was well worth the slow reveal. Her soft belly and round, womanly hips. The dark curls of hair that hid her sex from his gaze peeped out around the edges of her panties. Easing a hand between her thighs, he rubbed the soft skin there. Softer even than her dress, softer than anything he'd ever experienced. He longed to lock her long legs around his waist as he fed his shaft into her that molten core.

Releasing her nipple, he worked his way down, trailing slow kisses across her midsection. The scent of her arousal clouded his mind, and her muscles grew taut as he continued to stroke her leg. Was she wet for him? Rhys couldn't wait to find out.

12

If she closed her eyes, she could almost pretend this was still a job, that she was still a secret shopper and what was happening between her legs was only about physical pleasure.

Almost.

The way Rhys touched her, slowly and reverently, was as far away from the practiced kink of the other men as dawn was from dusk. One heralded the last spectacle of the day and the other brought forth hope for a new beginning.

"Rhys," she whispered, and tunneled her fingers through his hair. Red, she thought, it should be red. For a moment her mind superimposed the vivid color before transferring back to Marshal's midnight locks. "Do you think this is wrong? Using Marshal's body like this?"

"I doubt he would object." He moved her thong to one side, and cold air caressed the folds of her woman's flesh. Rhys rested his forehead against her belly, his breaths escaping in shallow pants to fall on her saturated sex. One finger dabbled at the opening to her body, spreading her juices around. "You feel magnificent, Gen."

So did he. All of her anxiety seemed very far away as he played with her body. Using two fingers, he teased her aching clit with soft, light touches that made her want to beg for more. He turned his head and kissed the inside of her thigh. Swirling, delving until she wanted to urge him on. Which was probably his plan.

God, the way he studied her, staring intently at her cunt and then shifting his gaze up to meet hers, those green eyes taking everything in. No wonder she'd fooled herself into thinking he cared about her before; such intensity couldn't be feigned.

"Do you want to know what I was thinking about when I stroked my cock earlier?" he asked almost offhandedly, like he might ask her for the time. The image of him working his thick shaft before the fire made her channel clench in frustration, aching to be filled by his hard flesh.

She bit her lip and nodded, hoping he would show rather than tell. Praying it would end in a spectacular release. Her clit begged for the first contact of his tongue, practically vibrating with the memory of remembered pleasure.

He moved faster than she could comprehend, lifting her legs up until her thighs draped over his shoulders, his big hands cupping her ass cheeks to balance her. His tongue delved into her snatch and swiped upward, dragging through her folds as though he wanted to relish every drop of her nectar.

He supported her weight completely, and in some distant part of her mind, she thought she should feel uncomfortable because the position left her too vulnerable with her back pinned against the wall, thighs splayed open and no possibility of moving away. But his broad shoulders looked more than capable of supporting her weight, and she felt sure he would stop instantly if she asked.

The word spilling out of her mouth, however, was *more*. Which she punctuated by breathy gasps, rocking her hips as best she could in his viselike hold. Knowing he really tasted her this time. The growls of male satisfaction in reaction to her lube sliding down his throat brought her right to the brink.

He was relentless, licking her over and over, tracing every fold with a heavy drag before lashing her clitoris. Then back down to feast on her core again, driving his tongue inside until she bucked against his mouth. His fingers kneaded her ass cheeks, spreading her wider to receive the sensual assault. So different than the sweet kiss they'd shared, but she craved both, the tenderness and the demand. He fit her perfectly, matching her mood, giving her exactly what she needed before she understood it herself.

Gen teetered on the verge, torn between the siren's song of release and the urge to wallow in this hedonistic pleasure forever. He made the decision for her. Opening his eyes, he stared right into her soul. Gen froze up, afraid he would try and manipulate her emotions again.

Sensing her mood change, Rhys pulled away slowly, his chin wet with her juices. "What's wrong? You were close and then you just shut down."

She exhaled a shaky breath. He already knew exactly how she felt; he may as well know the why of it. "I don't trust my feelings."

Thick dark eyebrows drew down, but he didn't let her go. "I'm not sure I understand."

"How can I tell the difference between when you work me over emotionally and what I'm really feeling?"

His thumb stroked over her inner thigh in a distracted caress. "I don't know if there is a way to tell. Does it matter?"

She took him in as he studied her. He probably wanted to get back to the action, but she doubted she'd be able to come while wondering if these feelings bouncing around the inside of her skull were genuine. "It does to me."

Nuzzling her pubic hair, he murmured, "What if I vow not to disturb your emotions unless you ask me to? No more empathic tricks, just a man loving a woman. Would that help you relax and enjoy?"

She bit her lip. Could she trust him, at least that far? "You mean, you won't interrupt anything I'm feeling, no matter what it is? You won't try to control it?"

"I only need the energy from your feelings. Although I must admit there is an addictive new edge I find delicious when my actions are the cause of them. When I touch you like this . . ." He suckled at her core, his tongue trilling around the sensitive skin at her opening. She let her head fall back against the wall. It connected with a dull thump, but she was too blissed out to notice.

He laved deeper, dragging his tongue sideways, the edge tormenting her clit, then pulling away again. "No, sweetness, I don't want to manipulate your feelings. Not when playing with your body can create them for us both."

Catching sight of his throbbing cock, which looked ready to burst, she asked, "What about you? Don't you need to come?"

Rhys grinned, his eyes alight with lust. "I want to come between your sweet lips. Like in your fantasy."

When her sex squeezed again with remembrance, he shook his head. "Later, after I make you come."

"Inside," she panted. "I need you inside me."

He rose up, shrugging his shoulders until her splayed legs rested over the crooks of his elbows. The grace and power in the move made her even hotter, something primal recognizing that this man could fight for her, deserved her as his mate. He leaned in to kiss her, that huge shaft rubbing between her sensitized folds. The urge to deactivate her germ shield so she could feel him, taste her essence on his lips, almost overwhelmed her. Had she lost her mind?

Rocking his hips against hers so his sex stroked hers, he stared into her eyes. "I promise, it's all you. Take me in when you're ready."

His cock slid easily against her slick flesh in another of those wicked caresses that made her want to roll her eyes back in her head and let him have his way with her. But Rhys knew better, and he waited for her to take control.

Reaching between their bodies, she gripped his cock tightly. Breath exploded from his lungs when she thumbed the slit. Her health guard dispersed the bead on the tip before she could slick it onto his shaft. So hard, yet the skin was smooth, almost velvety in texture. Wrapping her fingers around the thick stalk, she guided him to her opening.

The head slipped inside, eased by her arousal, and she withdrew her hand to firm her grip on his shoulders. She expected him to lunge inside her hard, but he eased his way, staring into her eyes as his shaft delved deeper inside her body.

When he was about halfway in, he looked down, watching the thick stalk disappear inside her. She tried rocking her hips to speed him up, needing him to stretch her completely, but he held her still.

"Please, Rhys, I need—"

He cut her off with a deep kiss. His tongue plundered her mouth the way she wished his cock would take her body—hard, instant, and unrepentant. Hers met his eagerly, and she was so caught up in the moment she barely noticed when he lifted her away from the wall and settled on the couch with her astride him.

She broke the kiss, and he flicked her ear with his tongue. "Take whatever you need, sweetness."

Gen sank down onto his hard shaft, throwing her head back as he filled her completely, stretching the walls of her sheath. Tears leaked from the corners of her eyes, and he brushed them away with his fingers.

Reveling in the feel of him inside her, she gyrated her hips, letting feelings wash over her. He seemed content to let her move how she would, while his hands roved her body in a slow exploration.

"Your colors amaze me," he breathed. "Almost iridescent. Tell me how you feel right now."

Her head swung back and forth, unable to put into words the magic that had taken hold of her body. "Overwhelmed. Greedy for more."

He made an indecipherable sound as she rose up and slammed her hips down, needing more forceful contact. She saw the heat in his face, the lines pulled taut. "I need to give it to you."

She nodded once, and again he moved like lightning, pulling out of her so he could lay her back onto the couch. Placing an ankle on each shoulder, he guided his cock into her saturated opening with a hard thrust. She gasped as he withdrew and did it again, this time with more force.

He stared down at her as he rode her hard and fast. The head of his cock pressed against her G-spot with every advance and retreat, a teasing pressure deep inside her slick passage. Her muscles clenched every time as if to hold him there, but his determined lunges overpowered her. She wanted to bow up to meet him, but the angle made it impossible.

Practically delirious from the need to come, she shook her head. "You have to . . . I need . . ."

"Do it yourself."

Her brows drew together. "What do you mean?"

The smooth crown of his shaft pressed up against her womb as he reached for her hand. Guiding her fingers to her mouth, he urged, "Suck on them."

She did and he rewarded her with a smile as he moved her slicked digits to her clit. "Take charge of your own pleasure. Don't be afraid to demand what you need. Trust me, I won't be insulted."

She bit her lip, unsure if she could with him watching her like that. But her wet fingers were already there, and with her channel gripping his cock, the temptation proved too strong.

Trailing a slow circle over her clit, she teased the stiffened nub from its hood.

His eyes glowed in the dim lighting, and his breathing grew shallower when she caught it between two fingers and tugged lightly. He jerked as her sheath contracted in a series of spasms. Hips pistoning, Rhys drove into her hard and fast while she worked her tender nub hard, letting go of all of her inhibitions and reveling in the pleasures of the flesh for the first time with another person.

Approval and appreciation for her mingled with the lust on his face, the tendons on his neck standing out, articulating the strain. His teeth ground together audibly. Though he said nothing, Gen knew he wanted her to go over first, and he would fight his own orgasm until she did.

But she needed this little piece of control, needed to assert her power over him, to know it was really her he craved and not just the nearest available warm body. "Rhys . . . kiss me."

Sweat dripped from his chest and sizzled against her health guard. His shaft seemed to grow inside her as he dropped his hold on her ankles to lean forward to claim her lips.

The instant he moved forward, she wrapped her legs around his waist and rocked her hips up, squeezing him with her inner muscles, demanding his release. He yelled out against her mouth and bucked against her.

The feel of his cataclysmic orgasm and the satisfaction from her own power sent her soaring. Their bodies locked together in a tangle of shaky limbs and thundering pulses. Her germ shield disposed of his jizm, but for a moment she imagined what it would be like to be flooded with his seed. To feel his child growing within her.

But it wouldn't really be his, because Rhys was in Marshal's body. Keeping track of all of this was making her nuts. Reality encroached on the afterglow as he slid his cock from her. Still half hard, his phallus was slick and shiny, wet from what her body yielded. A cold chill gripped her lungs. It was bad enough they had engaged in half-unprotected sex, but the choice really hadn't been Rhys's to make. Marshal had been willing to screw her before, but from behind the safety of his health guard. He'd had no choice in Rhys's takeover or what was done to his body now. Boil away the unusual circumstances and the two of them had essentially raped Marshal. Gen's stomach lurched. *Dear God, what have I done?*

His brows drew down and he reached for her. "What's the matter?"

Shoving him away, she rushed to the bathroom before she lost her breakfast. Slamming the door between them, she wished she could hide from this problem forever.

Rhys knocked on the bathroom door. "Gen, are you all right, sweetness?"

The only answer was the sound of her retching.

Shaking his head, he went to the other washroom to clean his—Marshal's—body. While he waited for the water to warm, he reflected on the most erotic encounter of his life and how he'd still been swimming in the golden sea of tranquility when the thick dark storm clouds of Gen's revulsion buffeted against him.

Stepping into the tub, he cleansed his host body with the fragrant soap that smelled similar to Gen's skin. What had gone so horribly wrong? He needed to talk to her yet felt sure she required some time to herself. Maybe the avalanche of feelings had been too much for her to endure.

They would have plenty of time to sort out their differences over the coming weeks. Rhys had once heard a man profess that visiting the empath's solar system was a monthlong sojourn. So, figuring half the time to reach the moon where he'd been captured, it would take them at least two full weeks.

His cock hardened at the thought of two weeks with nothing to do but explore her magnificent body. Discover every secret little hot spot with his fingers, his tongue, his shaft. Letting her do the same to him . . .

He'd just gripped his renewed erection when something pounded on the bathroom door.

"The weather is getting worse. If we don't leave for Albany now, we'll never make it to the spaceport before it shuts down." Her voice was brisk and matter-of-fact, and white-hot tension radiated from her, so strong he could feel it through the door.

Grunting, he rose and let the water out of the tub. There would be plenty of time to indulge himself soon enough.

13

"Took you long enough," Gen muttered when Rhys climbed inside her rental. Not wanting to arouse suspicion at Illustra, they decided to leave Marshal's vehicle at the cabin. Returning it early might send up a few red flags, and she needed time to figure out what she was going to say and do. Should she go with Rhys, to ensure nothing bad happened to Marshal's body? She couldn't help but feel responsible for Marshal's well-being, even if he was the evil bastard Rhys claimed. But going with him meant staying with Rhys, and that didn't seem smart, regardless of what her runaway hormones wanted.

Gen eyed him as he settled into the safety harness on the passenger's side. Watching him made her uncomfortable, so she stared at the layer of snow coating the other rental. If Marshal ever got his body back, he'd have one hell of an overdue fee on his hands.

"Why are you so angry?" Rhys turned to stare at her. White flakes littered his dark hair, making him look as though a halo encircled his head.

Gen backed out of the driveway, careful to avoid the low-hanging limbs of the fir trees weighted down with heavy snow, and pointed the car toward town and the highway. "Do you really need to ask?"

His tone was patient as he explained, "I'm an empath, not a mind reader."

"I really don't want to talk about it right now. How about you let me in on your travel plans?"

"We need to get to the Mars Outpost and from there book passage to the outer rim."

"You're shitting me, right?" She risked a glance at him before paying closer attention to the push of the wind against the vehicle. Rhys wore the expression she recognized when he didn't understand her colloquial speech—part puzzled, part annoyed. "Do you have any idea how many credits it takes to get to the rim?"

"That won't be a problem." He waggled his palm at her. "This one's on Marshal."

A hearty gust blew the car too close to the trees on the right side of the road, and it took some serious engine revving for her to correct their course. "You're determined to violate him in every possible way, huh?"

He had the nerve to wink at her. "Just keeping up with the precedent you set, sweets."

Gen cleared her throat, tamping down a fresh wave of guilt. "Touché. Okay, can you tell me where on the rim we're heading?" She winced at the implication that she'd be going with him.

"One of the moons in the Omicron Theta system." Rhys didn't elaborate further, and Gen was tired of pulling information out of him a thread at a time. She'd be better off plucking all the gray hairs from her head one by one. At least then she'd appear less frazzled.

Rhys touched her arm lightly, making her jump. "You need to leave this at the spaceport, maybe even in storage. We don't want to provide them a way to track us."

She made a noncommittal sound. Here she was with a handsome man, asking her to run away with him and leave all traces of her previous life behind. Fantasy was not all it's cracked up to be.

Despite the inclement weather, they made decent time to the spaceport. Before returning her rental, Gen phoned Amelia, one of her contacts at a local travel agency. "Hiya, Ami."

"Gen! Oh, girl, I heard about what happened to you. A damn shame losing your job over such a small thing."

"I lost a person. That's not exactly a small thing, Ami."

Amelia snorted. "Ornery old bat had it coming if you ask me. They found her holed up at one of the mining settlements, drunk as a star sailor on leave. Found herself a new husband too. You're practically a matchmaker. Bet you'll get an invite to their wedding."

Gen snorted. "Not holding my breath on that one. Can you book a trip for me?"

Her friend squealed and pivoted to start typing on an invisible keyboard. "You're doing the right thing here, honey, taking a trip with your man and getting away from it all."

"He's not—"

Rhys made a quick slashing motion with his hand, and Gen thought it through. Probably better if it looked like she was taking a trip with a lover, at least from a records point of view. Customs beyond the casinos on Saturn's rings were not as stringent as they ought to be. Having Marshal/Rhys traveling as her significant other made their trail murkier for anyone who might want to follow.

"Not what?"

"Not stingy with anything. No expense spared. That's my man."

Rhys grinned appreciatively.

Ami typed in a few requests. "When do you want these for?"

"The sooner the better." Gen cracked her knuckles and waited.

"I've got two last-minute cancellations on the Farewell Star cruiser heading out first rotation in the morning. It's cutting it a little bit close, but your shuttle should get there in plenty of time."

"Excellent, Ami. I owe you one."

"Do you want me to book return passage now?"

"Sure. Whatever you have returning, in about a week." Rhys could get what he needed to accomplish done by then or he was on his own.

A low hum as Amelia queued in the reservations. "All set. How do you want to pay for this?"

Ignoring the charge that raced through her body at the unshielded contact, she took his hand in hers. Splaying his fingers, she pressed the pad of his thumb against the screen of the comm unit. "Credit scan should be coming in now."

"Acknowledged. You are good to go! Have a fantabulous time!"

Gen smiled until Amelia's image faded. "Do we really have to do this?" She winced at the underlying whine in her voice.

"No," Rhys surprised her by saying. "I have to, but the choice is yours. Consider what you'd be turning your back on if you don't come with me now. I want you with me and not just because you make me stronger."

Frustration welled in her. "I'm no hero, Rhys. I don't know how you expect to bring down an entire corporation, no matter what they are doing. We should just go to the authorities."

Green eyes burned with a passionate resolve. "Do you honestly think your authorities would care? Our system is isolated and produces nothing of trade value. We don't have a seat on the embargo council—don't want a voice under the flag of free commerce. No, the only way to get your government to acknowledge what the board at Illustra is doing is to show them how it will impact their lives."

He opened the car door and retrieved their bags from the back. "You don't have to help me, Gen. But please consider what would happen to this world if Illustra succeeds. No more rational thought, everyone being governed solely by their emotional drives and impulses."

She stared out the windshield at the parking lot full of hovercraft. "I'm not sure it would be so different."

He tilted his head to the side, obviously studying more than just her facial expression. "So you're willing to let your people be emotionally manipulated into making decisions?"

"I didn't say that. I'm not questioning the validity of your argument, Rhys. I'm just wondering if there's anything I can do to change the outcome."

"Not if you don't get out of the car." He slammed the door in her face.

Gen continued staring out at nothing, her mind whirling. What was waiting for her at home? No job, no man. An empty apartment. Even worse, Nana and her litany of questions. Was a trip to the rim really such an imposition?

Gen's moral compass had always pointed in a different direction from the norm. She worried over things her peers dismissed or ignored altogether. Yet when compared to Rhys's absolute conviction, she felt as shallow as a puddle.

He promised her nothing and asked for her help over and over, even after she'd refused him before. Pride didn't matter to him, nor did he feel shame—just a burning determination to continue on his quest. He wanted her with him, though she still didn't understand why. *And you'll never figure it out just sitting in the car either.*

Gen tossed the key to the sloe-eyed rental steward and scurried across the icy blacktop after her empath.

"We're going to miss it." Gen's knee bounced as she stared straight ahead. Rhys turned from the vid screen where he'd watched the blur of warp space to survey her nervous mien. Her colors formed a sickly yellow shield around her body.

Reaching forward, he placed his hand on her knee. "Why are you so anxious?"

Though he'd intended it as a gesture meant to soothe, she jerked away as though he'd scalded her flesh. "Hands to yourself, please."

"Why, when my touch brings you pleasure? Why would you deny yourself?"

"Habit," she muttered. The knee resumed bouncing.

Her actions continued to puzzle him. He'd taken an enormous chance by leaving her in the parking lot to make her own choice. It had been a calculated risk, one that had worked in his favor. Gen could no longer claim she had been coerced into coming with him. Perhaps her agitation was due to their time table. "We will not miss the cruiser—we are actually several minutes ahead of schedule."

She nodded once but kept up her agitated movements. The woman across the aisle looked at her twitchy actions before catching his eye, her aura shining peach with understanding insight. "Nervous spacer?"

"I've never been up before," Gen responded automatically. Rhys's eyes went wide at her admission.

"But I thought you worked in the off-world travel industry?"

Her complexion appeared waxy. "I arranged vacations for other people. Never had enough time or credits to take one myself."

The woman tsked. "You'll get used to it after the first couple of days." She offered them a smile and returned to her portable reading device.

Rhys took the woman's calm assurance into himself and was tempted to let it flow into Gen. But he had vowed not to impact her emotions without her express permission. "Let me ease you."

Her eyebrows drew together for an instant, but then she leaned away from him, as though the physical distance might keep her safe. "I don't want your emotional mickey to mellow me out, all right? Just let me feel what I'm feeling when I feel it."

He glanced at the nearby passengers before pitching his voice low enough to barely be heard over the roar of the warp drive. "Don't those emotions taste bitter to you?"

She frowned and cut a glace at him. "Feelings don't have any taste at all for me. They do for you?"

He nodded. "It's why I like to see you happy. The resonance from your joy is so much sweeter than this agitation."

She snorted. "Figures. You only want me to be happy because it makes *you* happy."

Her irritation chafed at him. "Why does that offend you?"

"It just does." Her knee bounced double time.

The warp engines' droning faded to a low hum. Out of his view screen, he saw the chalky red surface of Mars, Earth's nearest neighbor. Though the planet remained uninhabitable, the space station in elliptical orbit around it teemed with life. Several star cruisers and large freighters were docked along the cylindrical tubing that made up the lower levels of the space station. He reached forward and retrieved the pamphlet stuffed in the seat pocket in front of him. According to the printed material, the upper levels housed lavish restaurants that revolved within in the station alternately overlooking the planet and the vast expanse of space beyond.

Gen leaned over him, careful not to make direct contact, and sighed with regret. "I always wanted to dine at one of the restaurants. The views must be breathtaking."

She smelled divine, like a combination of winter blossoms that peeked out of the snow on his home world and the fresh clean mountain air at the abbey. And something else inexplicable but just as alluring. His cock grew hard as he recalled the taste of her on his lips when he licked the tender folds between her thighs. How he wanted to do that again, to see the sparks erupt from her skin as she climaxed while he feasted on her pleasure.

Though she had asked him to keep his hands to himself, he couldn't help but touch a strand of her dark hair, silky tangles that fell forward as she craned her neck for a better look.

She jerked away abruptly. "Back off, loverboy."

"Why do my attentions unsettle you all of a sudden?"

Her lips compressed into a thin line. "It's not right, what you're doing. To Marshal, to me. We're just tools to you, like you were for Illustra."

Anger flared deep, and it took all his mental composure to hold his tongue. "You don't know what you're talking about."

"Wouldn't be the first time. Two wrongs don't make a right, Rhys. It's not okay to hurt people because someone hurt you. To use me to hurt him. He didn't consent to what we did, and in my mind that spells rape."

That's what had been troubling her? "Gen, I'm not hurting Marshal in any way. Neither have you. Sure, he wouldn't be happy not being in control, but it's not a grave offense, especially considering he was responsible for the ruination of hundreds—if not thousands—of lives!"

She crossed her arms over her chest. "That still doesn't make it right."

"Sweetness, try and understand. He's from my world, not yours. Fluid transfer during sexual encounters is perfectly acceptable to our people. I'll admit that I need his body and I need your emotions. But I have not harmed either one of you to suit my own needs."

She still appeared wary, though the stubborn angle of her jaw seemed less severe. He rubbed a thumb over her cheekbone. "Once I get my body back, I'll release Marshal into his and turn him over to the high council for trial. No harm will come to him while I'm in possession of his body. You have my word as a spiritual leader."

Gen nodded. "Okay. I guess."

Sensing he'd made progress with her, he leaned back against the seat. "Why did you agree to work for Illustra?"

She blew out a breath. "Thinking I could do that was beyond ridiculous. Have you ever wanted desperately to be something other than what you are?"

Rhys swallowed, remembering the night he'd fled his home world for the sanctuary of the abbey. He could still smell the coppery tang of blood, could still hear the man's screams. Shaking off the unwanted memory, he focused on Gen. "I have," he rasped.

She met his gaze as the engines shut off altogether. The shuttle shook as the station's docking gear engaged. Though she'd been in a hurry only moments ago, now she seemed compelled to explain herself, and she moved in closer to him as the other passengers stood to disembark.

"Ever since I was little, I've been . . . different. I like to blame it on what happened to my parents, that I was forced to grow up quicker to help Nana and Gramps with Tanny, but I have these memories from before. I worried over things normal kids don't even think about."

Despite her earlier protests, he took her hand, lacing his fingers through hers. "There is nothing wrong with you, Gen. You care about the welfare of others, not just yourself. It's why you came with me, isn't it?"

She searched his face, almost desperately. The intensity of her need gripped him hard. He didn't know what she sought, but he felt compelled to provide whatever it might be. "I don't know why I came with you." Her confession was low and tinged with frustration.

"I'm glad you did. Come on, or we'll miss our connection."

His hand still clutching hers, he led her to the tunnel, a grin plastered on his borrowed face.

14

Gen thought she might keel over from exhaustion, but no way in this universe would she miss the bon voyage send-off party at the observation deck, even if Rhys had to prop her up like a dysfunctional marionette amid the falling balloons and confetti.

"It's tradition in our culture to wave good-bye to our loved ones while the ship pulls out of dock." Three blasts from the ship's airhorn rocked the dock slightly as the cruise ship disengaged. Rhys grabbed her around the waist to keep her from pitching into the viewport.

"But you don't know anyone here." His tone, patiently indulgent, washed over her, the same way his touch made her long for things she'd be better off dismissing altogether. Off to the stern, the Mars station grew smaller and smaller as they headed to the Alpha Centuri hyperlane.

"That's not the point." She set her chin at a stubborn angle. "It's a farewell to what we knew before, whether it is another person, a place, or a way of life. It provides closure."

He remained silent for a moment, and she watched the station grow smaller through the viewport. "Humans are funny about closure. You seem compelled to identify concrete endings and beginnings," Rhys mused, studying the people who hollered and chortled around them, a cacophony of voices united by excitement. "Always marking the passage of time, yet wasting so much of it."

Gen turned to face him, scowling. "How do we waste time?"

He inclined his head to an elderly group of matrons chittering away around the banquet table. "Small talk, for example. What is the point of speaking when you have no information to relay?"

Gen watched the women fawn over each other's fine dresses and upscale coiffures. "Talking helps us feel connected to one another."

He raised an eyebrow. "I thought that's what sex was for."

A young mother passing by cast Rhys a shocked look and hauled her toddler farther down the deck.

"Lower your voice," Gen hissed. "People are staring at us."

He tilted his head in confusion. "Why?"

She groaned. "You're like a child, you know? Why, why, why? *Because*, Rhys, there are certain things we don't discuss out in public, where anyone can overhear."

He didn't bat an eyelash as he repeated, "Why?"

She huffed out a breath. "Look, I get that you don't think much of humanity on the whole because all you've seen are horny people who want to come. That's a strong drive, but it's not all we are. We have relationships that have nothing to do with sex."

Rhys scowled. "Of course you do. I'm not stupid, Gen. I understand about different kinds of connections. What I don't understand is why you all hide the sexual part of yourselves."

"What, like you would go talk to your sister about the intimacies we've shared?"

He shocked her by nodding. "If she required the information for some reason, yes."

Gen blanched and grabbed his hand. "Come on."

"Where are we going?" He let her tug him down to the connection tubes that ran between levels.

"To our cabin. If you insist in delving into these personal subjects, we need privacy before I kill you in public and we both end up with our faces on the evening news vids."

Thankfully, Rhys remained silent as they descended into the belly of the ship. Since their reservation had been last minute, their assigned cabin didn't have a private viewport. She'd probably sleep the whole time anyhow. Gen yawned and pressed her thumb against the scanner. The door slid open with a small hiss.

Struggling out of her jacket, she entered the cabin, dragging Rhys in her wake. "I cannot believe you'd feel comfortable discussing the intimate details of our sex life with your sister! Or anyone else for that matter! That sort of thing should be private."

He stepped toward her, reaching out to hold the jacket she struggled to remove. "Not on a world full of empaths who can sense your desire the moment you feel it. There is nothing shameful about pleasure, Gen. Everyone needs it, craves the touch of another's hands on his body. As I am craving yours right now. One of the many reasons I wanted to get you alone."

Now it was her turn to ask, "Why else?"

"Being around so many people . . . disturbs me. I am unused to crowds, and the barrage of emotion was overwhelming. I apologize if I acted inappropriately." He reached out to stroke her cheek. "Besides, you need to rest."

His consideration touched her. "You're right. And I'm sorry if you were uncomfortable." Tilting her head to the side, she winced at the crick in her neck.

"Let me massage the tension from you," Rhys offered.

A massage sounded heavenly; so much rigidity had bunched her muscles, and fatigue made every twinge sharper. But could she really stand his hands on her body again? "I'm not sure that's a good idea."

"Why not? Do you not trust me to keep from touching you intimately without your invitation?"

She stared into his eyes, gauging the risk and weighing it against the benefits. "No sex. Underwear stays on."

He nodded in agreement. "Get undressed and lie on the bed." Before she could ask, he offered her his back.

A real gentleman? Though she wouldn't admit it out loud, Gen loved the fact that he didn't feel entitled to view her naked body, even though he'd caressed almost every inch of it in some form or another. It made her want to show it to him all the more. What was her damage?

She stripped down to her panties—of fracking course it had to be a thong—and settled facedown on the large mattress. "Okay," she mumbled into the pillow.

Rhys bent to rummage through Marshal's duffel. He produced a bottle of the coconut verbena oil.

She smiled at him. "Where did you get that?"

His grin warmed her. "No sense leaving everything in the cabin, right?"

"I just hope my grandmother doesn't get it in her head to go there and discover all that stuff. She'll never let me live it down, and I shudder to hear what all she'll do with it."

Rhys poured the oil on his hands and rubbed them together, activating the warming agent. He started by running his palms along her spine, working in smooth circles outward, his touch light and tender at first, then going deeper, kneading the muscles beneath.

Gen couldn't keep her moan of bliss inside if her life depended on it. "Oohh, that feels wonderful. . . ."

"So, where does touch like this fall in the spectrum of human relationships?" Rhys asked, running his palms along her sides.

"Any kind of touch is intimate but is not necessarily sexual in nature. Some people actually provide massages for a living."

He didn't say anything for a time, working deeper into her

shoulders and neck. She gasped when his thumb discovered a particularly tight knot. "On my world, this kind of contact is reserved exclusively for lovers."

She stiffened a bit, but when he didn't try to mess with their dynamic, she relaxed more fully. "Any special reason for that?"

"You can ask a straight man to touch a member of the opposite sex and not have a physical response to it, but the outcome might be disappointing. It is too difficult to separate touch from sex. Lovers are supposed to know each other's bodies, inside and out, to increase the pleasure output for both."

"You mean they feed off of each other, like you've done with me?"

He made an irritated sound. "Putting it crudely, yes. It is all about filling needs for each other, wanting to give of one's self and have someone who wishes to give back equally. A real connection, unlike that hollow display above us or the sham Illustra offers."

An awful thought manifested in her gray matter, and she needed the answer as much as she dreaded it. "Do you have one? A lover back home?"

His hands stilled. "Of course not. My people bond for life. I was still young when I sought refuge at the abbey. Being with you, Gen, is the closest I've ever come to having someone to connect with on that level."

She let out a relieved breath she hadn't even realized she'd been holding. "What is it like, bonding like that?"

He took a deep breath and moved down to massage her lower back. "There is no way to describe it in your language. No ceremony or official record. To bond is to let go of yourself entirely, merge with your lover and re-form as a stronger unit, two halves to the whole."

She sighed at his description. "It sounds lovely."

"My father and mother have been bonded for many years. I

envied their bliss." He took a deep breath. "I find myself . . . frustrated, Gen, because I cannot fulfill you the way you need."

Her heart rate increased, though his hands remained soothing, almost impersonal where they touched her. Had she gotten it all wrong? Here she believed Rhys was using her, and in a way he was, but not because he wanted only to take from her. She'd denied him the chance to show her affection almost every time, thinking distance would keep her detached. "Why do you want to do that?"

"Because you have given me so much. I wish to give back, yet you refuse to let me pleasure you or see to your needs."

"I'm sorry. I don't know any other way to—"

"Shhhh, relax." He swept her hair to the side, rubbed her scalp. "You are human—it's all you know how to be. I didn't tell you this to make you feel guilty or press demands on you. I only want you to better understand how I feel because you cannot sense it. Sleep now, talk later."

Sighing, Gen surrendered to oblivion.

Rhys covered her with a blanket and settled into the armchair across the room to watch over her. Every time he looked at her, she seemed to grow lovelier. If she had been of his kind, he was certain the bond would have settled between them already. The warning signs were all there. Growing attraction, reorganization of his priorities, and a desperate need to pleasure her body and feed her soul in every possible way. All symptoms indicated he had started to think of her differently than any other woman he'd ever been intimate with.

Bonds were sacred, not something one entered into lightly. Several potential life mates in modern society refused to bond at all, instead choosing to stay together in a less demanding relationship. Rhys had been taught from birth that bonding was paramount to happiness—a belief only made stronger with his time spent in study and worship. A bond was not necessary to life, but it made life worth living.

Gen wasn't an empath. From what little he'd witnessed, humans didn't stay with one partner for very long, sometimes not even until sunrise. He couldn't bond with her, because he had no kind of future to share with her. His mission had to be his top priority, and Gen deserved more from a bonded mate. Could she even accept the sort of commitment that level of intimacy entailed?

As he watched her sleeping form, an idea took root in his mind. He'd promised Gen he would not try to emotionally influence her, but he'd said nothing about reading her emotional state. When they'd talked on the transport, she had admitted to having a burning desire to belong. And she'd also admitted pleasuring Marshal had unnerved her because she felt loyalty toward Rhys. Perhaps she was capable of bonding, even if her peers weren't.

He waited until the captain of the star cruiser announced they had entered the first warp current tunnel. She'd slept several hours already and lay curled on her side facing him, her breath coming out in little puffs of air. *Forgive me, sweet, but I have to know what you really think.*

Rising from the chair, he stripped off his clothes and climbed into the bed beside her, molding his front to her back. She snuggled in deep, murmuring something incoherent.

Swallowing, Rhys focused part of his attention inside himself, listening to Marshal's heartbeat, steady and true, and focused the rest on the heat of the woman in his arms.

His essence divided neatly, one part holding down the fort in Marshal's body and the other flowing into Gen. This time he didn't try to seize control, just shared the space with her, happy to float nearby.

Who's there? her voice asked, so strong and clear.

Rhys.

He'd expected some sort of resistance and was stunned

when she lit up, clearly excited to have him within her again. Her body snuggled into his as her mind whispered, *I missed cohabitating with you.*

Really? The part of him still in Marshal's body grew hard, wanting to be inside her in every way. *I like being within you, hearing your thoughts, sharing your feelings.*

Her body grew wet with need. He felt the ache in her breasts, and his hands moved to cup them.

Oh, so good. She sighed, relaxing against him. He dabbled with her hardened nipples, tugging, rolling the nubs until she squirmed.

Will you let me make you come?

Oh, yes, she breathed. *I'd love that.*

I'm going to activate my germ shield—otherwise you'll be angry with me when you wake fully.

He maneuvered her onto her back and her legs fell open. Trailing his fingers down the center of her body, he took his time exploring her curves, while inside he shared her delicious anticipation.

How does this feel? His fingers parted her labia, the middle digit caressing the soft skin revealed between the outer lips.

Her hips rocked up slowly, seeking to increase the contact. *I ache, Rhys.*

For me? His thumb swirled over her clitoris in a light caress. *Do you want only me?*

In this state, halfway between dreaming and awake, she didn't even hesitate. *Yes.*

Good. He stroked her harder, until she gasped. His index finger delved into the slick channel, exploring her wetness. *I want only you, Gen. I don't even want to share you with Marshal, but I'll use him to pleasure you like this until I can retrieve my own body, bury my cock deep inside you. Do you want that?*

She bucked her hips wildly. *Yes, oh yes, Rhys.*

He slid a second digit into her, increased the rhythm. *Say it, say that you are mine.*

I'm yours, Rhys.

So caught up in the heat of the moment, Rhys almost asked her then and there to bond with him. He couldn't, though, not like this. Her conscious mind wouldn't even remember it. Rhys had gotten his answer. Gen obviously could accept a bond with him, despite everything he'd put her through and the limitations of her humanity. He didn't know whether to be thankful or disappointed.

Let me feel you come, Gen. I want to know what an orgasm feels like to you, so when I do bury my cock deep in here—he thrust his fingers in hard—*I'll know exactly how I make you feel.*

She shuddered, her body giving over to her release. The explosion engulfed both of them, and he lost track of where he was as they rode the waves together. His shaft ached, full of seed, but it was distant compared to the shattering delight swallowing him whole. *Bliss, sheer bliss. How can you stand it?*

You get used to it. More, rub a little faster, right—

He felt it then, too, another one building. More ecstasy on the way. Groaning, he pressed down on her clit with the pad of his thumb, felt her feminine muscles clutch his fingers as it hit, drowning him in a sparkling sea of divine rapture.

The tide receded and he became aware of himself once more. His erection was pressed firmly against her ass, hips rocking, seeking a way to penetrate her body and lose his seed deep within.

You can if you want to. Dazed from her orgasms, Gen offered herself up, the baby lamb sidling up to the starving wolf. This version of her didn't care about what happened next, the ramifications of another union. Here in the dream world, she was raw and honest. An ache developed inside his chest, the smoldering need to protect her, even from herself.

I can't, my sweet. You are not awake and I promised no sex. You won't even remember what happened. It feels all right to give, but not to take from you when all your defenses are down.

Silly man. Let me ease you, then. Her unconscious mind maintained so much control—she actually managed to grasp the bottle of lube he'd left on the shelf behind the bed. Squeezing some onto her right hand, she offered him the bottle. When he hesitated, she pushed. *You know I want this, Rhys. I want to pleasure you. Why do you fight it? No one is going to abscond with Marshal's body—no one even knows you are in there. Let me do this, please.*

His lips settled over hers, and he took the bottle from her hand. *A beautiful woman, begging to make me come. Is there any way in the universe I can say no to this?*

Not if you want to keep your man card.

He worked the liquid over his straining erection, making it slick. The seed had already ascended halfway up his shaft. *This won't take long.*

Gen's hand closed around him and gave a slight tug. Rhys groaned and flopped back, doubly flummoxed because she truly did enjoy this contact, liked touching him, pleasuring him.

Her other hand slipped down to cup his sac as she thought, *Come for me, Rhys. Show me what I do to you.*

With a groan he did, coming all over her hand and belly in a white sticky mess.

His eyes went wide. *Her hand, shit.* She hadn't activated her health guard, and his seed had marked her. *Sweetness, I'm sorry.*

I don't mind, Gen thought, but he knew she would as soon as she woke and realized—

The ship rocked, tossing him out of bed onto the cold metal decking. Sirens blared and red warning lights flashed. Gen awoke just as a second hit upset the ship. Bare-breasted and covered in his seed, she stared at him, her gaze burning with betrayal.

"What the *hell* is going on?"

15

Rhys looked guilty as hell, sprawled naked on the deck. Considering, that she was coated in what most definitely was *not* tapioca pudding and that his little star sailor saluted her at halfmast, she connected the dots with horrifying ease. He'd lulled her into a false sense of security and then taken liberties with her unconscious body. *Sick bastard.* Tears burned the backs of her eyes, but she'd light herself on fire before she went all weepy in front of him again. How many times did he have to betray her before she understood? *Why did I ever think I could trust him?*

"You can trust me," he answered her unspoken thought.

Lights flickered overhead a few times before drop-kicking them into darkness. A low whine as the massive engines shut off and the ship listed to the starboard side. Gen landed on top of him, her breasts surrounding what she thought was his face. Strong arms wrapped around her. Violently, she shoved him away. "Back the hell off, Rhys."

"It's not what you think, Gen. I know you're angry, but I

need you to hold still for a minute." He spoke levelly, which made her feel hysterical by proxy.

"Why, so you can finish manhandling my body?"

His tone was calm, and it pissed her off all the more. "I need to get a piece of me out of you."

"You *what*?" It was worse than she thought, having believed his perverseness had been confined to the physical. Was there no limit to how far he'd go, how deeply the betrayal would run? She struggled to hit him and managed to knee him solidly in the nuts, but he refused to release her.

"Be still, sweet. You can punish me all you like later, I vow it. For now, I need to be whole before we encounter whatever is out there." He jerked his head toward the door.

Distant thuds sounded and Gen forgot her ire, listening. "It sounds like the ship is docking."

"Or being boarded." Gripping her hair in his fist, he rolled until he had trapped her beneath him and pinned her wrists above her head. Despite his recent orgasm and her punishing blow to the twins, his erection pressed into her belly.

With words as her only remaining defense, she blurted, "How could you, Rhys? I trusted you!"

He shifted to hold both of her wrists with one hand and clamped the other over her mouth. "Quiet."

She bit his palm, but he didn't even flinch. Her body shook, not from fear but from rage. Being scared of him would be the sensible reaction, but Gen was too busy feeling hurt and angry.

Something tugged inside her head, and she gasped at the bizarre sensation. Rhys muttered, "Damn," and leaned down closer to her. "You have to let go, sweetness."

She mumbled into the palm of his hand. He removed it and she snarled, "I'm not holding on to anything."

"Not consciously, no. Your unconscious mind doesn't want me to leave."

As her pupils adjusted to the darkness, Gen could make out the silhouette of his face. The jut of his stubble-covered chin, the sharp aquiline nose, the firm lips she still—in spite of everything—wanted to kiss. *It would serve him right if I smashed him with my forehead.* She didn't, just continued to stare up at him.

A scraping sound like someone had taken an industrial-size can opener to the side of the ship echoed in the metal corridors. "Please, Gen, there is no time."

"I don't even know what the fracking hell you are talking about! What can I do?"

"Stop resisting me. You're torn in two, between doing what you think is right and the pull of your heart's desire, and it's making you unreasonably tense." One hand stroked along her cheekbone. "Please, trust me."

She blew out a breath. A hell of a thing to ask, especially coming from the man who'd just perved off all over her unconscious and unshielded body. He wouldn't hurt her, though, at least not physically; she still felt relatively certain of that. The warmth of his hand beckoned her, a sweet invitation as well as the ultimate promise of bliss. She could almost hear him plead, *Believe in me.*

By small increments, her body relaxed and this time the sensation felt more like a gentle sweep than a hard yank. Rhys sucked in a deep breath, his big body shuddering for a protracted moment before his weight left her.

He helped her to her feet and commanded in a low tone, "Get dressed quickly."

"I need to clean up first," Gen hissed, stumbling toward the sani-facilities. She felt around in the dark until her hand touched the cool metal spigot. Wetting a cloth with warm recycled ship's water, she did her best to remove all traces of the massage oil and his seed from her body. "Don't think all is forgiven here, Rhys."

A soft clanging sound told her he'd refastened his belt. "I wouldn't dream of it."

She shivered and picked the first item out of her suitcase, a sleeveless dress with a built-in bra. The fabric had just settled around her hips when the door to their cabin disintegrated. Gen winced, the bright red emergency hallway illumination a painful contrast to the darkness.

"Hands where I can see 'em!" a man's voice commanded, shoving the barrel of a sonic pulse pistol under her chin. "Name and occupation."

"Genevieve Luzon, former off-world vacay coordinator," she responded automatically.

Rhys didn't answer, and she cut her gaze to where he stood shirtless, with a weapon trained on him. The frightened screams of other passengers echoed through the ship. Gen swallowed and the barrel of the gun pressed deeper into her throat. *What the hell is he waiting for?*

Gen's captor yanked her over so she stood facing Rhys and aimed the weapon to her temple. In a low voice he said, "Tell me what I want to know or you'll be scrubbing her brains from your face."

Rhys's gaze fixed on hers, and his look said, *I'm so sorry, Gen.*

Oh, God, he wasn't going to reveal his identity. They were going to shoot her! She might as well kiss her extra-large ass good-bye.

"Now, that ain't no way to treat a lady." Another voice, strong with the authority of command, rang out behind Gen. "He's the one we want."

The gun moved away and Gen risked a look over her shoulder. The man in the doorway was huge, with shoulders so massive he had to turn sideways to enter the cabin. His clothes were simple—leather boots, pants, and an open leather vest he wore without a shirt under it. Though she couldn't make out the exact color of his eyes, they glowed in the dimness. He wore his hair in a long dark braid, like a hunk of rope snaking down his back. He moved forward slowly, deliberately, and stopped beside Gen.

"Marshal, you slippery sonofabitch. What was your great plan, hide among the humans until I forgot?" He made a tsking sound and shook his head before turning his attention to Gen. "Hole up behind the protection of a woman's skirts. Not very chivalrous, now, is it? Who is she?"

"No one of consequence." Rhys spoke in a bored tone that Gen knew he didn't feel. Damn it, he'd snatched the wrong body, one that had crossed a space pirate! Some days she really shouldn't bother hauling her carcass out of bed.

The man touched Gen's cheek, sending a shiver through her entire nervous system. "Funny thing, if I traveled with someone I cared for and was forced to face a bunch of brigands with weapons, I'd pretend she don't matter none too."

"You know who I am. Do you really think I'm capable of feeling anything for another?" Rhys took a step forward and the man holding the gun on him smashed the barrel of it against his skull. There was a hideous crunch, and he crumpled to the deck. Gen shrieked and moved to help him, but Mr. Large-and-In-Charge hauled her back against his chest.

"Nice try, Marshal, but she's coming too. For entertainment value."

Rhys hadn't felt the primal urge to hurt another living being in years, not since before his time with the brotherhood. But as he came to in a small, gray room that could only be a prison cell, he wanted to end Marshal's existence once and for all. He'd swapped places with the bastard and he was *still* imprisoned against his will. The only difference was the addition of a splitting headache.

"Gen?" he called out, but didn't know whether she couldn't

hear him or chose to ignore him. He probed the surrounding area but didn't detect her emotional signature, though several others were nearby. They must be on board the pirate vessel. *Marshal, you dumbass, what did you do?*

Groaning, Rhys sat up and took in his surroundings. The force field hummed low and steady, one voice in a chorus of them. The cell across the way from him sat open and empty, perhaps waiting for Gen. Where had they taken her?

He didn't allow the panic he felt to overcome him, though it threatened, waiting in the wings, ready to trounce him at a moment's notice. Sucking in a deep breath, he locked his emotions away, knowing this situation called for a level head, not knee-jerk reactions. Only Gen's safety mattered now.

"Hello?" He stood, swaying slightly, and shuffled his feet forward until the electrical current from the force field made the hair on his arm stand on end. If he touched it, no doubt he'd receive a shock strong enough to render him unconscious, perhaps even stop his heart. "Is anyone there?"

Rhys?!?!

He breathed a sigh of relief to hear her voice in his head once more. If she could project her thoughts like this, Gen must be asleep. Considering how she'd reacted to what her sleeping self had done with him earlier, he doubted Gen even knew she was a telepath. Her abilities were buried deep down in her subconscious.

His education on the emotional strengths of humanoids hadn't prepared him for dealing with a telepath. It had been easy enough to talk to her when he was inside her body. Distance didn't matter to conversations of the heart, so the same might hold true for those between linked minds. Picturing Gen, he thought, *I'm here, sweetness.*

Are you all right? Gen asked. *They hit you so hard, I thought your skull would cave in.*

He touched the sore spot on the back of his head, wincing. *I'll be fine. Do you know where you are?*

She sniffled. *The big one took me to a bedroom on the pirate ship, sealed the doors before he left. I kept shouting for you, and one of the guards came in. Knocked me out with some kind of tranquilizer.*

Do they know I'm not Marshal? That might be their only advantage.

I don't think so. Rhys, is the candle with you?

He glanced around, but Marshal's bag wasn't there. *No. I'm in some sort of cell. Gen, you need to be very careful. Don't do anything else to anger these men in any way. They are violent by nature, and your safety is my top priority. I'll kill Marshal for endangering you like this.*

The alien thought formed and left his head, and before he had a chance to sooth his rage, he heard footsteps in the corridor. *Someone's coming.*

Her panic washed over him like an icy wave. *Rhys, don't leave me!*

He had to haul in his temper. Rational thought, not hot emotions, were his only hope for rescuing Gen.

"You're awake." The large man, who seemed oddly familiar to Rhys, nodded and deactivated the force field to the holding cell. "Good. I hate waiting."

Rhys recognized the lie. This man radiated patience from the inside out. His black leather ensemble creaked as he ducked to move inside the cell.

"What, no guards?" he asked.

The man raised an eyebrow, his mien confident. "I think I can handle one rogue empath."

Considering his feelings had been bottled up tight, Rhys wagered he could. "What have you done with the girl?"

"And here I thought she didn't matter to you none." Clasping his hands behind his back, the pirate squared off, facing

Rhys at parade rest. "She is a looker, I'll give you that much, but I never would have thought you capable of tender feelings, Marshal."

This is bad, Rhys thought at Gen. *He knows Marshal, not just in passing but specifics of his personality.*

What are you going to tell him?

The truth? Rhys wouldn't rule it out, but he needed to know more about his adversary.

Be careful, Rhys. I need you.

Warmth bloomed from deep in his soul at her heartfelt confession. If only he could get the conscious Gen to admit to the same need.

"You know you don't have to stay in the hold, Marshal. I could just as easily move you up to share the room with your woman. I even have your bag of tricks." He smirked at that.

"Something amuses you?"

"Let's just say I never thought you would lower yourself to become some human's love slave. You must have been very desperate to hide from me."

"How did you find me anyway?"

The pirate waved his hand in dismissal. "Makes no never mind. We had a deal."

Rhys lifted his chin. "Refresh my memory."

A hand cracked across his face before he realized the other man had moved. "You want to play games? We can bring your woman down here, play a few rounds with her. I'll take her first, then pass her around to my boys for a little bonus. Fitting for the mistress of a whore, wouldn't you say?"

Rhys thought furiously but couldn't find any way around it. He had to tell this man the truth. "I'm not Marshal."

He braced for another blow but received only a skeptical glance. "You look an awful lot like him."

Rhys held his captor's gaze. "Aren't my eyes a different color?"

The pirate shrugged. "Contacts. The technology is over a century old."

"If you'll hear me out, I'll tell you exactly what happened."

The man stared at him for a beat and waved his hand. "I'm always in the mood for a story."

Rhys sent up a prayer that he'd find some way to explain what he didn't fully understand. Sucking in a deep breath, he glossed over the reason for going to the abbey in the first place but told the rest in vivid detail, including his time as a slave and what Gen had done to help him steal Marshal's body.

"If this is true, then where's the real Marshal?"

"Trapped inside a candle."

The pirate rose and paced the floor. "You know, I've flown from one side of this damn galaxy to the other, have seen scores of unbelievable stories, heard lies in every color of the rainbow, and this still takes the cake."

"It's not a lie, I swear—"

The second blow knocked Rhys unconscious before he hit the deck.

16

"What did you do to him?" Gen snarled as two of the overly muscled thugs dragged Rhys's unconscious form into the room where she'd gone out of her mind imagining all sorts of horrific things. The men ignored her and dropped him at her feet. She sank down to check his pulse and mumbled at their retreating backs, "Cretins."

"They're not so bad, once you get to know them."

Gen glanced up. The mammoth-sized leader clad in black leather gazed down at her, his expression blank. "He told me an interesting story. I wanted your take on it."

Rhys's pulse felt strong and steady, though a big red splotch decorated the right side of his face. He'd have one hell of a shiner in a few hours. If they lived that long.

She glanced up into the midnight eyes of their captor. "Who are you? Why did you take us hostage?"

Her questions seemed to amuse him. "My name is Zan, and technically speaking, you are not a hostage. I've got no plans to barter you—you can leave anytime you like. Though I'd recommend you put a coat on. It's cold outside." He chucked his thumb to the view screen and the vast expanse of empty space beyond.

"Sick bastard." Gen rose to her feet and squared her shoulders. "What gives you the right to yank us off of our vessel—"

Zan raised his index finger. "Truth be known, it wasn't your vessel, just a vessel you happened to be traveling aboard. And it had something I wanted, so if that doesn't give me the right to board it, I don't know what would."

His absurd spin on logic pissed her off. "What are you, two? You can't just take what doesn't belong to you!"

"Why not? I wouldn't be much of a pirate if I paid for my spoils and waited patiently for my turn. I seize what I want, the moment I want it. And right now, I want his skin as a throw rug on my cabin floor." His finger stabbed at Rhys.

Bile rose in Gen's throat at the description. "What did Marshal do to you?"

Golden eyes narrowed on her. "Ah, so then he is Marshal."

"Why would you think he isn't?"

Zan moved across the room and shook her by the shoulders before she even registered his intent. "It ain't bright to play games with me, little girl. Marshal failed to deliver and for that disappointment he will pay with his life. After I make him suffer. A. Very. Long. Time."

With no clue as to what Rhys had said to Zan, all Gen could offer him was the truth. "His name is Rhys. Illustra used him and others like him to control people emotionally. I helped him trick Marshal into abandoning his body and Rhys shut him out." Unintentionally, but she didn't figure he wanted to know all the gory details.

The pirate's eyelids didn't even flicker. "So where is the real Marshal?"

"Trapped inside Rhys's candle. We had it with us, in our luggage." She sent him a scathing glare and bitched, "If you'd been reasonable, we could have proven this to you *before* you abducted us."

Zan stared at her for a beat, telegraphing no thoughts whatsoever. Then, he removed a small metal device from his black leather vest.

Gen took a step back. "What the hell is that?"

He held the object up to his face and clicked the end like a mechanical pen. "Worried?"

"Should I be?" she shot back with venom.

A grin split Zan's face. "I like you. You remind me of someone very special. She refused to take crap from me too."

With no idea what to make of that statement, Gen offered him a weak shrug. The door behind him hissed open and a small droid zoomed in, carrying their luggage on its back like a pack mule. She raised her gaze to Zan.

"Waste not, want not, right? Besides, I wouldn't be much of a pirate if I didn't loot and pillage." He crouched down and unlatched the black duffel containing Marshal's personal effects. The candle sat right on top, as Rhys had tossed it in on their way out the door. Zan picked it up and held it in front of his face. "This our boy?"

Slowly, Gen nodded.

"How do we talk to him?"

"Rhys says he can hear everything when bound to the candle. It's how he learned English."

Zan tapped his chin, his golden eyes focused at the wall behind her head. "This seems anticlimactic somehow. I can't hurt him when he won't feel it—there ain't no point. Shit, I can't even threaten his body with another man in there. Wouldn't be sporting. You'll have to get him out, make them swap places again."

Fracking hell. "It's not that easy."

He rose and handed Gen the candle. "It never is. But if you

don't want your boyfriend to suffer through the gauntlet of pain and humiliation I have in store for Marshal, I'd suggest you find a way to simplify the situation. You have one hour."

Gen swallowed hard and watched as he left. "Shit, fuck, damn, hell, steaming piece of fracking crap."

"Hark, Juliet speaks." Though his eyes remained closed, a small smile tilted the corners of Rhys's mouth.

Gen flew to his side. "Are you all right?"

"Not even in the same galaxy as all right." He tried to sit up, failed, and groaned.

Gen braced her hands on either shoulder, keeping him in place. "Stay still, dummy."

"No, there isn't much time. I've got to get you out of here."

"Rhys, don't take this the wrong way, but unless you can morph into a personal space cruiser, I don't think you can do anything except bleed."

He opened his undamaged eye and looked up at her. "He'll hurt you if he doesn't get what he wants. He's not an evil man at heart, but he won't tolerate letting Marshal go. I vowed I wouldn't let any harm befall him. There's only one alternative left to us."

Gen swallowed. "I'm afraid to ask."

"Light the candle. We're going to need Marshal awake for this."

Rhys remained flat on his back, sprawled on the metal deck while Gen retrieved the candle, still arguing. "I still don't think this is a great idea, you and him sharing space together. Why don't you go back into the candle?"

He let his lungs expand with air and released it on a slow exhale. She still didn't understand the hell of being bound to the candle. He prayed she never would. "I won't return there unless given no other choice." Before she could protest further, he set about lowering the defenses he'd erected, preparing the body for another inhabitant.

"You could always come back inside me."

Her offer, so sincerely made, kicked him in the chest and not just because of the double entendre. "Thank you for the thought, sweetness. But I'm in a better position to protect you here. Remember what I told you?"

She cleared her throat. "Light the candle and run to the other side of the room."

"And no matter what, don't have sex with me."

Laughter effervesced from her, thrilling him with the genuine unexpectedness of it. "I'll try to restrain myself."

She crouched by his side, lighter in hand. "You ready?"

He looked up at her and nodded once. "See you soon."

The last thing he saw was the wick flaring to life before his eyes slid shut. *Come on home, you bastard.*

Gen bolted across the room. "Anything yet?"

He opened his mouth to respond, and all the air rushed out of his lungs. Struggling for oxygen, he arched up off the deck, smashing his fists against the grate. The son of a bitch was trying to kill him!

You got that right, cocksucker. Marshal's disembodied voice sounded in his ears, wrath personified. *Had your whore trick me right out of my own skin.*

"Don't do this," Rhys pleaded, expelling the little breath he had left.

"Rhys, what's the matter?" Fear coated Gen's question.

Yeah, Rhys, beg for our girl to come save your sorry ass. I'll stuff you down so deep the only thing you'll hear will be her screams as I do to her exactly what she did to me, over and over. Fuck her until she's raw and bleeding, then kill the both of you at once.

Marshal was rightfully furious, but Rhys would not allow

the other empath to bait him into losing his temper. It would only weaken his own position. "That won't save you from Zan," Rhys wheezed.

The pressure on his lungs eased slightly. *Isn't it bad enough that you stole my body, but you had to deliver it to the one man in the galaxy who wanted to maim it? You think I liked being the fuck buddy to the elite, screwing countless twats with barely a clue as to what to do? No, damn it, I was lying low. And you come along with your self-righteous streak and cock it all up!*

"Marshal," Gen spoke up over the silent war going on for the only viable territory. "I know you're pissed, but he's doing this to help get you out of here. Please, let us help you."

Rhys lost control of vision and vocal cords all at once. His and Gen's anxiety made Marshal stronger. *Don't do me any more favors, bitch. I learned the first time not to put pussy in the driver's seat.*

"You can't tell me you didn't like it. I won't believe that. You were begging for it, to find someone as strong as you, to take charge and save you from yourself. It excited you, the way I bossed you around."

Marshal's grip loosened, and Rhys could see Gen through flickering vision. Shoulders squared off with military precision, hands on hips, fear nowhere in sight. His goddess, trying to give him the home field advantage. No way would he let her gift go to waste.

Surging up, he wrapped his essence around Marshal and took them both down hard, pinning him in his own mind. He struggled anew, but Rhys expected it this time. "Do what I say or Zan will win. You'll never get a shot at vengeance if we are both dead."

We're dead anyway. Marshal sagged, all the fight evaporating like dew off a space-bound hull. *You don't know Zan. He is no lightweight we can dupe, and there are too many to fight.*

"Then we come up with a new plan." Rhys eased his hold—

just enough to allow Marshal to believe he had an opening, in case this was a trick of some sort. Nothing happened, but for Gen's sake, he would stay on alert.

"Tell us everything you know about Zan. Is he human?"

No, neither is he empath or telepath, or any other race we've encountered. He doesn't belong in this galaxy, maybe not even in this universe.

"How did you meet him?"

He found me. I'd absconded with a two-man ship from our home world, with no plan in mind. The story I told you at the abbey, about my daughter's death, was the truth. I just wanted to find someplace quiet and die.

Rhys didn't bother to hide his skepticism. "Yet you lived on, to betray your religious leaders and all the innocent people on that moon."

I didn't want to, damn it! I was just drifting in space, waiting for the end when a wormhole opened and this damn pirate ship came out. Zan picked me up, offered to take me with him if I helped him find a way home.

"What went wrong?"

Nature. I'd been alone, deprived of any emotional reso-nance, and as soon as they brought me on board, I glutted my-self. Killed three of the crew, including the pilot who had flown him here. They are not like humans—they have no natural de-fenses against empaths.

Though Rhys might have been imagining it, he thought he heard a tinge of regret in Marshal's words. "How did you es-cape?"

Jettisoned myself out of the airlock right before they jumped into hyperspace. Nothing between me and the void but a space suit. You see, no matter how strong my will to die, my survival instinct has always been stronger. Bitterness oozed from every syllable.

"So when did you sign on with Illustra?"

One of their ships had been scouting the nearby solar system. They picked up on Zan's wake and came to investigate. Second time I was unintentionally rescued. His laugh sounded hollow. My curse—I can't do anything right.

"If you think this will change anything—"

Marshal mustered enough strength to shut him up. *I don't give a shit how you feel about me, Rhys, or about much of anything. I don't want to live, but I feel compelled to keep it up, no matter what cesspool I face-plant into. My existence is parasitic, totally selfish.*

Enough of these self-indulgent recriminations. "Spare me the highlights of your personal pity party. If you want to live so badly, tell me how to get us all out of here."

Best chance is to abandon the girl. His gaze slid to Gen, though whether Rhys or Marshal controlled the action he didn't know. *She's a liability, will slow our escape. Fucking her blind might soothe Zan long enough for us to make a clean getaway.*

Through gritted teeth, Rhys growled, "Not an option."

You can't always fix it so everybody wins, O Holy One. What distinguishes the winners from the losers is the ability to outmaneuver their peers. She's an asset. Let's use her.

"I said it's not going to happen."

Then we're all going to die.

17

Watching Rhys / Marshal argue with himself, the conversation only half out loud, was the most unnerving spectacle Gen had ever witnessed. Considering the events of the last week, that really said something. He remained sprawled on the floor, head bent at an awkward angle, eyes flickering from brilliant green to fathomless black, attention totally trained on her. *Eerie much?*

Her nerves had formed a conga line and were proceeding through her stomach at a breakneck pace. "Hey, could I have a vote in whatever decisions are being made? Is that all right with the two of you?"

Black orbs narrowed at her. "No."

Her throat went dry. "Rhys, a little help here?"

The creepy eyes closed and he thrashed violently. "I never thought you were such a defeatist, Marshal."

His skin seemed to ripple as though he stood in a wind tunnel. Gen had heard of being at war within one's self, but this brought the old adage to a whole new level. Why did Rhys have to be so damned noble? From what she could tell, Marshal didn't have a problem leaving her behind to rot. After what she and Rhys had done to him, why did that surprise her?

A small, scared part of her mind wanted to beg Rhys to leave Marshal's body so they could turn him over to Zan and save their lives. Locking the cowardly sense of self-preservation down was harder than she'd expected. The only thing that held her tongue was imagining the disappointed look on Rhys's face if she even suggested it. Marshal had made his bed, and the time had come for him to lie in it, but her empath wouldn't see it that way. He wouldn't be Rhys if he didn't try to save the entire universe. The least she could do was support him.

That refrain seemed oddly familiar somehow. A severe case of déjà vu washed over her in a torrent. The truth dawned like a rising star, burning away the haze as it ascended to its rightful place in the sky. The least she could do was absolutely nothing except what Genevieve Luzon wanted to do.

What did *she* want? More than anything? The answer was so simple she felt like a nitwit for not figuring it out sooner. To be loved, by one man, who put her needs first, who held her hand and comforted her when she felt sorrow or fear. To not be placed on the back burner, her very life threatened because he had Important Things To Do. The problem with heroes, they were so busy trying to save the universe that they didn't have anything left for the ones who supported them but a quick roll in the hay or a pat on the head.

No one could save her better than she could save herself. Because no one had quite the same motivation. "Hey!" Gen pounded on the door with closed fists. "I wanna talk to Zan!"

"What are you doing?" Rhys's—or maybe it was Marshal's—question held an edge of panic.

She didn't turn around. "Bailing my own fat out of the fire." Footsteps echoed in the corridor, and she kept her insistent pounding up until the door opened and the barrel of a laser pistol was shoved in her face. Her hands went up, but she stood her ground.

"Take me to Zan."

The guard smirked at her, his piggy eyes sizing up her cleavage. "He's busy. How about I play with you for a little while instead?"

Gen smiled sweetly. "Sorry, I don't do charity work."

The butt of the gun slammed into her cheekbone, and a starburst of pain sent her to her knees. Air rushed past her, followed by a grunt and a dull thump and the guard hit the deck with a thud. Cupping her sore cheek, Gen stared up into green eyes blazing with the fires of the damned. Rhys had taken over, and he didn't look happy. "What was that?"

"A plan," she lied without batting an eyelash. She took his hand but released it the moment she found her balance. The laser pistol had slid to the open doorway, and she bent to retrieve it, but he yanked her into his chest. "Hey!"

Eyes flickering from green to black, he stared at her unblinkingly. "I ought to kill you right here."

Shivering involuntarily, she watched for his deep inhale as fear ran rampant through her. "You won't."

He squeezed her arm tighter. "Don't think because your boyfriend has been using me to fuck you means I give a shit about your welfare."

She kneed him in the sac. He grunted and reached down to cup himself. Scooping up the gun, she pointed it at him. "No, you want to feed off of me, and for that to happen, you need me alive. My rotting corpse won't sustain you."

The malice written on his face faded, and he sucked in an audible breath. "You're right on that score, little she-devil. Want to let me in on the rest of your plan?"

"No." Gen peeked her head out into the corridor. "Where do you suppose the captain is?"

"Bridge probably. I'd suggest we make our way to a cargo bay, see if they have any two-person crafts we can borrow."

Gen stopped at the end of the dimly lit hallway and poked her head out, checking for any sign that the crew knew they were on the loose. "Let's say there is and we actually manage to launch it without killing ourselves in the process. What's to keep Zan from blowing us out of the sky?" She arched an eyebrow and waited.

Marshal crossed his arms over his chest. "Truly, if you have a better plan, I'd love to hear it."

She scuttled partway down the hall, keeping low, Marshal right behind her. Who knew what kind of tech the pirates had on board? They might be able to fry her where she stood, duck-walking because it made her feel more discreet. "I'm going to create a diversion while you and Rhys emotionally manipulate the crew into taking us where we want to go."

His voice was rougher than Rhys's, more gravel, less whisky. "What sort of diversion?"

"Don't worry about it. Just get yourself together so you can take over without killing them, if at all possible." Voices drifted down the hallway, and she flattened herself against the bulkhead.

Rhys touched her arm. She could tell it was him by the tenderness in his caress, even before she saw his eyes. "There are too many of them. I sense at least half a dozen souls on this vessel, and two empaths can't manipulate them all at the same time."

"How many can you handle?"

His gaze focused inward as he thought it through. "Perhaps four, provided they are not all as focused as Zan. And that is not for an infinite period of time. A few hours at the very most. Depending on where we are in the universe, it might not be enough to change our situation and then we are all at their mercy again."

Gen blew out a breath. "What do you think, Rhys?"

His green-eyed gaze burned into hers. "Tell me how you plan to distract Zan."

"I'm going to seduce him."

"No." Rhys shook off Marshal's grasping bids to regain control. The traitor liked the idea, but Rhys refused to entertain it. "I won't let you."

She cast him a withering look. "Not your call. I want to do this."

It felt as though she'd stabbed him in the heart. His mouth hung open before he rasped, "You don't mean that."

Gen tilted her head, and he winced at the angry purple mark on her cheek. "Why not? How is this any different than what I did with Marshal?"

He gripped her shoulder. "It *is* different, damn it. Zan could kill you."

"Is that really what you are worried about?" Her eyes searched his face, and for a moment he wondered if she could read him as well as he could her. "Be honest with me, Rhys, for once. What do I mean to you?"

I'm ready to hear this. Marshal stopped his desperate bids for control, and Rhys could envision him leaning back, his feet up, waiting for the fireworks to begin. *Just how much does she mean to you, this woman you fucked with my cock? Can't be that much.*

Struggling with his own mixed feelings, Rhys muttered, "This is neither the time nor place to—"

Gen held up her hand. "Message received."

Panic threatened to overwhelm him, and even though she stood directly in front of him, he felt her slipping away, her colors diminishing. What had he done to put out her fire? "What does that mean?"

She ignored him, studying the alien script decorating the

walls. "Get Marshal back up here. He's been on this ship before, and I need his help finding the bridge."

"Please rethink—"

She glared at him. "Rhys, either you lead, you follow, or get the hell out of my way. Do not obstruct."

He bowed at the waist. "As you wish." Slinking to the recesses of Marshal's brain, he let go of his control over every sense but hearing. In truth, her plan might work. At the very least, they had no other options. What was his guilt when compared with her life?

Don't worry, old chum, I'll take good care of her, Marshal sneered as he regained control. Rhys didn't bother with a response, the threat left unspoken. Vows of nonviolence aside, if Marshal betrayed Gen or failed to protect her, Rhys would annihilate him.

"Bridge is on the top level." Marshal spoke low. "Captain's quarters directly below that. Main engineering is at the stern, with auxiliary power adjoining the cargo bay. We're somewhere in the crew dorm area."

"My best bet is to catch Zan alone. I don't think he wants to kill me, but if I approach him in front of his men, he'll be distracted by their reactions."

"Don't underestimate him. Zan isn't bloodthirsty, but he'll do what he has to in order to get what he wants," Marshal cautioned.

"Noted." Gen's tone had picked up a brisk, businesslike efficiency, reminiscent of Alison. A woman on a mission. One that no longer seemed to include him.

He'd been unable to read her feelings since the pirate's attack. Was something blocking him out of her mind, or were his own feelings for her getting in his way?

The sound of Marshal's footfalls told Rhys they were in motion. "Quit with the sulking already. You're depressing me."

Rhys didn't know if the words were meant for him or Gen,

and he didn't really care either. Marshal could think whatever he wanted. He didn't seek the other empath's good opinion the way he did Gen's.

Why was she so angry? Every time he felt as though they'd made a bit of progress, something happened to offset it. Now he wasn't looking out for her; she was saving him. Maybe she just wanted to bed Zan. Variety being the spice of life and all that. Her emotions shifted too fast under the adrenaline coursing through her veins, and he had seen her with the space pirate. Was this her way of putting distance between her and him? Any sort of relationship between them was too complex, too many variables to predict what might happen in the future. Would they even live to see the start of a new day? Rhys didn't have any guarantees to offer her—he didn't even have his own body to help him demonstrate how he felt about her.

The one thing he did know—he couldn't lose her.

"Hands where I can see them!" a new voice ordered.

What's going on? Rhys fought to regain control, scrambling against the slippery resistance Marshal put up. *Marshal, let me see.*

"Stay where you are," Marshal muttered, though whether he spoke to Rhys or Gen was anyone's guess.

Rhys ignored him and fought like a wild man. Did the newcomer hold some sort of weapon? Was Gen in danger? *Why did I back down so easily?*

"Drop your weapon!" the stranger ordered. Rhys snatched Marshal's eyesight just in time to see Gen pointing her pilfered laser pistol at a young pirate, who looked no more than sixteen. They were in a medical chamber, judging from the healing pods on the floor. Panic radiated from him like heat from a newly formed star and his hands shook.

"I don't want to hurt you." Gen's tone was calm, her grip steady. "But I won't let you shoot us."

"I . . . I must report this to the captain. He'll be furious if I don't." His voice cracked on the last word, the bright yellow of nerves and a sickly green tinge coating him.

"I'm going to try and calm him," Rhys whispered low, so only Marshal could hear. "Pool your energy with mine and maybe we can catch him off guard."

Just let her shoot him. Marshal made a disgusted noise. *Her weapon is set on singe.*

"No one has to get hurt." Rhys spoke louder so Gen and the young pirate both heard him. The boy's gaze shifted nervously to Rhys, his grip on the weapon tightening.

Moving slowly, so as not to spook him, Rhys sent out a calming wave, drawing on his own inner reserve. *It'll all be fine. Just put the gun down.* The message buffeted against the colors of the boy's aura. Tension leeched from his shoulders, though he kept the weapon pointed at Gen's chest.

You don't want to hurt her. She is beautiful, unique, a treasure to be cherished. He projected his own vision of Gen, hoping the boy would see how she glowed, revel in the way her dress fell over lush breasts and womanly hips. *You cannot damage something so fine.*

"What are you doing?" Gen asked out of the corner of her mouth.

Rhys took a reading on the boy's state. "Helping him see your value. It goes against nature to directly harm that which brings us joy."

The boy shook his head. "Stop it."

You're losing him! Marshal made a desperate grasp for control, ready to drain the boy dry of all feeling, but Rhys shoved him back, snarling, "I can handle this!"

The child fought Rhys's onslaught, his will stronger than anything Rhys had ever experienced. Holding on to the threads he needed was akin to gripping oiled snakes. "You're trying to trick me!"

Rhys dove at the same moment the boy pulled the trigger.

18

Marshal intercepted the laser blast aimed for Gen's chest at point-blank range. He barreled into the young marksman and knocked him off his feet before crumpling to the ground. The kid's eyes were wide as his laser pistol clattered to the deck. Gen's heart skipped a beat. Smoke emanated from Marshal's body, the smell of burned meat and singed hair making her gag. Still, she kept the presence of mind to command, "Put your hands up, now."

The kid's panicked brown eyes fixed on her, as shaking limbs extended at a perpendicular angle to his body. "I didn't mean to—"

Gen took a roll of gauze from one of the supply cabinets and stuffed it into his mouth.

"Don't play with weapons if you don't mean to hurt people," she snapped, and wrapped another roll around his head to keep the gag in place. Methodically, she tied his hands behind his back and bound his feet at the ankles for good measure. The entire universe had slowed to one heartbeat at a time. Dread filled her when she imagined turning Marshal over, seeing the damage the weapon had inflicted.

Rhys. The sorrow she didn't actively express threatened to overflow the part of her mind not aimed toward survival. She needed to stay numb, to be cool and levelheaded, but reason became murkier, harder to hold. *Why did you do that?*

The question was pointless, totally irrelevant. She knew why he'd thrown himself in front of her, shielding her with his own body. That's what heroes did in real life.

Die.

Look at him! The shrill voice came from somewhere deep inside her, and even as Gen shook her head, she reached forward to touch his bare shoulder.

Biting the inside of her cheek, she turned him to face her. Marshal's dark eyes stared sightlessly up at her. A sob broke out of her thin-skinned emotional prison, followed by another when she took in the gaping hole burned into his chest cavity. White ribs were clearly visible, the ends charred black by the heat of the laser. The thick metallic tang of blood caught in the back of her throat.

No one deserved to die like this.

Grief slammed into her like a ship caught in a planet's gravity, sucking her down to the dense core of madness. Two lives gone, two men dead with the twitch of a nervous trigger finger. "Why didn't I stun the kid when I had a clear shot?"

Because you are not a killer, Gen.

Her mouth went dry as hope welled. "Rhys?"

I'm here, sweetness, inside you.

She shuddered in relief, scarcely able to believe that he was still with her. "Are you all right?"

A long pause, long enough that she started to panic on his behalf. God, what if he was dying on her?

I am . . . undamaged. But I cost a man his life, Gen. Rage coursed through her, a helpless gut-churning fury with no outlet. She sensed him struggling to suppress it, locking it back in those hidden depths deep within his psyche. His admission was filled with utter despair. *I don't know what I'm doing. With Marshal, with you . . . it's all been a horrific mistake.*

She flinched at the last. His spiritual foundation had been badly shaken. "I'm sorry," she whispered, not knowing what else she could say to him. "But I'm glad you're alive."

He didn't respond. Leaning forward, she passed her hand over Marshal's eyes. "We had fun, didn't we, you evil bastard."

Marshal let me do it. He wanted to save your life. If he'd truly fought me, I wouldn't have been able to. . . .

Eyes misting over, she finished the thought for him. "To save me. Thank you, Rhys."

She glanced down at the kid, whose eyes almost bugged out of their sockets as he watched her have a conversation with herself. "What do we do now?"

With Marshal dead, Zan has no reason to hold you here, Rhys thought in a sullen tone. Some part of him had died inside Marshal, his light noticeably diminished.

"Can I do anything for you?"

No, sweetness. I need to pray for Marshal's empathic light. Meditate for a few hours.

So much for their great escape plan. She couldn't help but feel abandoned, shoved aside when she became inconvenient to him. Why did he have to shut down on her? She'd gladly help him through whatever crisis of faith he was coping with. In that moment, she accepted that watching out for Marshal had been an excuse that allowed her to follow her heart after Rhys on his madcap mission. And look where it had brought her.

Gen sighed. She was truly on her own now.

"What's going on here?" Zan had the standard villain timing down pat. She said nothing, well aware that Rhys couldn't do anything more to help her and that her leverage was sprawled dead on the floor. Closing her eyes, she concentrated on taking deep, calming breaths.

The creak of leather marked Zan's progress into the room. His hand brushed over hers sensually, taking the weapon from her grip. She didn't fight him. Even if she killed him, she held no hope of getting away. Marshal might have shot himself out into the cold embrace of the universe, but Gen didn't want to live that badly.

"And your man?"

She cracked an eyelid and found Zan squatting down to examine the corpse. His big, leather-clad thighs bulged with well-developed muscle. Funny the things she noticed at a time like this.

A tear streaked down her cheek. "He's just a friend." She spoke the words clearly, giving Rhys plenty of time to challenge her statement, afraid he would but more afraid he wouldn't.

The corner of Zan's mouth kicked up. "I meant, what happened to him?"

She couldn't stare him in the eye and lie, say that Rhys was no more, so she turned her head away, letting all the loss she felt show in the slump of her shoulders. Let the pirate make of that what he would.

He moved toward her then, offering her a bow. "My apologies. I would have liked to meet him in the flesh. Come to the mess hall and have a drink, soothe the jagged edges. Little indulgences help to quell the grief."

She didn't protest as he led her from the medical chamber, afraid to give herself away with the slightest inappropriate reaction.

Rhys stayed quiet, meditating probably. She wanted time to talk to him, to plan out a strategy of what else they could do, but whatever he was going through seemed to demand all his attention. He'd abandoned her to her own devices.

She wished she could stop allowing him this power over her.

As her bare feet padded woodenly across cold metal grating, Gen came to an understanding.

No one else had her back. Though Rhys might have cared if she died, it meant no more to him than the fall of his enemy. His stringent system of beliefs dictated that he hold all life sacred, regardless of personal connection. She didn't know whether to laugh at her own absurdity—because she had thought she meant something to him—or cry because she was so damn desperate for someone to give a shit.

Zan steered her into a small, poorly lit room. The large viewports boasted a magnificent view of the stars, and Gen wanted nothing more than to stare out into the endless reaches of space until she crumbled into dust.

"Here." Zan handed her a cup made out of some transparent material she'd never seen before, more sturdy than glass, colder than metal. The liquid inside was an amber color and twinkled like the stars as it settled. "Really, it ain't poison. If I wanted you dead, I'd use my hands."

"Good to know." She stared into it, mesmerized by the play of light, like liquid fire. Tipping the cup back, she let the beverage slide down her throat. Her tongue didn't pick up any sort of taste at all, like water from a fresh stream. The concoction warmed as it went, burning her esophagus raw. The heat spread through her chest, lighting her up from the inside out. She coughed heartily and then wheezed, "Damn, that's got a hell of a kick. What's it called?"

He refilled her empty cup. "Risgalie. It's brewed on my home world and exported across the cosmos by freighter pilots who will then barter it for other . . . favors." His gaze went unfocused.

Gen drained her cup again. "I know that look. Who is she?"

Zan scowled. "I don't follow."

"The woman you're pining for. What's her name?" Though

her thoughts had grown fuzzy, she still recalled the time with Javier and Steven. "Unless it's a him?"

Zan stared down at her before knocking back his own drink. "No, you were right the first time."

She changed her tactic, wanting to keep him talking so he wouldn't ask her questions. "So, is she waiting patiently for you to come home, keeping the fires burning and all that warm-fuzzy shit?" A hiccup escaped.

Zan threw his head back and laughed. "No, not at all. She was not one for home and hearth, more of a shoot-first-and-let-God-sort-out-the-details type."

Was. Oh, ouch. "I'm sorry, I didn't mean to dredge up painful memories."

Zan raised an eyebrow. "Loving her was the biggest mistake of my life."

Gen laughed. "I hear you. Love is a sick-bitch mistress, never satisfied and always willing to take another strip off your hide."

He seemed to like that, his eyes warming a fraction. "Takes one to know one, yeah?"

She scrunched up her face as she tried to determine if he'd just insulted her. "Whatever you say, Zan."

"I like the sound of those words." He took the glass from her hands, set it down on a nearby table. "You know, I think it's about time I find a new sick-bitch mistress."

His intent was obvious, but in her inebriated state, it took a moment for his meaning to register. "Where do you suppose you can find one out here on the edge of nothingness?"

His thumb stroked over her cheek, the point of her chin. "I'm a pirate, remember? I take what I want."

She stared into his eyes. "I'm not her."

Golden gaze burned hot, penetrating her, just like the booze. "And I ain't him."

Gen shrugged. "So, if you can't be with the one you love—"
His mouth claimed hers, cutting off her droll quip. *Love the one you're with.*

Rhys said nothing.

Rhys wished he'd been the one to die. Forget his all-important mission, his people, his sister. He'd cost another soul his life. The price for his freedom was too high, and he doubted he deserved to exist outside the candle.

And he certainly didn't deserve Gen.

She was attracted to the space pirate. And Zan wanted her, had wanted her from the moment he'd seen her. His lust was sharp, a splinter in Rhys's mind. Here was a man who could give Gen everything Rhys couldn't. Zan wouldn't hesitate to kill another to defend her life. Rhys's ideological belief that all life should be preserved had almost gotten her killed.

Just like he had killed Marshal. He was no one to judge what the other empath had done. Yet Rhys had acted as his judge, jury, and executioner. Gen deserved so much more; her bright colors needed to be matched with an intense personality, not Rhys's slashes of rage and guilt. Always the guilt pressing on his shoulders, weighing him down.

He'd lied to her, practically kidnapped her, and coerced her until she helped him. Invaded her body in every way possible. He didn't deserve the memories of her soft touch, the heat of her body, the scent of her lustrous hair. No, he had stolen those bits of her sweetness and would cherish them always.

He sensed her pause, trying to clear the alien alcoholic fog from her mind. She wanted him to object, to tell her not to enter the pirate's lair. Not to share herself with him. Her hurt when he didn't respond tore him up inside.

Allowing that he was a bastard ten times over for breaking his promise, Rhys found the pleasure center of her brain and pulled on her need. Manipulating her emotions once again. The light pink cravings flushed as he stoked her fire, letting it build slowly, naturally, as the best part of himself turned to ash.

Her time with Zan would be his punishment. Tonight he would silently endure the sensation of his woman's body being loved by another. If a more potent kind of torture existed, he couldn't think of it. Tomorrow he'd proceed with his mission and let go of Gen for her own good.

Rhys prayed he would be strong enough, but he worried his conviction was no match for his aching heart.

19

The doors to Zan's cabin whizzed shut with a hiss, cementing the fact that they had been sealed in together. The noise cleared some of the alcohol-induced haze lingering in Gen's mind, and she tensed in the dimly lit room. Zan hadn't touched her since that deep kiss, and he kept his distance between their bodies. She wished he wouldn't; she didn't want the time or the space to think—to remember what she had been struggling so hard to forget.

"Do something for me?" Zan murmured. The pulsing green light of his cabin cast him into a stripe of shadows, dark slashes masking the extent of his expression. She had planned to seduce this man? Gen could have laughed at her own idiocy. It was like a young virgin trying to entice a jaded whore. Yet Zan still seemed to want her.

He handed her another drink, and she debated a moment, wondering if more booze was the answer. Was there even a right answer? "What's your pleasure?"

"I got something real special I want you to wear." The corner of his mouth kicked up, and her eyebrows climbed practically to her hairline.

"What, some sort of sexy costume?" Maybe it came with boots. Heat pooled in her belly at the thought of being fucked in fuck-me boots. Wasn't that why she continued to buy them, the constant hope that maybe someday a man she was with would say, *Leave 'em on, babe. They really do it for me.*

He didn't respond verbally, just moved over to a high alcove. There was a sharp click, and the bulkhead behind him slid away. Zan beckoned her to follow and stepped through the uneven passage.

"Whoa, Mama." The lighting in the room matched its sparkling interior. Gold, silver, and jewels of all colors, shapes, and sizes ate up the enormous space. Gen spun around, trying to take it all in. "I thought pirates were supposed to bury their treasure."

Zan threw back his head and laughed. She enjoyed the sound all the more because she doubted he did it often. "Where some poor slob could dig it up and win the jackpot? I need it on hand to spend whenever we reach quasi-civilized space. But not too civilized—they want no part of me, and I want less than that from them."

She pivoted, somewhat drunkenly, trying to take it all in. "So you stole all this from luxury liners?"

Zan moved closer and tipped the drink to her lips. "Not all. Something like that is a special and rare circumstance. Too high-profile because now there will be an alert out for us, for this vessel. We need to avoid the Milky Way galaxy for a long time. So you see, I can't exactly bring you home."

Gen turned to him, narrowing her eyes. "Was it worth it, to see Marshal dead?"

He shrugged. "I took no pleasure in his death. Some people just need killing, especially if they've harmed me or mine. If I hadn't hunted him down, my crew would mutiny, simple as that. Demonstrations of might and ruthlessness earned me my rank, and I ain't willing to jeopardize that position for no one."

His tone held warning as well as explanation. Gen shivered.

Zan reached out a hand and hesitated, letting his fingers drift an inch from her skin. "Have I scared you off? Am I too evil for you?"

Her heart thundered in her chest and her head swam. He smelled of dark spice, exotic and mysterious. "I'm starting to understand that what I once thought was evil is just the necessity of people trying to scrape by. I'm in an odd position here, Zan. Alone without the connections or resources to get home. If I say no, will you have me killed?"

Slowly, he shook his head. "Not for that."

She could read between the lines. There were other reasons, other missteps she might make that would result in her death at his hands. Zan wasn't offering her immunity or protection, just physical comfort, a few moments of bliss. Knocking back the rest of her drink, she closed the gap between them, leaning into his caress. Golden eyes lit with lust took her in, reflecting the stacks of wealth around them.

"What did you want me to wear?"

His thumb stroked over her cheekbone twice before he took her empty glass and set it on a golden table. Bending at the waist, he scooped up something and turned, offering the object to her. "This."

She frowned. "A mask?" An exquisite mask to be sure, woven of fine golden threads and decorated with rubies and sapphires. It was designed to cover the top portion of the wearer's face, from forehead to nose. "Is this so you can pretend I'm someone else?"

"No, Gen. I know exactly who I want to fuck." Circling behind her, he slipped the mask over her face and then led her back to the other room. "The illusion is for you. Something to help you forget who you are, so you can enjoy."

He was right, she realized as she touched her fingertips to the valuable covering. She felt like a different person behind the mask, someone bolder, braver, hotter, and demanding. Someone who had no trouble unfastening her dress and letting it pool around her ankles. Bare to his gaze, she stepped forward and trailed a long fingernail down the dark exposed skin revealed by his leather vest.

He gripped her hand as she touched his naval. "Rules first."

Her hand tingled where he touched her, like his hand was a conduit for electrical current. Zan was . . . intense, and hidden behind the mysterious mask she craved another hit.

Her body called the shots now, thrumming and throbbing with need; all her worries and concerns waited elsewhere. The freedom was heady and a little bit frightening. "I'm not really a whore, and I don't expect payment. And I'm going to utilize my health guard, no matter what you say or do."

He nodded. "Fair enough. Now, there are certain parts of my body I won't permit to have touched in any way. Can you live with that?"

She licked her lips. "Just tell me where and I'll avoid those spots like the space pox."

Tilting his head to the side, he surveyed her hungrily. "My hair, my feet, and my ass, all off-limits."

What a strange combination. She wanted to ask why but doubted he would tell her. "Agreed. Anything else?"

He pushed her back onto the mattress. Encouraging her to splay her thighs, he then gazed down on her body. "It's been too damn long since I've had a woman."

She spread her legs wider for him, reveling in the way his golden gaze fixed on her sex. "Should I give you a refresher course?"

Without waiting for an answer, she slid her hands up to cup her breasts, pinching the nipples until they stood at attention. His hot breaths tightened the bud of her clit and made her ache all the more. Slowly, she trailed her hand down over her stomach, creeping lightly over her mound to circle the throbbing nub.

His gaze transfixed, Zan shifted, shrugging out of his vest and pants, his eyes never leaving her body. She opened her mouth to remind him to lube up but then stopped. He wasn't from earth, didn't have a germ shield in place. While she wouldn't receive any of his genetic material, he would be coated in her lube. Unshielded sex, half of the forbidden thrill she'd witnessed with Steven and Javier. That she'd felt with Rhys/Marshal. Her channel clenched at the thought, her fingers working her clit harder, faster. Viciously, she shoved all thoughts of Rhys to a corner of her mind and slammed the door. Rhys had made it clear they had no future together. With no hope of a future, there could be no relationship, and with no relationship, she was a free agent, even if she didn't want to be. He'd had his chance to say something, but he'd been too busy sulking. Was she really just going to pine for him for the rest of her life? The way her libido worked, she doubted she could, even if she wanted to. This man wanted to touch her, and she wanted to be touched; there was nothing more to say.

Kneeling between her spread thighs, he continued to watch, consuming her with his hungry gaze. Rough hands started at her ankles and slid up over her calves, massaging behind the crook of her knees and up to stroke the inside of her thighs. He licked his lips, and she groaned when he finally touched her, dragging one blunt finger through her wet folds.

Circling the opening to her body, he spoke on a low murmur. "Did I get you into this state?"

She knew what he wanted to hear—yes, he and his massive cock had worked her into a frenzy. But she respected him too much to lie. "No, I'm just catching up on too much time spent repressed and distracted, ignoring my body's needs."

His gaze lifted up to her face, piercing her with that ruthless intensity. "What does your body need, Gen?"

Wearing the mask made her bold, allowed her the freedom to talk dirty, the way she'd always wanted to. The words forced themselves out on a breathless gasp. "To be fucked, hard, until I come."

He groaned and rose to his feet, aligning his throbbing shaft with her sex. Spreading her legs until her knees rested over his elbows, he nudged forward, impaling her. She gasped as he slowly filled her, the precum beading at the crown of his shaft causing her germ shield to snap up his genetic material before it could touch her. Her channel was slick enough, though, and he closed his eyes as he surged forward in a sharp thrust.

She could feel him, that large cock throbbing deep inside her, every muscle pulsing as she made room for him. Her eyes slid shut when he withdrew and then rocked back into her slowly. "What happened to hard and quick?"

"That ain't what you need." His voice sounded sure, and he continued his slow and steady advance and retreat, dragging his staff out of her sheath and moving slowly back inside.

The way he held her, she had no leverage, couldn't slam her hips to his or wrap her legs around him and pull him inside. She was totally at his mercy. No matter how she writhed or tried to spur him onward, he kept up the slow, brutal strokes.

She cursed at him, using words to enrage him into giving what she couldn't forcibly take. He smiled and withdrew altogether, his greased staff bobbing at the mouth of her womb. He turned her over, pushing her facedown into the mattress and clambering up behind her.

"Would you just get on with it already!" she shouted at him.

Zan leaned over her, pressing his front to her back so he could cup her breasts. "So damn impatient," he murmured while his fingers pinched her nipples. "What's your hurry?"

She opened her mouth to say something snotty, but she didn't have a concrete answer for him. Why *was* she trying to rush this? Not like she had anything better to do.

His rough palms scraped across her skin, and his prick bobbed between her splayed thighs. He rocked again, just as he'd done inside her, and the tip of him nudged her clitoris in a sharp stab that made her buck.

"That's it," he crooned in her ear as her body fell into rhythm with his, her hips undulating so the head of his cock swirled over her throbbing bud more on each pass, dancing, lingering, reveling in hedonistic glory. The contact was small but intense. She focused on each meeting of their flesh, aching for more. Again, he speared her and she came in an unexpected rush that erupted from her molten core like a solar flare.

"Now you're here with me," he growled in satisfaction. His fingers delved into the wetness she'd yielded. "Now I can fuck you hard and fast until you come all over my cock."

He surged inside her on a brutal thrust, catching the end of the rippling wave that still washed over her. Fisting the sheets, she could do nothing but hold on for the ride. His hands left her breasts and clamped onto her hips, holding her wide open to his invasion. The way he held her, greedily, possessively as though he would never let her go, made her moan.

Sweat beaded under her mask. Her mouth hung open as she panted and gasped as he drove into her, again and again. The sharp tang of sex filled her nostrils because even though she was protected, their fluids mixed on his body.

"This is only the beginning," he said. "I am going to take you all night, in every position I can imagine till you beg me to let you rest."

Sounded sublime to her, but she wasn't about to cave so easily. "And if I don't?"

He released her hips so he could fondle her clit again. "A woman always breaks first. You aren't made to withstand the sexual torment I could rain down on you."

She squeezed her inner muscles, clamping down on him as he tried to withdraw from her.

"Tough words. I'll believe them when I see them."

A hand landed on her ass in a light stinging slap. "You gonna fight back?"

This time when he plowed into her, she shoved back. "Count on it."

He withdrew and flipped her over again. "Ah, Gen, you are just what I needed."

His lips met hers as he thrust into her again. The crispness of his dark pubic hair rubbed against her clit as he ground into her, stirring his cock inside of her channel.

Wrapping her legs around his waist, she took him deeper still, bucking as the head of his cock stabbed against the sensitive spot inside her until she cried out in another release.

His hips bucked in a wild, erratic pattern, and his golden eyes slid shut as he found his own slice of paradise.

Her germ shield sizzled as they lay twined together. Hesitantly, she ran her hand up along his back, tracing the deep cuts of well-defined muscles. She waited for guilt to assail her, guilt that she'd betrayed Rhys, had given her body over to Marshal's murderer, but nothing happened.

Maybe she'd already done her stint in purgatory?

Zan lifted himself off her. "Are you all right?"

Leaning up, she kissed his lips, chastely, an odd response considering he was still semi-erect inside her. "Thank you."

Dark slashes came together over the bridge of his nose. "For the sex?"

"For not letting me get away with faking it."

He chuckled and rolled off of her, pulling himself out. His hand went to his hardening cock, stroking the moisture over the growing shaft. "Why in the six shades of hell do women do that?"

Her hand joined his on his quest. "It seems like a good idea at the time."

His fingers closed over hers, showing her the exact amount of pressure to use to please him. "I think it's an interdimensional conspiracy between women to keep men in check."

She slithered down until she could breathe onto his cock, "Not all men."

He bucked as she took him between her lips, sucking on his cock until the head hit the back of her throat. His hands fisted at his sides as he watched her. She closed her eyes. He touched her face, right beneath the mask. "No, I want to see you."

She released him to ask, "Why?"

"Because it turns me on to have a beautiful woman suck my cock. Tonight is all about pleasure, right?"

She nodded.

"You sorry about this? About what we've done together?"

She thought about it, still idly stroking his shaft. "No, not sorry. I kind of wish things hadn't happened in the order that they had. I'm a twice-over kidnapping victim who's been emotionally manipulated. I've seen things I didn't want to see. Done things that I'm sure will horrify me in the light of day."

He smirked at her. "Doll, that's life. You can't have everything just as you want it."

Her lips curled up. "Oh, some things I think I can."

He didn't question her anymore as she licked and sucked him until his body bowed off the bed. Again her germ shield gobbled up all the foreign matter, and she was almost sorry because she wanted the taste of him in her mouth.

But not enough to break all the rules.

Some things were just too deeply ingrained.

She dozed for a while and woke to the feel of strong masculine hands parting her thighs. "I want you again," Zan murmured, fingering the wetness between her legs. "Do you yield?"

Silently, she nodded, planting her feet to lift her pelvis up to meet his questing fingers. He played for a time, swirling over her nub, gathering her wetness to coat her flushed sex. She was more than ready by the time he came inside her, riding her hard and fast. She didn't orgasm this time, but she didn't fake one either.

Progress was progress, no matter how small.

20

Well, that happened. Gen didn't want to open her eyes and face the world of hurt waiting just beyond. Everything ached and throbbed, centering in her skull and radiating outward. Damn foreign booze. If this was what arthritis felt like, she didn't know how Nana could stand it.

Stretching her cold, stiff, naked body, she bumped into Zan's sleeping form. Now she had to open her eyes, to stare down at the man who'd shown her the stars last night. He'd found peace in his sleep, and she wanted to believe she was part of the reason for that. She'd certainly done her damnedest to wear him out. And he'd returned the favor, with interest.

Good morning, Rhys offered in a perfectly civil tone.

Gen opened her mouth but then snapped it shut again because she didn't know what to say. She didn't owe him any explanation for her actions. Plus, she didn't want to wake Zan up just yet.

I'm not your judge, Gen. You are free to do whatever you please, with whomever you wish. Though you might want to have a psychologist look into your tendency for falling into bed with your abductors. It's not a healthy habit.

"Neither is jumping in front of a laser pistol," she muttered, scooting out of bed. "Didn't stop you."

He remained quiet as she used the facilities, then gathered her clothes, ready to put him back in his candle and have some space for a change. Maybe without him in her head, she could breathe and begin to think clearly again.

Plus, she didn't want Zan to see her first thing in the morning so soon. Sex on a first date, fine, but morning after was more of a fifth date kind of deal.

Wait, you want a relationship with the pirate now? What about our mission?

"*Your* mission," she corrected, squinting down the halls, trying to find the room where they'd left their bags. "I'm putting you back in the candle and washing my hands of you for good."

Sweetness, please, think about this for a moment. I understand you want to punish me—

She laughed hollowly. "This isn't all about you, Rhys! Stop trying to guilt me into taking on your hopeless quest! I'm not a hero, and it's not wrong that I don't want to die helping you kill yourself."

My sister, Gen. I don't know whether she's been captured, and it's killing me. Her and millions of other children across my planet will be enslaved if I do not find a way to stop Illustra. I need you.

His plea cut her to the quick. He needed her, but he didn't want her. Not enough to speak up and stop last night from happening. The night before he'd left her raw and bleeding, and because he was Rhys, he would be the only one to see it. "What would you have me do? Steal a shuttle and get blown up? Use my body to manipulate Zan? I doubt I could, even if I wanted to. How about opening a vein as a distraction? Tell me, Rhys, in your spiritually enlightened opinion, how much is too much to ask for?"

He didn't answer, and it was just as well, because she couldn't find the damn room. Every turn on this space bucket looked exactly like the one that had come before it and the one after. Several of the pirates cast her knowing smirks as they passed by.

Brings walk of shame *to a whole new level.* But the thought came from her, not Rhys.

Finally, she found her door and stepped inside. The guard they'd overpowered was long gone, but the candle still burned on the dresser. Securing the door, she walked over to it and knelt down, cupping her hands around the flame. Heat leeched into her, and she let everything out, all of her sadness and fear, the hopeless despair she associated with caring for Rhys. Let him have it all. Sure wasn't doing her a whit of good.

A hand landed on her shoulder. She looked at it, so foreign and familiar all at once. "He won't ever love you. His heart is impenetrable."

She stared up into Rhys's face, taking in the red-gold curls, the green eyes that could see so much. "Neither will you."

His head shook back and forth slowly. "No, you're wrong there, sweetness. I do love you. Just because I have something else I must do doesn't negate that in any way. I can't be what you need, can't offer you much of anything, not even my body."

Her eyes narrowed. "You know what, Rhys? That's a load of bullshit excuses."

"You're angry," Captain Obvious stated.

"You haven't given me anything except marching orders and a few pretty words. There's no trust between us, Rhys, and I'm sick of being used!" Shame warred with indignation because she'd used Zan.

Though he didn't appear to mind at the time.

Unlike so many other men, Rhys refused to look away from her furious face, taking the heat of her words full force. "What would you have me do to prove my sincerity to you?"

Give up your mission. She wouldn't make that demand, though, not when she knew how much it meant to him. Deep down in the honest part of her, Gen knew the reason she was falling for him so hard was because of his noble streak, that unwavering determination to do what was right, regardless of the personal cost. He'd destroy her if she let him.

His mind had gone in another direction, though. "Would you have me take you now, your body still warmed by the touch of another? If you asked it, I would be inside you in a heartbeat, claiming you for my own, pleasuring you in ways you know only I can." He gripped her hair, yanking back in a firm tug. "I'm not the hero you make me out to be, Gen. I'm a murderer and a bastard, and I can't ever seem to do what's right."

Rhys didn't wait for Gen to respond, just slanted his mouth over hers in the brutal, punishing kiss that he knew she craved. Being with her, being inside her head and heart last night, had redefined torture for him. All this time, he'd believed that the uncertainty over what might have happened to Sela was the worst sort of misery. His sister's well-being remained in the forefront in his mind, until the space pirate had invaded his territory.

How was her time with Zan any different than what she'd done with Marshal's body, for his own pleasure? Rhys had had several hours to brood on it and stew in his misery until the scent of failure was all he could smell. He'd failed Marshal, sacrificed the man's life for Gen and then pushed her away too. All the lessons he'd been taught at the abbey about cultivating tender feelings, using love and joy to heal, and still, look at the damage he'd wrought.

Her hands splayed across his chest, poised to push him

away. Rhys accepted she had every right to, but until she said the word *no*, he would do his best to convince her that his feelings for her were sincere. He wasn't punishing her with the bruising kiss but himself for being so complacent, for believing she was like a boomerang he could toss away time and again and still she would come back to him. However, he'd seriously miscalculated the human heart being more difficult to interpret than anything he'd ever encountered. Her attachment was not to his quest, to right or wrongness of what Illustra did. Gen was no freedom fighter; she'd done it all for *him*.

And he'd driven her into another man's arms.

As he explored the sweet recesses of her mouth, his hands trailed down to her round ass, pulling her against him, his shaft throbbing, ready to plunge inside her. If the urge to claim her was so strong in this form, he would probably die when he reinhabited his body.

Her emotional aura sparked with purple and gold flecks of excitement. He pinned her against the wall, reaching between her cheeks and exploring her wetness. She gasped and shivered when his finger invaded her core, making his cock twitch in anticipation. *Soon.*

She tore her lips from his. "No . . . wait a minute."

"Let me," he rasped, spreading her slick lube around her sensitized folds. Her hips bucked once, and he leaned in to take her mouth again. "I know you want this. I want to love you, Gen."

"I said stop, damn you!" Her forehead flew forward, bashing him in the chin. His teeth slammed together, stunning him from his intent. He released her and backed down. Her eyes narrowed on him, her hair wild, her body quaking under the intensity of her emotions. "This is another one of your games, right?"

His jaw cracked a few times as he stretched its hinge. If he'd been in his flesh-and-bone body, she probably would have dislocated it. "I have not been playing games with you, sweetness."

"Bullshit." Hands clenched into fists, she stalked toward him. "You've been manipulating me from the moment your wick ignited. You think I'm a moron, that I don't know what this is all about? Another man dared to play with your toy, making her feel things you didn't put there. Nothing you can say or do will convince me to help you anymore, Rhys."

"I'm sorry I didn't say anything. I thought Zan could give you what you needed, but if I hadn't—"

Her eyes blazed. "What? Rhys, what did you do?"

He ground his teeth together, wincing at the remembered soreness, and nodded once. She already suspected and he wouldn't lie to her again. "I'm sorry, I broke my vow. I manipulated your emotions so your pleasure overwhelmed your sadness."

She looked away, her shoulders stiff. "I knew it would happen, that sooner or later the temptation would be too much. Face facts, Rhys. You're an addict. Can't seem to stop yourself from playing puppet master and yanking my strings so I dance for you. You're just as bad as Marshal."

Her words cut him deeply, her lack of faith in him as unsurprising as it was heart wrenching. "It's not like that! I wanted you to find happiness. Without me. And I'm so, so sorry."

Her eyes flashed fire. "Goddamn you straight to hell, Rhys. The only difference between last night and every other sexual encounter of my life is that you were faking it for me!"

"You forget, you never had to fake it with me, love." He moved in close, forcing her to back up until her knees hit the edge of the bed. "Are you really seeing a forever with the space pirate? Even if his life span does exceed the projected thirty-four years, you know you're only a shadow of what he wants—a woman he can't have."

She blinked twice, her mouth hanging open. "Wow, you

unimaginable bastard. I cannot believe you just said that to me. On top of everything else, do you really need to rip me to shreds in every way you can imagine?"

Rhys didn't understand where her hurt came from, when he spoke only the truth. "Why be Zan's second choice when I want you and no other?"

She shoved him, hard. "This isn't a competition to discover who wants me more! I get to choose what's best for me. And you know something? There are several options out there other than you or Zan." Her eyebrows drew together as though she mulled over some new information.

Frustration gnawed him from the inside out. Though she stood only a few inches away, he felt the yawning chasm separating them, growing with every breath. The obstacles piled higher every second of every day. "Genevieve—"

She held her hand to his lips. "I need to be alone for a little while. To think, sort through my feelings."

He nodded, though he wanted to howl. "This has been too hard on you. I understand." He couldn't leave her like this, though, with everything so unsettled. Taking her in his embrace, he buried his nose in the soft dark strands of her hair. "I'm so sorry. I was only doing what I thought was right. It was hell for me, Gen. A hell I deserved—but you don't. I want what's best for you, sweetness."

She sighed, accepting the hug. "I know. It's why I haven't murdered you. This isn't forever. I just need space."

He pulled back, stroking his thumb across her cheek. "You're in space, sweetness."

She cast him a withering glance. "You know what I mean. Time and a little bit of quiet on my own."

Fear congealed into an iceberg in his gut. "Promise me you won't go back to him without talking to me again."

She wanted to say no. Rhys could see it in her eyes. By all rights she ought to tell him to go screw himself and his mission.

Hurt emanated from her like heat from a star, and he realized in that endless moment that if she refused him now, he'd have to leave her be. The decision must be hers.

What came out of her mouth was, "Okay."

"Thank you," he breathed. Heaving one last sigh filled to the brim with relief, he stepped away. Letting go of her powerful emotional pull, he permitted his resonance to fade back into the candle's flame.

Where he would wait.

Gen sniffled as he vanished, truly alone for the first time in days. Damn, it had been so hard to say no to Rhys when his alpha switch had been flipped to overkill. But hopping into bed with him would be only a temporary fix. He was still on a mission, one she felt obligated to help him with, if only so she wouldn't be shrouded by guilt for the rest of her life.

First order of business—she needed a damn shower. Good thing the pirates didn't keep birds on board the ship; they would have all nested in her hair by now. A small cubbyhole-type room adjoined the bedchamber. Stripping off her clothes, she headed for it. The lights turned on as soon as she crossed the threshold, and the door whizzed shut behind her. Hopefully she could figure out how to open it when she'd finished.

The foreign controls took some getting used to, and instead of water falling from an overhead spigot, it was forced up like an indoor sprinkler system, arcing overhead before running back down the drain again. Gen waited for the temperature to reach comfortable levels and stepped inside.

The shock from the forced water on all those hard-to-reach areas made her jump, but she soon grew accustomed to the pulsing jets between her thighs. That bit of her anatomy had seen more action in the last week than it had in her entire life, yet she was still amazed at how a little bit of water could make her crave more.

Spreading her legs wide, she took her time cleaning herself, enjoying the utterly decadent sensations, not thinking of anyone or anything in particular. She scrubbed her hair with a viscous purple compound that she really hoped was shampoo or soap. Suds dripped down her arms and torso, and she flipped her head forward to rinse. The waterspouts chugged away, drumming relentlessly against her sex. Her breasts felt full and achy, and she squeezed them, letting the water penetrate as deep as it could go. *I could really get used to this.*

"Thinking of me?" A low male voice startled her from her play.

Gen flipped her head back and dodged the water. "Zan!" *Shit, shit, motherfragging shit.*

He stood there, naked from the waist up, those colossal Arms crossed as he leaned against the doorway. "You slunk out this morning without saying good-bye."

She slammed her palm against the water controls and the jets stopped. Shivering, she stepped from the shower, glancing around for a towel or any sort of covering. "Sorry, I was craving a shower."

The corner of his mouth kicked up, his golden eyes alight with interest. "I can see that." He reached over to tweak one stiffened nipple. She leaped back, still dripping wet, and skidded into the wall.

One dark eyebrow went up. "Not in a playful mood?"

Arms wrapped around her chest, she nodded. "It's been a rocky couple of days, and I need a little space."

"You're in space."

She rolled her eyes. "Men."

Taking pity on her, Zan snagged something small and silvery off the shelf. He shook it out half a dozen times, and with each shake, it grew larger and sparkled brighter. He handed it over to her. "To dry off."

She wrapped it around herself, totally astonished at the

amount of fabric. "This is so cool. Too bad you don't have clothes that can do the same thing. Would take all the stress out of shopping, with one size really fitting all. Especially shoes. God, I had this pair of boots and it took me forever to find my size. . . ."

Zan's eyes had glazed over. *Stop with the pointless babble already, Gen. He doesn't care.*

"So, did you just come here to chastise my morning-after etiquette, or did you want something?"

His grin returned, and Gen silently cursed herself. How easy to fall into witty banter with this man. Pirate. Whatever. It would be so simple to just let nature take its course, to fall back into bed with him, satisfy her body if she couldn't satiate her heart. The small, spiteful part of her wanted to see if he could make her come without Rhys's little nudges.

But she'd promised Rhys, and though she didn't hold out too much hope for them, he was right that she had no future with Zan either.

"Actually, I wanted to take you up to the bridge. You ever flown a spaceship before?"

Her heart actually leaped at the thought. "Two days ago I'd never even *been* on one before."

He winked at her. "Get dressed and I'll let you take the helm for a little while."

She waited until she heard the outer door hiss shut. Hmm, maybe she shouldn't dismiss Zan so abruptly. Obviously some interest remained inside him, even sober, and the fact that he'd let her pilot his vessel was a major gold star next to his name.

Don't be a dumbass, her rational mind lectured while she scurried into a clean skirt and a blousy shirt. *Zan is still in love with a dead woman, and you are emotionally attached to another man. Giant slut bag, you promised!*

She shook her head at her reflection in the mirror. "From

famine to feast." Without glancing toward the candle, Gen sashayed out of the room.

Zan stood at parade rest outside the door. He didn't smile at her, but from what she could tell, he was of the still-waters-run-deep variety. She could look forever into the golden orbs and never quite see the bottom. The fanciful notion made her shiver.

Luckily, Zan didn't seem to notice. "You all set?"

She nodded and he marched off down the corridor. Scurrying to catch up, Gen took the time to notice details of the ship that stress had made her oblivious to. The hard metal grating shimmered as the built-in deck lighting bounced off it, almost as though the ship preened for her perusal.

"What's the ship's name?" she called out to Zan.

"Name?" He didn't slow his pace.

Lengthening her stride, she matched his speed. "You know, like a designation? What do you call her?"

"*He* never told me."

She grinned until she realized he was dead serious. "You mean it's alive?"

Zan nodded. "Although not what you might term *sentient*. My people have developed a symbiotic relationship with this kind of space-faring creature. We help them find food, and they take us where we want to go."

She looked around with a newfound respect and swallowed. "What does it eat?"

He caught her drift. Small lines of mischief appeared at the corners of his eyes. "Not people, if that's what you're thinking. These creatures are not organically based life-forms like we are. They can ingest any form of energy to convert to useable fuel. Having us detect the highest concentrations of power in a particular system allows the ship to fill itself up, not having to spend all its energy seeking more."

"Wow." Gen reached out and touched the bulkhead. "And he knows that we are here?"

Zan shrugged. "We aren't sure how aware it is beyond the need to eat."

Gen thought it through. "That makes no sense. How do you tell it where to go if you can't communicate with the creature?"

They came to a metallic walkway that spiraled up like a slide. Zan gripped her by the elbow and propelled her in front of him. "Hold on."

Opening her mouth to ask what she ought to hold on to, she lost her breath when the spiral was sucked upward, straight to the bulkhead. Throwing her arms over her head, she let out a squeak and braced for impact. It never came. Before she could inhale enough air to scream, the wild ride halted. They stood in another room, one she hadn't even suspected sat above their heads. "What was that?"

Zan released her arm. "Security measure. Don't ever try to come up here without me or one of my bridge officers, or the bulkhead won't disappear."

She flinched, imagining the splat of such an impact. It would probably break every bone in her body. "Thanks for the warning."

The bridge looked completely different than the other parts of the ship she'd seen. The walls effervesced with a pulsing green light that spilled over four bedlike chambers. Two of the "stations," as Zan called them, were occupied with men who appeared to be lost in a deep sleep. Tubes and wires were attached through several ports to the bed and ran down into the deck below. Two other men sat in chairs facing a bank of monitors where screens displayed the men's life signs as well as other information she couldn't decipher.

"What are they doing?" Gen asked, taking in the bizarre scene. She kept her tones low, as it seemed rude to shout while men slept on the job.

Zan indicated the two upright chairs. "Those are our nav stat readers. They scan the area, searching for decent-sized sources of energy and keeping an eye on the contact going on with the fliers. Make sure everyone is healthy, things like that." He indicated the sleeping men.

Gen stared at the unconscious figures. "So, they are flying the ship while they are sleeping?"

Zan nodded. "Exactly. You asked how we talked to the ship. This is how. They study the information from the readers and then feed it to the ship through their own minds. Then, it's up to the ship where to go. We can make requests, but they are sometimes ignored. It's how we ended up so far from home in the first place."

That seemed beyond risky to Gen. "Can't you ask it why?"

Zan shivered, though the room seemed plenty warm to her. "Believe me—you don't want the ship to talk back to you."

"Why ever not?"

"Because when it tries, it drives the fliers mad."

21

Gen stepped away from the beds. "Does that happen often?"

"No." Zan caught her hand before she could scurry back down the ramp from hell. "This ship was born to a domesticated ship and has never once tried to talk to the fliers. It's perfectly safe, if you want to take it for a spin."

Fear warred with curiosity. Did she trust Zan? Of course not, but she figured if he wanted to hurt her, he'd do it himself, not concoct some weird scheme. And she really wanted to know what it felt like to fly the ship. "What do I need to do?"

"Here." He helped her climb into one of the empty beds, attaching the small disks to her bare skin. Slipping a small wire into her ear canal, he moved to one of the seats and spoke softly. "Is the transmission clear?"

It sounded as though he was whispering in her ear. "Perfectly."

His gaze seemed to study her. "Lie down and try to relax. I'll be your reader, feeding you the coordinates to give to the ship. It'll take over from there."

Gen nodded and closed her eyes. The bed felt unbelievably

comfortable, molding to her every contour. She inhaled slowly through her nose, bringing the air deep into her lungs and breathing out all her tension. The light throbbed around her, pulsing with a rhythm she instinctively knew, and she matched the speed of her breaths to the soft *lub-dubbing* of what sounded almost like a giant heart beating.

Tranquility seeped in through her pores, and Zan's voice was like a caress as he spoke low. "You're doing great, Gen. Perfect first run. He likes you."

Her lips tilted up at his words. "How do you know?"

"Because, according to my instrument panel, he's already accepted you into his inner data matrix. Try giving him a command."

"Like roll over?" she muttered.

"Would rather you didn't. There's a white dwarf star not far from here. Relay these coordinates." Zan rattled them off.

Gen repeated them, opened her eyes, and let the glow from the ship sweep through her until light seemed to pulse from her fingertips. Her heart rate picked up as the ship pivoted in space, expending the minimum amount of energy to reach the star. "He's so hungry."

"Why makes you think that?"

"I can feel it. The thought of food makes him giddy, and he wants to race over there, but he's not strong enough. When was the last time he ate?"

She heard the frown in Zan's voice. "Earlier today."

Gen shook her head, knowing it for a lie. "No. He hasn't eaten in a very long time. He's starving."

Zan said something in a foreign language, but from the urgency, she felt sure it was a curse. The soothing tone he'd been using disappeared as he switched back to English and called out, "We have a nutrient leak somewhere. Pin it down, now!"

The poor ship. Even as she heard the sharp voices of the worried crew, Gen allowed herself to drift, feeling her way through the corridors, searching for the source of weakness. Before she realized what she was doing, she breathed the question, "Can you tell me where it hurts?"

"NO!" Zan shouted. With her mind elsewhere, she couldn't be sure, but she thought he might be trying to shake her awake. Then she lost contact with him altogether.

Yessss, the ship hissed, guiding her conscious mind through seemingly solid bulkheads and even a few people to the below-decks area. *Here, hurts here, friend.*

Gen carefully studied her surroundings. There was nothing but dark tubing as far as the eye could see. "How can I help fix you?"

There was a pause, as though he considered carefully how best to answer. *Patch. Feed. Better.*

Well, that seemed relatively straightforward. "I need to tell Zan so he can patch. You keep going toward the star and get ready to feed. You know Zan, right?"

The ship didn't respond aloud, but she felt sure he understood. "I'll do whatever I can to help you."

Hurt friend. Goooo.

Gen went, her mind traveling at the speed of thought. She pictured the glowing bridge and the next second opened her eyes, staring into Zan's slightly crazed ones as he shook her shoulders almost violently. "I know where the leak is."

To his credit, Zan recovered quickly, not asking how or what had happened. The dark knowledge resided there, and he feared she would snap at any moment. "Show me."

Taking his hand, she hauled him to the gateway and together they slid down several decks. Picking up her pace to a sprint, Gen led the way to medical to retrieve the organic sealant used to doctor flesh wounds.

Zan raised an eyebrow but didn't comment. She gave his hand a quick squeeze for reassurance. "I'm not losing my mind. Well, any more than usual."

"That's what all the crazies say." His hand went to his laser pistol. "This is your warning—if you go nuts, I will shoot you."

She didn't doubt it for a second. "Understood." One final quick stop in her cabin and they were good to go.

"Hold this and pass it to me when I'm through." Gen thrust the lit candle at Zan so she could squeeze into the small access panel. If her hips fit, she'd be in the clear, but no way could Zan's massive shoulders angle inside.

From the pinched look around his eyes, he knew it too. "Mind telling me what this is for?"

Struggling for a toehold, she avoided his suspicious stare. "It's dark in there."

"If the ship knows you are coming, he'll power up so you can see."

"The ship needs to conserve power." True enough. And maybe Rhys could enlighten her in more ways than one. She tried not to put too much thought into how soon she would see him again. Her hurt over his high-handed maneuvering still throbbed, but in a sick and twisted way, she could almost understand his reason.

Besides, this wasn't for her; it was for the ship.

Damn it, no more cheesecake. I mean it. She'd have to grease herself to fit through this thing. Perhaps some of the pirates were smaller, but that leak needed to be fixed as soon as possible.

A bit more frantic struggling and some chaffed skin on her hips but she made it. Her feet landed in liquid with a plop, and she reached up for Rhys.

Zan didn't give her the candle right away. "Can I trust you?"

She stared straight back at him, unblinkingly. "Can you afford not to?"

He handed her the candle.

Taking several steps in what she hoped was the right direction, Gen let all of her adrenaline-charged feelings flow into the flame. "Rhys, I need your help."

His answer was immediate. *What is it, sweetness?*

"The ship is damaged. I'm trying to repair it."

To his credit, he didn't ask why she had been tasked with the job. *What do you need me to do?*

"Can you feel him? The ship I mean. He's alive and he's in pain."

Not like this, no. Is it safe for me to take corporeal form?

Gen glanced back at the hatchway but couldn't see Zan anymore. "Yes."

Think about how you feel when I have my head between your luscious thighs.

Heat flooded her face. "Not now!" she hissed. But of course she couldn't not picture the way he'd appeared, his red-gold locks trailing over her pale skin as he dipped his head to take her in his mouth, green eyes blazing with intensity. . . .

"We need to do that again soon." Rhys touched her shoulder, stark naked and as radiant as ever. "Pleasuring you is such an emotional high."

She bit her lip to keep from smiling. "Keep your eye on the prize here, you junkie, or you won't get a chance for your next fix. Can you feel it?"

He closed his eyes, shook his head. "Still nothing. Tell me exactly how you found this out."

Gen described what had happened on the bridge as best she could, considering she didn't understand it herself. "I was connected to it, through these tubes. Normally they talk to the ship, but it can't talk back without making them crazy. But I heard it, talked to him, and I don't feel any crazier than usual."

Rhys touched her arm, just a quick brush of his fingertips over her skin. Nothing overtly sexual about the gesture but it warmed her insides. "I think I know what is happening. Your grandmother is a telepath, correct?"

"No, Rhys, she's *the* telepath, like the most powerful to ever live."

He nodded. "And at least one-quarter of her DNA was passed down to you."

Gen's mouth fell open. "Are you saying *I'm* a telepath?"

"Not in the strictest sense, no. You won't be able to read the minds of anyone in your vicinity, but if there's an emotional connection made first . . ." He trailed off and focused on her face. "Are you all right, sweetness?"

Was she all right? What Rhys said made perfect sense; she should have been a telepath. Her mother had been one, and Tanny showed signs of the gift too. Gen never had. "I thought that maybe it skipped me, that my brain couldn't handle it."

He reached out and cupped her chin. "There is nothing wrong with you, love. Stop worrying."

Looking into his vivid green eyes, Gen decided to put a pin in this new little nugget and study it under a microscope later. "So any idea how to proceed?"

"Perhaps if I come inside you, I can find the ship's resonance."

Gen nodded. "Hands down the best line ever. 'If you don't let me in you, we're all gonna die.'"

His laughter lingered in the air as his energy melded with her own.

Being inside Gen, sharing her energy, felt like coming home to Rhys. The hours he'd spent in the candle with nothing to do but brood had dragged onward, the relentless passage of time and nothing to mark it. He had started to equate time in the candle with the twilight years of an old man's life. Nothing to do but ruminate on what could have gone differently, if only he'd been smarter, braver, less selfish.

When she'd come for him and he'd heard Zan's voice, panic had seized him. What if she didn't follow her heart but followed that razor-sharp mind of hers and hedged her bets on the pirate?

Would he ever be able to recover? This little emergency was the best thing that could have happened, at least for his nefarious purposes.

Inhaling deep to fill her lungs, Rhys commanded her eyelids open. Her worry for the ship was pungent, skewing his senses a bit, but he could detect the dwindling presence of a creature in pain.

"I think it's this way." Candle in one hand and tube or organic sealant in the other, Rhys stepped carefully through the ankle-deep liquid.

"Gen!" Zan's voice called out. "The ship is nearing the white dwarf star! We'll need to seal this area off in five minutes or we all risk radiation poisoning!"

Some days, I wish I didn't bother getting my happy ass out of bed. Gen sighed.

"We can go, now—"

No! Rhys, don't you even think it. I promised him I would help. And if he dies circling the sun, how much longer do you think the rest of us will live?

He wanted to argue about the possibility of another ship coming along, but deep down he knew she was right. "I just wish it were someone else risking his neck here, sweetness. You have four minutes and then I'm going back."

Dodging several giant cords and piping that carried more plasmalike fluid, Rhys narrowed in on the sharpest point of pain. He squinted into the gloom and saw the broken line, which had to be the source of the leak. "There, I think I've found it."

What the hell are you waiting for? Let's haul ass.

Stepping over to where he could inspect closer, he commented, "You said this ship is not a carbon-based life-form. Will an organic seal hold?"

Do you have a better idea? Even her thoughts sounded defensive. He sensed her fear, wanted to soothe it, but refused to tread that shaky path again. What he needed to do was respond like a nonempathic male. Bring her stress down with words, instead of abilities.

"Don't get snippy, Gen. We don't want to put the poor creature through this again. But you are right; we are without an alternative so . . ." He set the candle down on a large outcropping bulkhead before pinching off one end of the leaking tube. Holding the other, he prepared to seal it. The ship shuddered.

Wait! I have an idea. Let me have control over my body. We'll need more than one pair of hands for this.

The countdown in his head had just passed the two-minute mark, and he accepted they didn't have time to argue. He breezed out of her, solidifying in time to grip her shoulders as the ship lurched again.

She shuddered. "He's excited because the star is so close. There's a knife in my boot. Take it out. I need you to do exactly what I say, Rhys." Fear had been replaced by steely resolve. Whatever course she had set, she was intent on it.

Bending down, he retrieved the knife. "Now what?"

She sucked in a deep breath. "You're going to have to cut a strip of skin off me."

Horror filled him at the thought. Maybe she *had* gone crazy. "No—"

Her gaze held steady. "It's the only way to ensure the seal will hold. We need to wrap the cut in organic material first. Take from the outside of my upper thigh. It's the only place you can get a long enough strip of skin."

Did she have any idea what she was asking of him? Requesting he inflict pain on her. His hands shook.

She leveled her gaze on his, an apology written clearly on her beautiful face. "Pain is better than death, Rhys. I wouldn't ask you, but there is no one else. If you don't do this now, I will die."

Overwhelmed by the fierce emotions she projected, he sank to his knees and rucked up her skirt. A muscle jumped in her jaw as she gritted her teeth against the coming ordeal.

He stroked a hand over her perfect, unmarred flesh. "I'll try to take as much of the punishment for you as I can."

She looked down at him, her eyes swimming in unshed tears. "I know you will."

Leaning forward, he kissed her leg in gentle tribute. "I love you."

The knife slashed down and he cried out with her, taking the white-hot agony into himself. *Always me before her; always let me spare her hurt.*

He worked quickly at his gruesome task and removed the strip of skin, tying it around the cut line. Hands trembling and coated with her blood, he took the sealant from her.

"Don't waste it on me—"

"Nonnegotiable." He ground the word out. "You need to run to make it out of here."

Mercifully, she quieted and let him patch her. Rising to his feet, he murmured, "Hold it still, sweetness. We have less than a minute to go."

After her sacrifice, there was no way he would botch this. Squeezing the tube in a serpentine pattern, he worked the bonding agent over the patch twice before dropping the empty tube and gripping her hand. "Time to move."

She stumbled at his first tug, and now that the detail work was done, he drank her pain in huge swallows, losing his focus as the magnitude overwhelmed him. Adrenaline coursed through her veins, and between that and his efforts, Gen moved with fluid grace. He heard her heartbeat thudding in his own ears.

"Keep the candle with you!" he yelled as he boosted her over the last obstacle. The access panel was in sight, and he merged with the flame, sucking everything from Gen but the need to run.

"Ten seconds!" he heard Zan yell. "Give me your hand!"

Rhys forced his will for her survival into her and drew strength from Zan to urge her on. Chanting a prayer for fortitude, Rhys barely noticed when the candle slipped from her hand and the wick snuffed out, his power fading. Gen screamed his name once before he was sealed in the bowels of the living ship, alone in the darkness.

22

"Staci, try to contact Gen again. I need to talk to her, ASA—" Alison's voice died in her throat as she entered her office to find it already occupied.

The man with his feet propped up on her desk made a slicing motion across his throat and gestured to her comm link. Absently, she shut it off and stuffed it into the pocket of her suit jacket. He didn't acknowledge her movement as he turned his head to face the window. Alison clenched her hands into fists to hide the tremors. No, it was too soon.

"The board has heard a rumor." His voice was thin and dry, like a snake slithering through dead leaves. "I am here for an explanation."

Alison stared at his reflection in the pane of unbreakable self-cleansing glass. She had seen him before, lurking in the shadows during Illustra board meetings. The assassin had no name, and to hear his voice was to hear the sound of death. Her stomach clenched in a knot as she looked upon the face of her executioner.

His long hook nose was the only remarkable feature on an

otherwise ordinary face. His brown hair had been slicked back against his head, and he wore head-to-toe black, including a pair of black faux leather gloves covering his steepled fingers.

Her mind raced. Was there any hope for a reprieve? It depended on how much the board knew. "I am handling the situation."

He turned to face her, his expression devoid of any emotion. "Marshal is dead. The tracker I put on him personally alerted me the moment his heart stopped beating."

Shit. Alison felt as though he'd wrapped those gloved hands around her neck and started to squeeze. Dispatching Marshal as one of Gen's boy toys had been a calculated risk. For Gen.

Alison had wanted to know if Gen had any of her grandmother's considerable telepathic ability. Though Gen had never shown any signs that she was a mind reader, Alison had hoped that sending an empath to her would help reveal her talents. Never in a million years would she have guessed Gen would have been capable of killing Marshal.

She licked her lips and opened her mouth to reply, but he took his feet off her glass-topped desk and rose to his full height. "The concerning aspect is not that the informant is dead but where he died."

"Where's that?" Alison pivoted to keep him in her sights.

If he noticed her discomfort, he didn't give any indication. "Outside the Alpha Centuri Lanes. You were there when he was requisitioned, Alison. Do you remember the conditions for his help?"

"That he would never have to leave Earth." Though she couldn't remember the why of it, Marshal had insisted on staying planet-side in exchange for lowering the defense grid on the empath's moon. The board had agreed immediately. They had approached the empathic people several times to request volunteers for the emotional interactive program, but the empaths had refused. Finding Marshal—who not only provided them with access to hundreds of empaths but also a way to contain them—had been a major coup.

"The board has also learned that one of the monks might have survived."

Alison shook her head. "No, I oversaw their executions personally. Every member of the order was taken care of."

Idly, he leafed through the stack of info disks and personal communiqués on her shelf. "So your report stated. Yet we have received word of a man with red-gold hair and green eyes who has invaded dreams of several of our former targets. None but the members of the brotherhood had the knowledge to project their own images."

Her heart pounded. "Merely a coincidence."

He made a tsking sound. "I do not believe in coincidence. Neither does the board. It's an election year. The time is coming, Alison. Everything the board has been working to achieve is at hand. But you've created this problem. . . ." He stopped directly in front of her, tilted her chin, and stared into her eyes. "Why do you think I'm here?"

It wasn't a question. A stab of white-hot pain in her mind nearly blinded her. She cried out, but he held her firmly. She tasted blood, felt the wet stickiness spilling from her nose, her ears.

"Please," she begged as her vision dimmed. "I know who is helping him."

He released her, and she crumpled to the carpet in a sniveling heap, hating her own weakness. But what could she do against an assassin who killed with the power of his mind?

Removing a white cloth from his pocket, he methodically removed her blood from his hand. "It is not enough. The board wants action."

Wiping the blood from her chin with the sleeve of her suit, Alison fought to regain composure. "We'll move the slave bodies. Even if there is one strong enough to project his image, he is likely untrained and has no way to prove his tale. We move the slaves and then set a trap for them on the abandoned moon. Problem solved."

He stared at her for a minute, his thoughts unreadable. Her comm link buzzed, but she ignored it, waiting for his decision.

"Evacuation of the moon has already commenced," he said, almost as an afterthought. "A military escort has been arranged."

"Let me oversee the takedown," she pleaded. "I can be on the next shuttle off-world—"

He slid a small disk over to her. "Your flight leaves in an hour."

She reached for it, but he pulled it back. "For your sake, I hope I never need to come after you again, Alison."

By the time the door slid shut behind him, the tremors shook her whole body. Stumbling into the lavatory, she shucked her ruined white suit and stepped into the sonic shower. Wrapped in only a towel, she buzzed Staci.

"I want an inventory on all the candles in the facility as well as a list of those authorized to use them and any customer complaints about those professionals. Bring the information and a new suit to my office and cancel my schedule for the rest of the week. If anyone asks, I'm on a last-minute business trip."

She disconnected and stared out the window, wondering when she had sold her soul and if she could ever get it back.

"Rhys!" Gen cried out as Zan and one of his cohorts dragged her through the access hatch, ripping the patch from her throbbing leg. Blood spilled over her knee and ran down her calf, but she ignored it, fighting to go back for the candle.

"Seal that off, now!" Zan bellowed as he dragged her away from where the other man was working. Golden eyes went wide as he laid her back on the deck. "What the hell did you do to yourself in there?"

She struggled against his hold, her gaze glued to the sealed-off panel. "You have to let me go back. I dropped the candle—he's trapped in there!"

"Gen, it's all right. The ship can absorb the radiation from the star. We can't." Zan spoke slowly as if lecturing a child on the cruel realities of the universe. "Hold still so we can get you patched up."

She fought harder, filled with all the horrific possibilities of what might happen to Rhys alone in there. Could he die, cut off from all emotion? Would radiation melt the candle? *I have to go back for him.*

Zan swore in a language she didn't recognize and immobilized her upper body in a full nelson. She twisted, landing on her open wound, and hissed in pain. He held her tighter. "Damn it, girl. Don't make me trank you."

"Please, you don't understand." Tears spilled down her face. "I have to go get him."

Zan lowered his head so his lips brushed over the shell of her ear as he spoke. "No, *you* don't understand. Once that panel was sealed, a barrier was put up. We breach that now and we'll all get a lethal dose of radiation. Nothing you can do right now but lie still and let us patch up your hurt."

"Zan, she's fucked in the head." Finished with his task, the crony who had doomed Rhys to his fate stared at the two of them. "It's just like all the others. The ship talked to her and now she's a space case. Be a piece of kindness to put her down."

Gen stopped struggling, desperation morphing to despair. *Rhys.*

No answer.

"Mind your station," Zan snapped. "Don't you worry none about her. I'll see to our guest."

Gen barely paid attention as the man's footfalls receded, her eyes glued to the panel. "How long?"

Zan slowly removed his hands. "How long what?"

Though she didn't want to, she met his gaze. Zan was the

only one who might be her ally right now; she couldn't afford to alienate him, or worse let him "do her a kindness." He would, too, if she left him no other choice. "When can we open that back up?"

"Lie back," he commanded, and she did, barely feeling the cold metal decking against her back. He rose and circled around her to where her leg bled. He eyed the patch job that had been partially scraped off before meeting her gaze. "This is no accidental cut."

She shook her head. "The ship isn't organic. You said so yourself. I needed organic material to create a bond so the patch would hold."

He stared at her, no emotion visible. "So you cut a hunk out of your leg?"

"Not me. Rhys did it."

Zan's eyes narrowed. "Your man? I thought he was gone."

Reckoning time. Gen bit her lip, considering her choices. Either she admitted to intentionally misleading Zan before or she'd have to lie now. Rhys was a liar but she was, too, her falsehoods motivated by the need to survive. Didn't change the fact that she'd misled Zan, then gone to bed with him.

"He's why I went to get the candle." Haltingly, she explained how Rhys could cohabitate within her, how he'd sought her out after Marshal had been shot. "When I got back to my room, he returned to the candle."

She'd hoped he wouldn't put the timetable together right away, but apparently he was just like any other man—his mind leaped directly to sex. "As I recall, you took an overnight detour before returning to your room."

Forcing herself to hold his gaze, she nodded.

A muscle jumped in his jaw. "You're telling me that while you were screwing me, he was tagging along for the ride?"

She nodded again.

Off he went, swearing in that alien tongue again. Gen could

do nothing except hold her hand over her wound and bleed while he ranted. It took a full five minutes of Zan's uninterruptible chastisement before she could understand him again. "Here I thought I had done some kinky shit, but this, this beats all. Was it his idea or yours, this little revenge fuck? Mind telling me why the pretty women are *always* insane?"

She offered him a grim smile. "Too busy bleeding here."

With another mumbled curse, he scooped her up. "If I was smart, I'd space you out of the torpedo bay."

She didn't argue, figuring anything she said would only be fanning the flames of her pyre. Despite his gruff exterior and disreputable way of life, Zan didn't kill aimlessly.

He strode into the medical bay and set her down on one of the antigrav pallets. Punching in commands, he turned his back and scrubbed his hands up like a professional surgeon. "Are you allergic to anything?"

Her mouth opened and closed on a few false starts. Looking to mend her or poison her? She cleared her throat and forced out the words, "Not that I'm aware of, no."

Zan didn't reply as he set about sterilizing various instruments. To heal or to torture? Gen swallowed and murmured, "I'm sorry. I never should have led you on, especially while things were so unsettled with him."

He didn't respond, but she pushed on. "I didn't set out to seduce you for any reason other than I wanted to. Rhys and I have an impossible relationship. I know it, he knows it, and we torment each other nonstop, but I can't help how I feel."

Zan met her gaze, held up a hypodermic needle. "Local anesthetic." He injected it into her damaged thigh and tapped the skin a few inches above the wound.

She braced for another wave of pain but felt only a dull contact. "I didn't feel anything."

He nodded in satisfaction and set to work, cutting away the

semibonded sealant. Other than a few bizarre tugging sensations, she felt nothing. Her heart waited elsewhere, suspended in time.

After a while, Zan spoke in a level tone. "You don't need to make excuses. I'm not going to kill you over something that can't be undone."

The idea that he'd want it to be undone at all disturbed her. Even now she could not regret being with him. Zan was by turns a forceful and patient lover, taking his time to pleasure her as well as himself, demanding the most her body had to give. If she'd never met Rhys, she would have been more than content to explore him on a regular basis for the rest of her natural life.

Unfortunately, she *did* know Rhys, and craved him like air in her lungs, a light in the abyss. Tears threatened to overwhelm her again as she thought of him trapped in the dark, nothing to feel but his own fear and the residual traces of her pain.

"You really love him, don't you?" Zan's soft words broke her from her obsessive thought cycle. He'd flushed out the wound and applied a thicker coat of sealant, a stark-white strip of artificial skin running down her leg like she'd been detailed.

She wanted to grip his hand and squeeze hard, but refrained since they were coated in blood and sealant. "Yes, and it hurts like hell. I know you don't want to hear it, but you deserve the truth. We used each other, Zan, and I'm not sorry."

He let out a humorless laugh that didn't quite reach his golden eyes. "Want to do it again?"

Recalling the look of agony on Rhys's face when he'd cut her removed any temptation Zan's offer might have held. "I promised him I wouldn't, not until we broke it off for good."

His golden gaze seemed to bore into her head until it penetrated her mind. "I can tell you right now—that will never happen. Once you've given your heart away, it's gone forever. The best you can hope for now is to steal one from some unsuspecting sap and let the chain of hurt continue. It's why we'd be good together—we won't ruin anyone else."

She saw the logic in his grim thoughts. "Is that what you really want?"

He turned away, gathering medical supplies. "It's all I can have and a far better deal than most will get. The sooner you accept that, the happier you will be."

23

Rhys opened his eyes, surprised by the aches and pains throbbing through him. What had happened? Whose body did he inhabit now? He struggled to remember, but the pounding in his skull kept the thoughts from coalescing. Throat parched, he couldn't even groan, the sound coming out as more of a wheeze.

Turning was sheer agony, one of his ribs screaming so loudly that he felt sure it had been broken. The pain and effort were worth it, though, when he realized who lay next to him.

"Sela," he whispered, reaching out a shaking hand to brush her hair out of her eyes. Though his vision left much to be desired in the gloom, she didn't appear to be damaged, at least not to the extent he had been, but his focus was so blurry, he didn't trust it. She was asleep, her chest rising and falling with even, silent breaths, and it finally dawned on him what had happened. Whose body he resided in this time.

His own.

"Sarge, we got a live one in eight." The crusty voice came from the lit area at the edge of his field of view, and by the time Rhys managed to move his head in that direction, a white cloud of noxious fumes filled the tiny room. He choked, sputtering, unwilling to surrender to unconsciousness. His gaze fixed on Sela. "I will find you again." The words rasped out as the darkness claimed him once more.

He floated in an endless void, tethered to nothing, swimming in starless space. Cold, alone, detached from everything he knew, separated from those he loved. How he wanted to die; his existence brought only pain to his sister, to Gen.

What spirit had possessed him to believe he could single-handedly end Illustra's occupation of this moon? Their reach had obviously expanded beyond the monastery, and a chill crept through him as he realized they had somehow discovered his connection to Sela. Why else would she have been imprisoned with him? *They know I've escaped their direct control, know who I am.* If they connected the dots, figured out who had helped him, Gen's life might be in danger, the lives of her loved ones back on Earth too.

Warmth and light flared, pulling him out in a rush and dispelling the chill that had clung to Rhys's soul. Worry for her, alone with the pirates and no real protection from Illustra, had consumed him while he waited in the dark. With no emotion to feed from, his essence had diminished, shriveling like old fruit discarded from the vine.

Then, as if from a great distance, he sensed her, his woman, the one he craved, the one he needed. A sickly yellow concern cloaked her life force, and he pulled at it, desperate for feeling after doing so long without. Reaching out, he tried to touch her, to connect with her mind but hit a wall.

Let me in, sweetness.

At the sound of his voice, she opened to him, a flower blooming in the sun. He dove blindly, following nothing so much as instinct to join with her, please her in any and every way. Seeking the comfort that only his bonded mate could give him after realizing his worst fear had come to pass.

He felt her relief, chased by a new thread of worry as she asked, "Rhys? Are you all right?"

His corporeal form wavered and only the need to touch her, to assure himself that she was real, held him together. They were back in the bowels of the ship, the candle flickering in the gloom. "They have her, have my sister. She is as I am, a slave, her mind separated from her body."

Soft curves pressed against him, and he buried his face in her hair. She stroked his shoulders, his back in comforting touches. "You saw her."

He nodded. "Just now. Without any emotion to hold me here, I reverted back to my body. It should not be possible to do unless mind and body are relatively close together."

She frowned at that, worry lines creasing between her perfectly shaped eyebrows. "I thought your body was in the Omicron Theta system."

Thinking back over what he'd just seen, Rhys came to a conclusion that terrified him. "Unless they are transporting me on a ship."

Gen blinked at him. "What, you mean, we're passing by your body somewhere in space right now?"

"There you are." Several pairs of boots clanged against the metal decking. The space pirate strode down the corridor, a scowl etched into the lines of his face as if he'd been born with that expression. His eyes went wide as he surveyed first Gen and then Rhys in all his naked glory. "Who is this? What in the five shades of hell is going on in here?"

Gen cleared her throat and shifted slightly away, though he maintained his grip on her hand. "Sorry, I didn't mean to worry you. But when the ship told me we had moved away from the star, I had to go back for Rhys."

Zan raised an eyebrow. "Rhys?"

"Talk about awkward," Gen muttered low. Taking a deep

breath, she raised her chin and made the introductions. "Zan the pirate, meet Rhys the empath."

Before either of them could say a word, a loud Klaxon sounded throughout the ship. Shouting and the thunder of running feet sounded from an adjacent walkway. A blond pirate stuck his head through the doorway. "Captain, proximity alert! Aft scanners have detected a convoy of earthships headed straight for us."

Zan narrowed his eyes at the two of them. "You two know anything about this?"

Gen squeezed Rhys's hand. He waited for her to explain, and when it became clear she wouldn't, he struggled to his feet. Between Gen's worry and Zan's outrage, he was able to harvest plenty of strength to sustain himself. "Does your man know if the convoy is made up of private ships or military grade?"

Zan turned to the smaller pirate. "Do you?"

"No, sir."

"I reckon it might be a good idea to find out," Zan said in a deceivingly mild tone. Even without viewing his crimson aura, Rhys would have detected the fury barely contained by the other man's skin.

"Captain, I believe your man will discover that the convoy is actually made up of a military squadron escorting one prisoner transport." It was the only explanation as to why he could have awoken in his own body. Illustra knew he had escaped and that he posed a threat and had decided to move the bodies of all the trapped empaths before he could free them.

Zan looked him over head to toe, especially the hand still wrapped around Gen's. "And how does a naked empath who just appeared on my ship know this?"

Rhys didn't look away. "Because I'm the reason they're here at all."

* * *

Gen made a small, helpless sound as Zan gripped Rhys by the shoulders and shook him. "I don't like guessing games, boy. Now, either you tell me exactly what trouble you're bringing to my doorstep or I'll shoot your miserable carcass out into the deep. We clear?"

Rhys didn't look the least bit intimidated. "No need for theatrics, Captain. I'm willing to give you my full cooperation, as long as you vow to see Gen safely home."

Gen didn't like the sound of that, as if Rhys no longer needed her. "Do I get a say in this?"

"No," both men replied in unison as they continued to glare at each other.

"Men." She gritted her teeth.

The standoff ended when the young pirate, barely more than a boy, returned. "Scans report it is a larger passenger vessel. State-of-the-art with a full military escort, including one-man stinger patrols."

Zan nodded. "Take this man to the med bay and get him something to wear." He turned to face Gen. "Meet us on the bridge."

Her gaze slid to Rhys, and she saw the knowledge of her panic reflected in his bright green eyes. His body was nearby, but they were outmanned and outgunned. And knowing Rhys as she did, she doubted he'd be willing to kill, even to save himself and his sister.

"I will see you soon, sweetness," he whispered as Zan gripped her arm and propelled her forward.

Though his hold didn't hurt, she yanked her arm back anyway. "What are you going to do to him?"

"If I were in your shoes, I'd be more concerned with myself." Snagging her arm more firmly, he escorted her to the bridge. "My mama always said no good deed goes unpunished."

"Rhys's people are aboard that ship. His body and that of his sister. We need to get aboard."

Zan stopped in his tracks and pressed her up against the wall so he could glare down into her face. "Sweetheart, if you go aboard that ship, they will shoot you down like a rabid dog. As of right now, the only thing you got working in your favor is that they don't know he is on board. They start threatening my ship or my crew and that advantage is going away real quick. Do you feel me?"

She searched his face, looking for any sign of compassion and found none. "Illustra is enslaving his people, Zan. Using them to manipulate others who wield power and influence. They need our help."

"I ain't no hero, Gen. The only piece of the universe that concerns me is the corner I happen to be in at this very moment."

She lifted her chin and glared up at him. "I won't let you trade him to them."

The corner of his mouth turned up. "Funny, because from where I stand, you ain't got much of a say." He propelled her forward again, and she held her tongue as they made their way to the bridge.

The Klaxons had been muted, but orange warning lights flashed throughout the ship. Gen eyed the beds, but Zan pushed her toward the far wall.

"Can you stay here and be quiet, or should I bind and gag you?"

Wrapping her arms around herself, she muttered, "I'll do what's best for me."

Zan nodded once, then strode to the view screen. "Magnify sector two point two five."

One of the pirates touched the area of the grid Zan had indicated and stretched his hands wide, until the marble-sized gray splotch sprawled across the entire screen. From her place against the wall, Gen could see the transport vessel and the squadron of fighters buzzing around it like flies swarming a buffalo.

"What's their ETA to intercept?"

"Communication in two, energy pulse in less than five."

A quick sucking sound revealed Rhys in a borrowed flight suit, his hair slicked back in a ponytail. The laughter lines around his eyes were pulled taut with strain. He started toward her but Zan intercepted.

"We have no weapons that can take on that many fighters. If we can see them, they can see us. What are the chances they won't try and board my ship?"

Rhys responded, "None. By now the fact that I awoke mid-transport has been reported to the captain of that ship. They know my empathic essence is nearby, and they'll search every ship they come across until they find me—that is, if their orders are not to simply blow us out of the sky."

Zan studied him a moment. "I appreciate your candor. You know our situation. This ship is fast, but it can't outrun the stingers and can't outgun the transport. What would you have me do?"

Rhys looked at Gen, his eyes flickering in the glow of the living ship. "Trade me to them and see her safe."

"No!" Gen lunged forward, but one of the pirates at a nearby station gripped her arms. She struggled, but he held her in a viselike grip.

"Zan, you can't do this! Rhys, I won't let you! What about your people? You can't just hand yourself over to them!"

"Let her go," Zan told the other pirate. "Contact the leader of the stinger squadron and make the arrangements."

The pirate released her arms, and she slumped forward in defeat. How could it end like this?

Rhys strode toward her, crouched down beside her. "Gen, we have no choice. If turning me over to them can save your life and the lives of these men, perhaps I can be forgiven for the death I have caused."

He tried to embrace her, but she shoved against him. "Marshal was an accident! You said yourself that he let you save me."

He reached for her again, and this time she allowed his touch, half afraid she would never experience it again. "It's more than just Marshal. I killed another man too."

Her lips parted, though she didn't know what to say. Rhys was not a killer. She knew him, damn it. Her eyes slid across the bridge to Zan. He was perfectly capable of ending someone's life, but Rhys?

Before she had a chance to absorb this latest blow, one of the pirates looked up from his flashing console. "Captain, all attempts at communication have been refused. They have received our message that we are in possession of the empath, but I'm getting nothing back. "

Zan muttered under his breath, probably some of his alien curses. "Has course or speed on any of the ships changed?"

It seemed as though the entire bridge held its breath. Gen reached a hand down to the ship, stroking along the smooth glowing bulkhead. Was he afraid? Could he sense their fear?

"Sir, several of the stingers are breaking formation and increasing speed. They will be in firing range in less than a minute." The pirate turned away from his station. "They're forming an attack pattern."

24

"No," Rhys whispered, his hands clenching into fists at his sides. "They can't do this."

The stinger ships spread out across the view screen, blocking the pirate's living vessel from the transport ship.

"Someone should tell them that," Zan shouted as he strode toward one of the beds. "I need a fresh flier in here now!"

Gen released Rhys's hand. "Let me do it."

The flurry of activity on the bridge slowed as all eyes focused on her. Rhys was buffeted by waves of concern, both for Gen and for themselves. They knew she had talked with the ship, and most suspected it had driven her mad.

Zan stared at her for a beat before nodding. "Go ahead."

"No!" One of the pirates at the other station rose to his feet. Rhys made a motion to block him from rushing Gen, but Zan was faster. Pivoting and drawing his pulse pistol, he shot the man in the leg. The man crumpled to the ground, moaning in agony. Rhys moved to the man's side to ease his hurt.

Zan surveyed his crew. "Any other objections?" When no

one made a sound, he tucked the pistol back into the waistband of his pants and helped Gen into the bed.

Immediately, a white glow engulfed her, an aura of welcome and a show of peace from the ship.

"Explain to him what's going on," Rhys called from his position by the wounded pirate. "He might have a solution we haven't thought of yet."

Zan narrowed his gaze on Rhys. "Are you suggesting I turn control of my ship over to my ship?"

The wounded man lapsed into unconsciousness as Rhys finished binding his smoking calf. "You have been deluding yourself, Zan. He has always been in control and is merely allowing you and your crew on board."

Zan glowered at him but didn't refute his claim, nor did he try to block Rhys from moving to Gen's side and clasping her hand. "Talk to me, sweetness. Tell us what the ship thinks we should do."

Though her lips moved, no sound came out. The glow surrounding her spread to Rhys's arm.

"Gen, can you tell him to run?" Zan murmured.

"I've explained our needs to him. He has a solution, but he wants Zan's permission to take over from here."

A smile spread across the pirate's face. "Whatever he thinks will bail our fat out of the fire. I say go for it."

As the words left his mouth, the lights went out on the bridge. The ship listed to one side, and Rhys threw himself across Gen's body to keep her from tumbling out of the flyer's bed.

"Captain, there's some sort of rift opening up directly behind the ship. Sir, it's pulling us in!"

Zan pushed off from the floor. "Full reverse!"

All the flier stations except for the one Gen lay in went dark. The other pirates sat up. "We've lost contact with the ship!"

A great humming noise filled the air, and on the view screen Rhys watched the stinger ships break formation, trying desperately to get away from whatever had the living ship caught in its gravitational pull.

"Look!" One pirate pointed to the passenger vessel. Behind the mammoth ship, a great vortex had opened up, a swirling mass of colors pulling at the hull of the vessel like tentacles guiding it to its gaping maw.

"Is our ship doing this?" Zan shook Gen's shoulders. Her eyelids were still closed, her breathing even.

The droning noise increased until several of the pirates clapped their hands over their ears. Light flooded the bridge, but not the ship's natural bioluminescence. The blinding swirl of colors bled through all of them, and Rhys held tighter to Gen, needing to protect her from whatever was coming for them.

As suddenly as it had started, the sensory bombardment ceased. Rhys met Zan's eyes, and they both turned to look at Gen.

She smiled up at them. "All systems functioning, Captain."

Zan blinked and whirled to face his bridge crew. The shock and fear rolling through them hit Rhys like waves of seawater lapping against a huge open wound. Zan made a furtive gesture with his hand. "Well? Someone want to tell me what the fuck is going on?"

"Are you all right?" Rhys bent down and scooped Gen up against him.

Her smile was brilliant. "I'm perfect."

"Captain." The blond-haired crew member turned to face Zan. "All but one of the stingers has disappeared from our sensor range."

"Say what now?" Zan whirled to face the view screen.

One lone stinger dipped away from where it had followed

them in, flying directly back to the transport as if hell itself was on its tail.

"What did you do, sweet Genevieve?" Rhys whispered in her ear.

She laughed merrily, squeezing his shoulders in a reassuring grip. Truly this woman amazed him to no end.

"The ship, our ship, created two wormholes. Nothing happened to the other stingers. We were moved clear across the galaxy."

"Come again?" Zan's eyebrows drew low over the bridge of his nose.

Gen gestured toward the passenger vessel. "You're free to go aboard at your leisure, Zan."

Zan glanced from her to the empty view screen and back again. "How come I didn't know my ship could do this?"

Gen bit her lip and thought it over for a moment. "Did you ever ask?"

Zan threw his head back and laughed heartily. "Damn, now why didn't I ever think of that?" Regaining his normal confident composure, he clapped his junior officer on the shoulder. "Order one of the fliers to latch onto their energy reserves before they get their wits about them and fire on us. Prepare a raiding party."

Gen kissed Rhys on the cheek. "Let's go get your body back."

With the pirate vessel latched onto the passenger ship like a babe sucking greedily on its mother's nipple, the ship didn't have the energy reserves to mount a counteroffense. Zan and his pirates led the raiding party. Rhys wanted Gen to stay on board the living ship, but she refused.

"Don't you think it's time you tell me the whole story? I know you killed someone, Rhys, but I don't know why."

If nothing else, he owed her this. As they picked their way through the dark and damaged vessel, he gathered his courage.

"Sela is unusually gifted as an empath. She doesn't just have the ability to stoke the fires of emotion—she can also force her feelings on others. A man, one of our spiritual leaders, told my parents that she was bewitched by an evil spirit. They could sense his fear, though, and denied his request to cleanse her."

Gen paused. "He wanted to hurt her?"

"A cleansing is an archaic ritual that traps the evil essence, nullifying its ability to interact with others. They would have cut out her eyes and tongue before placing her in *lesternari*, the living death." The thought of that fate for his sister stirred the rage he had thought was long ago suppressed.

"He tried to do it anyway," Gen breathed. "And you stopped him in the only way you could."

Her sympathy washed over him. "I committed an act of great evil. The man was afraid. I should have helped him, but instead I ended his life. His blood is on my hands, Gen."

"No." Her tone held that stubborn ring he knew so well. "You are frustratingly high-handed, and sometimes obnoxiously self-righteous, but there is no evil in you. Just because your people can't understand why you did what you had to doesn't mean I don't. I admire you Rhys, and I'm glad I fell in love with a man brave enough to protect his innocent sister."

"You love me?" Hope and fear battled for control of his heart.

Of course, she picked up on his turmoil. "We'll discuss it later, once you are back where you belong. Don't give up on happily-ever-after yet, Rhys. We need to find your body."

Gen thought they would have met up with more resistance from Illustra's ground forces. But the few humanoids they ran across wore white lab coats in lieu of weapons. Whoever had ordered the empaths to be moved were obviously under the impression the military escort had been enough.

While Zan and his men secured the skeleton crew, Gen and

Rhys explored the containment rooms housing the bodies of unconscious empaths.

"There are dozens of them, hundreds maybe." Ice water slid through her veins as she saw helpless children hooked up to machines that kept their life processes operating while their empathic souls were forced to do God knew what to countless others back on Earth.

Rhys held her hand. "Their influence has spread out. They've discovered the younger ones are easier to keep trapped. All the older members of my order were slaughtered because they could escape the candle's pull."

Wiping tears from her eyes, she made a promise that she would find some way to not only free them all, but also to expose Illustra so this never happened again.

She crept around another corner and made her way into a dimly lit room. The power flickered ominously as the pirate's ship fed off the energy reserves. The hallway branched off in three different directions.

"Which way?" she asked Rhys.

He closed his eyes, shook his head. "I don't know. I can't *feel* anything. They must have set up some sort of shielding around the empaths after I awoke in my own body."

"Let's try from port to starboard." Easing forward, Gen approached the mouth of the first hallway. It was completely dark, and she held up the flickering candle, peering into the gloom.

"Let me go first."

Rhys pushed past her, and, swallowing, she followed him into the darkness.

He stopped in front of the first cell. "This is where they kept the stronger prisoners. See how thick the cell frame was? It's to add a dampening field to protect the guard's emotions in case someone managed the impossible."

"Like you did." She was proud of his strength, his perseverance against the challenges he continued to face. Rhys's bravery and need to do what he felt was right inspired her own. He made her want to keep testing those boundaries she'd lived with all her life.

He stopped in front of one cell door. With the energy field down, he could have stepped inside unimpeded. From the tension in his posture, Gen knew whatever he saw affected him greatly.

Moving up so she could see, she took his hand, looking at him instead of at what was inside the room. "I'm here."

He glanced down at her, studying her face for an endless moment before turning back toward the cell. Taking a deep breath of recycled ship's air, Gen stepped over the threshold.

Two cots had been erected amid a tangle of medical equipment. The smaller cot contained a girl, probably about fifteen Earth years old. A tube had been shoved between her pale lips, and her skin was waxy and clammy to the touch. "This is Sela?" she asked Rhys.

He crouched on the other side of his sister's bed, and she saw the tears swimming in his eyes. "I'd hoped they wouldn't find her. My parents must be dead or they would have come for her."

A sound of absolute grief filled the small space. But it did not come from where he stood on the other side of the cot. This noise broadcast again, a keening wail that came from behind her. Slowly she turned to see the other occupant of the room.

Her heart shuddered in her chest as Gen studied the still figure on the bed. His face was a mass of bruises, dried blood crusted in his hair. His body was as large as he projected himself, but gaunt and half-starved. She could count his ribs beneath the ashen skin. Tubes and wires snaked out from the cot, and his chest rose and fell in an artificial rhythm. Her heart ached as she studied the man she loved. "What have they done to you?"

She heard it again, pain and anguish made audible from the still form on the cot. She reached for his hand to offer what little comfort she could. The man she knew approached her from the side. "I won't know the full extent of the damage until I'm inside. These machines might be all that's keeping me alive, Gen."

All at once, she understood what he was saying. This might be the end; he might die as soon as his soul reclaimed his body.

He reached for her face, stroked her cheek. "This is what I've been driving toward the whole time. What I wanted. But now I find that I do not want to go."

She leaned into his touch. "You won't die. I won't let you." Even as she made the vow, she realized she couldn't affect it one way or another.

"I do not fear death, Gen."

Her eyebrows drew down. "Are you worried about the others? I'll make sure we get them back to Earth, reunite them with their bodies."

The tears in his eyes spilled over. "Such nobility you credit me for. In truth, I've barely given them a thought since we've entered this room."

Gen shook her head. "Help me to understand here, Rhys. What is it you're afraid of?"

He looked down into his own battered face, surveyed his wasted body. Then, turning back to her, he took a shuddering breath. "That you will no longer want me if I am forever broken."

Her lips parted and she blinked. Was he serious? "Rhys—"

Pulling her forward, he thrust his tongue into her mouth. She tasted his tears, mingled with her own. Her free hand ran through his silky mane of hair, freeing it from the holder until it spilled across both of their faces.

She gasped for air when he finally released her. Resting his forehead against hers, he murmured, "I will always love you, my sweet Genevieve."

Before she could reply, he turned to that shimmering gold-mist body. The flight suit he'd worn fell to the floor in a heap. Tiny sparkles hovered over the still form on the bed and slowly settled back into place.

The candle extinguished on an invisible breeze, leaving her alone in the dark.

25

Agony.

Rhys couldn't catch his breath, hadn't the wherewithal to gather his thoughts. Reentering his body felt like being sliced open by a thousand razor blades at one time. Madness gnawed at his mind, and if he'd had the strength, he would have clawed his own eyes out to make the awful burning pain stop.

"Rhys," someone whispered. A dulcet feminine voice that smacked of a longing he could no longer comprehend. "Are you in there?"

He parted his lips, but only a puff of air came out. It was too much, sensation overload. They'd hurt him more since his last visit. Something internal was badly damaged, vital life processes.

Had he reclaimed his flesh just in time to die within?

"Gen?" A male voice, full of command. Rhys recognized it, but his mind couldn't form the name. "How's he doing?"

A sniffle and he felt her fingers weave through his own. She didn't apply pressure, as though trying to minimize his hurt, but her gentle touch gave his mind something to cling to, a goal to move toward instead of flailing helplessly in the blackness.

"We need to decide what all's gonna happen from here." The man kept his voice low. "Me and my kind are ready to pull up stakes and move on. We need you to talk to the ship and get us home."

"I'm not leaving him, leaving any of them. Zan, you've seen them. They're totally defenseless like this."

The all-encompassing pain took him under before he heard Zan's response.

Later, he awoke to find Gen nestled up beside him. Judging by the machines and instruments as well as the overpowering smell of disinfectant, he'd been moved to some sort of medical treatment facility. The pain had dulled to a constant throb, and he suspected he'd been drugged.

Gen stirred beside him, lifted her head to meet his eyes. "Hey." Her voice was froggy from her recent nap and charmed him as much as her tousled hair. "How are you feeling?"

The pity and sorrow in her eyes was almost his undoing. Closing his eyes, he whispered, "Where are we?"

"Still on Illustra's ship. Though we've had to rely on the med bots to treat you and the others because the crew has been locked down below."

"Is Sela . . . ?"

She offered him a warm smile. "Her body is fine. They haven't hurt her in any way."

He struggled, trying to sit up. Even that small effort caused sweat to bead on his brow. He touched it in wonder, unable to believe he was back in his own skin for the first time in months.

Gen retrieved some pillows to help him maintain his upright position. "Try to stay still. The last thing you need is to hurt yourself more. You're looking at months of intense therapy as it is."

A lump formed in his throat. "I don't have months. Not when they're stealing untrained children and forcibly separating them from their bodies."

"We need to come up with a plan. I can stall the pirates only so long. Now that they know their ship can open wormholes, they're eager to return home."

Staring at his atrophied legs beneath the blankets, Rhys murmured, "You should think about going with them. I'm sure Zan would appreciate your company."

She drew back as though he'd struck her. "What the hell does that mean?"

He met her gaze; she deserved no less. "I'm a wreck, Gen. You said yourself it will take months for my strength to return. I cannot be the man you need me to be."

Her eyes narrowed on him. "So you're just going to make that choice for me? Don't I get a say in this?"

"I've ruined your life. The same way I ended Marshal's. You can never go home, as long as Illustra is in power."

"And you don't want me anymore. I get it. Now that you have your body back and have your own emotions to monkey with, I'm just excess baggage."

"Never." No matter if it was better for her to believe such nonsense, Rhys couldn't let her leave thinking she was without value. "If I had a choice, I would keep you by my side forever. But that choice was taken from me. I'm trapped now just as surely as I was within the candle. They turned my body into another prison."

"Stop feeling sorry for yourself," she snapped. "It's a total turnoff."

He laughed hollowly. "As if my wasted state and constellation of scars weren't enough? I feel as though I sold you a false bill of goods, Gen. Promised you a perfect physical specimen and was switched out with a broken-down junker at the last moment. I can't ask you to accept me as I am."

Gen glanced over her shoulder to the open door. Rising, she walked backward, holding his gaze the entire time. "Maybe I want to accept you as you are. Did you ever consider that your physical perfection intimidated me a little?" Behind her, the door slid shut to ensure privacy.

He couldn't believe what his senses told him. She was aroused, the red pulse of her libido unmistakable. Even more incredibly, his cock twitched with interest as her fingers moved to the buttons of her dress. She unbuttoned it to her waist and let the top gape open to reveal the creamy mounds of her breasts.

"My pleasure still gives you strength, doesn't it? I can help you. But you have to want me, to let me." Her gaze locked with his. "To trust me not to run away when we hit a wall."

He couldn't believe she would want this, with him as he was. "I can't leave my body right now, Gen, can't project myself as the man you've known." Even as he said it, his hands reached for her, eager to touch the smooth skin she'd exposed. To finally feel it with his own hands.

Her blue eyes glittered with passionate intent as she climbed up on the bed. "No one was asking you to leave. Don't you know by now that what I want, more than anything else from you, is the truth?"

Dipping her head down, she brushed her lips over his in a sweet caress. The contact jolted him, and he opened his mouth, wanting a deeper taste of her. She complied, sweeping her tongue into his mouth in a slow exploration, his flesh melding with hers for the first time.

Even with his hands attached to tubes and wires, he couldn't hold back from exploring her generous curves. Her nipples pebbled under his ministrations, and she arched into his hands so he could cup her more fully. Her sigh of pleasure went straight to his now-erect cock, and he rocked it against her, wanting to feel her there.

Panting, she pulled away, though her fingers continued to trace the scars on his chest. Poised on her knees, she held herself over him. She was careful not to press against him, still acutely aware of his physical state. "You need to tell me if something hurts."

"It hurts when you stop," he told her honestly.

She rewarded him with a dazzling smile. Scooting down, she tugged the blanket with her. "I bathed you, when you were unconscious. Did you know that?"

Her fingers trailed lightly over his chest. Unable to form a replay, Rhys shook his head.

"I needed to do it, to do something for you." Her soft hand worked lower, over the smattering of hair on his belly, loving everything she found with her touch. "So you don't need to worry about disappointing me. I already know what I've got and I want it. I want *you*."

As her fist closed around his erection, Rhys exhaled, shaky with excitement. "Then take it, take whatever you want. All I have is yours, my sweet."

She nuzzled his stiff prick, her hot breath falling on his throbbing erection a moment before she took him into her mouth. The warm, wet depths bathed his heated flesh, and he fought the urge to buck his hips and force her to take even more. No way would he jeopardize this moment.

Her eyes met his again, and he saw her pleasure as she took even more of him. Those gold and purple sparkles cresting out from her aura. The wet slide of her lips and tongue over his rock-hard cock, the way her hands smoothed down his thighs in a tender caress. She pulled back until just the tip of her tongue laved over the crown, tasting the moisture there. In that instant, he realized what was missing.

"You're not using your germ shield."

Smiling, she shook her head. "Not with you, Rhys. I want nothing between us."

Gripping his shaft, she bent down to claim him again.

* * *

He was hers. Gen could see the acceptance in Rhys's eyes, the way his shaking hands moved to her head while she sucked him deep into her mouth until his cock touched the back of her throat. She loved the taste of him, the salty tang of his seed, the musky maleness of his smooth phallus. This was the first blowjob she'd ever given without her germ shield, and she doubted she'd ever go back.

Seconds away from orgasm herself, she reached down to stimulate her throbbing clit so they could come together. His heavy-lidded eyes focused on her movements. "Let me taste your pleasure."

Dipping her fingers into her honeyed well, she then moved them to his mouth, all the while keeping up the steady suction on his pulsing shaft. His tongue parted her fingers, licking down one side and up the other, and she could easily envision him doing the same between her lips, hungry for more.

"Gen," he gasped, releasing her hand. "I'm going to come."

She sucked harder, needing all of him she could get. Rhys let out a hoarse gasp, his fingers tunneling in her hair. Hot jets of semen erupted in her mouth. Her sex clenched in response, wishing he filled her there so she could milk his cock dry.

Next time, she promised herself as his orgasm slowed, and he tugged at her hair, gasping and shuddering beneath her.

With one final lick, she let him go and crawled up against him. Sharp, ragged breaths tore from his throat, and he didn't open his eyes. Concern replaced the satisfaction she'd felt moments before.

"Are you in pain?"

He shook his head quickly and groped for her hand. "You overwhelmed me. As you always do."

Smiling, she settled down beside him. "I guess I don't need to ask if it was good for you."

"*Good* is too mild a word, sweetness." As his breathing evened out, he continued to touch her, a slow exploration as if relearning her every dip and curve. "I'm still amazed that brought you sexual satisfaction. And perhaps a little disappointed."

"Why?" She raised her head to look at him.

"Because I don't get to keep playing with you now."

She giggled, startled at how lighthearted she felt. They had so many overwhelming problems to deal with, but for now, this momentary slice of happiness was theirs for the taking. "You've got to earn your boons. Welcome to Gen's rehab program, phase one."

Tilting her chin up, he met her gaze. "It will be worth every moment of pain to know I have you to look forward to."

A knock sounded on the outer door. Sliding out of the narrow medical bed, Gen covered Rhys with the sheet once more. After fixing her dress and finger-combing her hair, she opened the outer door.

Her jaw dropped. "Gia? Where the fracking hell did you come from?"

Gia looked just as startled. "I didn't believe it when that bastard pirate told me you were on board. That was my stinger that got sucked into the vortex with you."

"Gen?" Rhys called out.

Gia tried to peer around her, but Gen blocked her path. Turning to Rhys she said, "It's all right, she's a friend. Get some rest. I'll fill you in later."

Shutting the door, she escorted Gia into the empty lab. The med bots were all stowed carefully in their rechargers until someone called for medical assistance.

"You look different," Gia remarked as she boosted herself up onto the desk. "Dare I say, happy?"

With a start, Gen realized she was happy. Sinking into the lone chair, she glanced up at her friend. "I know it sounds nuts, but I am happy."

"Because of him?" Gia chucked her thumb in Rhys's direction.

Gen considered it. "Partly. It's totally nuts, but I like this sense of purpose."

"Tell me everything," Gia ordered.

Gen did, filling her friend in on the events of the last week. "Having you order me a man whore really did change my life."

"Damn. And I got stood up that night, if you can believe it. Who would have thought you'd turn into a freedom fighter?"

"Well, the pay isn't as good as the secret-shopper gig, but you can't beat the benefits with a stick."

Gia threw back her head and laughed. Zan chose that moment to stride in, without knocking. He glanced at Gia but then focused on Gen. "I need to talk to you."

Gia glared at his back. "Rude much?"

Gen didn't want to have this argument again. "Zan—"

"We received a transmission from someone named Alison, directly to the captain of this vessel. She's bringing all the empathic candles in their possession to a prearranged rendezvous point. She'll trade them for you and Rhys."

"What?" Gen couldn't believe that her own stock had risen so much that she was worth all of those lives. "That's totally screwy. Why would she do that?"

Gia hopped off the desk. "It's a trap, Gen. She's baiting it with what she knows Rhys wants, hoping he'll act nobly and give himself up."

"Not just what Rhys wants." Zan glanced over at her. "The message also said she has your grandparents and your sister. They've already rigged the self-destruct sequence and abandoned the bridge. If we don't show up there in one hour, they'll destroy them all."

26

"Go easy, Rhys," Gen murmured as she helped him maneuver down the corridor in the antigrav straps. "Take it slow."

Her concern for him itched almost as much as the scarred tissue along his healing wounds. It came from her shiny pink love, though, and for that he would tolerate any discomfort.

"We don't have time for me to take it slow, my sweet." Until he built up enough strength to control his muscles, he would be forced to rely on others and mechanical devices. If he lived that long. "Are you sure we can trust this friend of yours to help us? She was working for Illustra."

"No, she wasn't. Gia's military, a stinger pilot. She was ordered to protect the vessel, but no one bothered to tell her why or who was on board. Now that she does know the whole story, she'll help us, even if it means dishonorable discharge. I trust her, Rhys, with our lives." Sincerity coated every word, along with the sapphire blue in her aura.

"And I trust your judgment." His movements were a little smoother now that he had practice working the antigrav strips.

The medical bots had done an excellent job of patching up his surface wounds. He needed to gain weight, rebuild his muscle strength, but he was unable to do anything about those deficiencies right now. If not for the fact that he floated horizontally a foot above his lover's head, he could almost imagine he was normal.

With Gen's help, he eased around the last corner toward the main conference room. She held him while he righted himself, reengaging the armbands to sync with the ship's artificial gravity. Gen gripped the front of his borrowed flight suit and stared into his eyes as she murmured, "You know they would have done this in the medical lab."

Taking a moment to compose himself, Rhys righted his body with only the slightest bit of unfortunate lurching. "They'd view me as a victim in there, not part of the solution."

Her worried gaze caught on his. "Do you have a solution?"

He did, though he didn't wish to tell her about it yet. "Everything will work out, sweetness. Trust in that."

Standing on tiptoe, she brushed her lips over his. "I trust in you." Turning her back, she headed into the conference room, leaving him to make his way under his own power.

Rhys swallowed hard. Did he deserve her trust? Not even a little. The lives of her beloved family members were on the line, and she expected him to do the right thing. He'd do it, too, in an instant, if he could only figure out what exactly it was.

The only thing that was clear to him was that Gen deserved his best. She'd left him to make his own entrance, to show their unlikely allies he could take control and see them through this mess. Teetering on artificial gravity out here in the hallway wasn't acceptable. Disengaging the antigrav strips altogether, he leaned heavily on the wall.

The pain had lessoned to a dull ache that covered his body. Reaching down into his spiritual reserves, he collected composure before pushing away from the bulkhead, remaining upright by sheer force of will. The doors hissed open at his approach.

Gen smiled at him as though she'd expected nothing less. Her expression of pride was worth the light-headedness, the burning in his atrophied muscles. Gia studied his every move as he crossed the conference room. Still dressed in her gray flight suit, she'd perched on the sill of the viewport, and he could tell from her colors that that move was designed for protection's sake. Even though she sat among friends, Gia would present her back to no one.

Zan sat at the head of the table, his leather boots propped up on the polished surface. "'Bout time you got your lazy carcass out of bed to do something. Tell your girlfriend to release the lockdown on my ship."

Rhys glanced at Gen, who sat on his immediate left. Bless her, she'd saved the closest seat to the door for him. Force of will could only extend so far, and it took every ounce of effort for him to not just collapse into the chair. "What is he talking about?"

Gen shot Zan a dirty look. "He's blaming me for his inability to communicate with his own ship. It's not my fault he would rather respond directly to another sentient being than take orders from people too scared to talk to him."

Zan pointed a finger, encompassing both of them. "Here's how it works. I tell the ship where I want him to go and he takes me there. There ain't never been a need for communication other than that. I've got nothing but a whole heap of trouble since I took you two on board."

Gia snorted. "Maybe that will teach you not to kidnap people."

Zan glowered at her. "I seriously doubt it."

Gia shrugged her slim shoulders and swung one boot-clad foot idly. "If you don't want to play by the rules, you shouldn't whine when things don't go your way. It wastes time and irritates people."

Rhys watched the two of them spar, saw the white-hot sparks of charged feeling flying between the two dominant spacefarers.

"That never worried me none. Besides, what else have I got to do?"

Gia rolled her eyes. "I don't know, learn the rules of grammar? Or maybe work on your personal hygiene? Just because all the other space monkeys throw their own sh—"

"This is getting us nowhere." Gen's quiet interruption was full of steel. "Hundreds of lives are in jeopardy, and we have to figure out how we can help them. *All* of us." The last was directed at Zan, who scowled but didn't contradict her.

Analyzing what little he knew about the man, Rhys offered the one caveat that might net them the pirate's willing participation. "On my home world, there is a treasure trove of valuable items. They are kept by the members of my order. You and each of your crew are entitled to any items of your choosing if you help us all return home."

Zan linked his fingers together and leaned his head back against his clasped hands. "And if we want it all?"

"Don't be an ass," Gia snapped. "It's part of their cultural heritage. You can't just abscond with that."

Rhys ignored the waves of outrage springing from Gia's small form, the first true emotion he'd sensed from her. Why was she so upset? "You may have whatever your ship can hold."

"I want it in writing." Zan sat forwarded, ignoring Gia's squawk of indignation.

Rhys studied the other man. "I'll draw up a contract, and Gen will give it to you as soon as we've accomplished the mission."

Gen's soft hand touched his arm, warming him through the

thin material of the flight suit. No way could he look on her as he stated his intentions, so he focused on the others as he explained his plan.

"I intend to set Gia's stinger on a collision course with the Illustra vessel. They can't destroy the hostage ship if they are already gone."

"What?" Gen's voice was low. Not a shriek of outrage, but more of a deadly displeasure.

Rhys turned to face her. "What other choice is there?"

Her eyes narrowed, all hope vanishing like matter through a black hole. "You don't know for sure that will even work. They could fire on you before you get close enough. Or the explosion could trigger the autodestruct codes."

"If you have a better plan, now's the time to voice it." There was no snideness to his statement, but Gen looked as if he'd slapped her.

Zan whistled low. "You really do have a death wish."

Rhys frowned at him. "Death doesn't scare me."

The pirate pointed to where Gen sat. "Yeah, but she should."

"Would you two excuse us for a minute?" Gen's voice contained barely suppressed rage. Gia and Zan exchanged a loaded look and as one moved toward the door.

"Hurry up. We can't wait on this much longer," Zan called over his shoulder. The doors hissed closed behind them.

"This won't take long," Gen muttered. As soon as the door closed, she was on her feet, pacing the length of the room. "You just can't wait to be rid of me, huh?"

The brilliant red from her anger almost blinded him. "Sweetness—"

Pressing her knuckles into the table, she leaned forward, her nose an inch from his. "Don't you dare sweetness me, you bastard. Again, Rhys, again with the deceptions and the lies. You'd think I would learn! But apparently I'm too fracking stupid to

figure it out. Rhys is on a mission. Period. Nothing else matters."

"That's not true. You know how much I love you. I'm doing
this for you, Gen, so you can have your family back and so that
what's left of mine will be safe. If there was another way—"

"You aren't even *looking* for another way. It's like you can't
wait to die."

He saw the tears in her eyes spill over and reached forward
to brush them away. "Let me love you now, just once in the
flesh and it will be enough."

Her hands were already working the fastenings on his borrowed pants. "It will never be enough."

Rhys silently agreed as he cupped the back of her head,
lifted her onto the table behind him. Her crimson dress rode up
her long legs, and as he captured her lips, his fingers explored
the silken flesh that was foreign and familiar all at once. All his
frailty was forgotten as he derived strength from their burning
passion.

Their tongues mated, and he groaned when her hot little
hand wrapped around his throbbing shaft. Unable to wait another second, he shredded her panties, eager to explore her wet
heat.

She tore her lips away as he thrust two fingers into her.
"Rhys, now. Don't wait."

He kissed the smooth column of her throat, nibbled on her
ear. "You don't have your shield up."

"No," she agreed, wrapping her legs around his hips. "And
I'm not putting it up either. You promised me once that you
would fill me, and that's what I want. Us, together, with nothing between our bodies. I want you to come inside me, fill me
with your seed. Mark me yours."

He couldn't hold back, not after her intense words of invitation. Yet he didn't want to rush, so he bent over her, slowly

feeding his cock into her body. Watching her puffy pink folds swallow his engorged shaft inch by inch. Her lube made him glisten as he pulled slowly out and then crept back inside. Her eyelids fluttered, her breathing hot, heavy, and she moaned his name.

Slowly, he withdrew again, but the tight grip of her legs locked around his waist wouldn't let him go far. "My beauty," he rasped, surging back into paradise. Her musky arousal filled his nostrils, the heady scent of sex making him slightly dizzy.

Her nails sank into his shoulders, her hips undulating beneath him. "Harder, Rhys. Please, I'm so close!"

Instead of complying, he rotated his thumb over her throbbing clitoris, gasping as she hugged his cock harder, demanding that he give her everything he had. He closed his eyes, held very still, clinging to his control. But it had been so long since his body had had this pleasure. "I wanted this to last, but I'm going to—"

Her heels pounded against his ass, spurring him on and shoving him deeper inside her. Willpower vanished and he pistoned into her wet depths, losing himself in the sweet heat of her body, the bold colors of her release. Her cries of ecstasy in his ears. "Yes, Rhys, oh yes!"

Her orgasm hit, a blinding wave of brilliant color that swept him up in it. No way to deny himself, he cupped her face and claimed her mouth, even as his seed spurted deep inside her. Perhaps it was irresponsible to hope, but he wished he planted a life there in her womb, something of himself that would love her always. As he would even beyond his dying breath.

He flinched. Something sharp was jabbing him in the hip. He glanced down to where she'd stuck him with a small hypodermic and then back to her tearstained face, still rosy from their union.

"It's not just about you anymore, love. You won't listen, so

I'm doing what I have to. To make sure all the people I love are safe."

Her face filled his vision as his sight tunneled into nothingness.

Gen had just fixed her clothes and arranged Rhys back in his when Gia returned.

"He wouldn't listen?" was Gia's only comment as she helped her friend activate Rhys's antigrav strips.

"You called it right." When Gia had pulled Gen aside while Rhys was dressing, she'd advised that Gen find some way to subdue the empath. At first Gen had balked, but when she'd discovered that Rhys had once again kept vital information to himself, she was glad she'd snagged the hypo. "How did you know?"

Gia raised one eyebrow. "He's a man in love. Reason is not his forte right now."

"Is everything set on board this ship?"

Gia nodded. "As soon as I drop him off, I'm heading out."

"Thank you, Gia." Gen didn't escort the unconscious Rhys back to medical, instead returning to the living ship, to the bridge where her link to the vessel was the strongest. Zan grumbled once again about trusting Gia. Closing her eyes, Gen sent up a silent prayer that her half-baked scheme would work, that she hadn't doomed all the people she loved.

Within moments, all three ships were ready to enter the wormhole.

A vast starfield opened up before them. Though no planets or moons appeared nearby, there was a giant asteroid field to the left of the screen. An old freighter hovered at the periphery, looking decrepit next to the pristine Illustra cruiser. Gen took it all in in seconds as Gia's stinger emerged from the wormhole.

"Hail the Illustra vessel. Tell them I want to talk before prisoner transfer," Gen told the pirate monitoring communications.

She waited and hid her relief when he reported, "They refuse to respond other than to retransmit the original message. They want Rhys."

"Makes two of us," Gen murmured.

Friend ready? Though he had traveled far and hadn't eaten in a while, Gen sensed the ship's eagerness.

I am. You remember what you are supposed to do? Keep the asteroid between us and the fleet so they don't use the opportunity to attack us.

The ship hummed in what Gen took as compliance. She stared at the gleaming chrome of the flagship, still unable to believe Alison had captured her family, betrayed her.

Just as Rhys believed she was betraying him.

Doubt churned up the acid in her belly. Gen was not an organized person, had never even pulled off a successful surprise party, yet here she was, mapping out military strategy. The entire thing was beyond absurd. *I'm the only hope for Rhys, and for his people.* They deserved more than her and a half-grown ship, but no one else had stepped up. Desperate times called for asinine measures.

"The stinger has landed on the asteroid," one of the crew announced.

Gen nodded. "How many life signs on that ship?"

"I can't get a good reading. Too much electromagnetic interference."

Closing her eyes, Gen lay back in the bed. *Can you sense the other vessel?*

The ship flashed her a picture of the passenger ship off their starboard side, lying in wait.

Begin travel sequence Gen 1.

The ship pulsed, firing up its engines, preparing for stage one.

"Contact the stinger," Gen ordered.

The connection crackled and she heard Gia's brisk, "Shuttle-craft here. Are we set?"

"Set for what?" Zan barked, coming up behind Gen. "Why is she in the stinger? Where's the empath?"

Gen ignored the pirate and checked with the ship. *Yes?*

The power he wielded flowed into her and she gasped, "Now, Gia."

"Stinger to transport, fire at my location, now!"

"At *her* location? Have you lost what little sense you were born with?" Zan roared over the whine of laser fire.

The wormhole the ship had built in the wake of the stinger's exhaust trail opened right in front of the other passenger ship's cannons, snaring the discharge and sucking it to the vortex to the other side.

"The flagship is under assault!" Gia reported with a whoop. "Readings indicate the wormhole opened up inside their shields!"

"What in the flaming depths of the great inferno is going on?!" Zan bellowed.

"Move in on the Illustra ship, Captain. I'll explain later," Gia responded in a clipped tone.

Begin travel sequence Gen 2.

The ship acknowledged her command, weaving yet another wormhole. A giant rift directly behind the fleet vessel.

"Transmission coming in from the flagship."

"On screen," Gen ordered as she sat up. On the bridge of the other ship, Alison was illuminated by flickering red lights. Her eyes blazed with fury. "What the hell are you doing, Gen?"

"You will release the autodestruct codes right now, or I will have my ship finish the wormhole sequence and suck your fleet through to the other side of the galaxy."

Alison's jaw dropped. "You're bluffing!"

"Gia," Gen said. "Fire another round."

Dispassionately, she watched the bridge of the flagship rock, and Alison was thrown onto her ass. When the noise from the explosion died away, she said, "I could kill you right now, but I'd rather make the exchange without bloodshed. Don't push me, Alison."

There was a pause, and Gen held her breath along with the rest of the crew.

"Fine," Alison growled. "Autodestruct terminated. But this isn't over."

"For me it is." Gen cut the connection. She turned to look at Zan, who had paled beneath his swarthy skin tone. "The ship is yours again, Captain. Please begin rescue operations for the passengers of the freighter. I've told the ship not to dock, just in case it's still rigged to blow, but using the stinger as a ferry, we can get everyone on board in no time."

She departed the bridge, landing on her feet at the bottom of the slide. Would Rhys ever forgive her for the deception? Would he even try to? She'd seduced him and drugged him, and it had all worked out, but things could have just as easily gone the other way.

Sinking down into a ball in a small nook, Gen let her tears flow freely. She'd done it, saved the day. In moments she would be reunited with Nana and Gramps, with Tanny. She'd have to tell them they could never go home, at least not while Illustra was still in power. And she'd have to face Rhys.

The tears slid faster. Even when she won, she still lost it all.

27

Rhys awoke in medical, his throat full of cotton. He stared out the viewport at the field of moving stars that pulsed by as the ship traveled at sub–light speed. The pirate vessel had to stop frequently and feed, which slowed the caravan's journey. Wormholes, apparently, demanded a great deal of energy.

The medical wing buzzed with activity, full of empaths reunited with their bodies and loved ones. Over thirty of his people had been retrieved from the freighter. Including Sela. Despite much grumbling, Zan had agreed to transport them back to his world. Rhys owed so much to the pirate captain, and even more to Gen. He planned to thank her privately for keeping him from making the biggest mistake of his life. As the days wore on, he bided his time, needing as much strength as he could collect before confronting her. He'd show his appreciation with hours of pleasure. Once he found her. She'd avoided him since she'd drugged him.

After hours of fruitless searching, he decided to wait her out in her cabin. What she had done for him, for his people, hum-bled him. There was so much to be done, but nothing was more important than discussing the future with Gen.

Exhausted after hours of counseling, acting his part as the spiritual leader to help others with their healing, he lay down on her bed. He'd just dozed off when the door hissed open.

"What are you doing here?"

"I love you," he replied, needing to get that out in the open.

She sat down beside him on the bed, shoulders slumped. "How the hell can you? I drugged you."

He reached for her, needing to connect with her however he could. "You were right to do it too. I was so determined to die for you that I didn't understand what you really needed was for me to live for you."

She stared at him, the colors of her aura shifting too quickly for him to assess. "I didn't think you wanted to."

"How can you believe that?" Even as he asked the question, Rhys understood how she could accept the worst about him. He'd lied to her from their first encounter, put her feelings second to his own goals and ambitions. "Gen, I promise, everything will be different now."

"You're right, it will be. I've decided to remain on board with the pirates."

A dull roar filled his ears, like the ocean before a storm. She would leave him, forever? "No." Pulling her down on top of him, he crushed his mouth to hers. Every bit of frustration he felt over the last three weeks rose up, needing her, wanting her to admit she needed him too.

Her lips parted as she responded immediately, welcoming him home with warm wet kisses and the slow lap of her tongue against his. Her tongue danced with his, her fingers sliding across his back. Passion, which always lurked right beneath her surface, whipped up as his hands cupped her face. "I want to bond with you."

"What exactly does that entail?" Gen's eyes sparkled as she

moved around the bed. Rhys caught a whiff of her intent, her emotions more delicious than anything he'd ever experienced. Considering the banquet she typically provided, that was quite a feat.

He reached forward and strummed her turgid nipple through her dress. "After tonight we can never be parted. According to our oldest scriptures, a bond transcends time and space—even death itself. Your telepathic abilities may add a twist to our connection, or it might not play in at all."

The corner of her mouth turned up in a sultry smile. "I meant, how do we make it happen? What exactly do we have to do to achieve the bond itself?"

His heart sped to a frantic tattoo. Was she considering it, or perhaps just curious? He'd made so many mistakes with her and felt almost paralyzed by fear at the thought of losing her for good. Moving aside the dark spill of her sweet-smelling hair, Rhys bent his head until his lips caressed her collarbone. "Everything. No holding back. Every fantasy you've ever entertained, you must share it with me. I need to do the same. The bond will not cement itself until absolute trust exists between us. Souls cannot be tethered together where reservation exists. Do you want to do this?"

Nodding, she eased her hands down his arms until her fingers twined with his. "I trust you."

Rhys hoped so. "Do you really? After everything?"

She searched his face and offered a small smile. "I love you. I always have, right from when you first appeared. For a while I thought I might be crazy for it, when you kept things from me. But I understand why you did, even if I don't like it. I know you would sacrifice everything to keep me safe. So, yes, Rhys, I do trust you."

Her heartfelt confession made his chest ache. He had so much to make up for, so much to be thankful for. She'd put her trust in him, yet he'd never really done the same. She deserved to know everything. Clearing his throat he murmured, "There is one other thing. If the bond doesn't take tonight, there is no second chance for us. We can never attempt this again. Not with each other. And for me that means never, because you are the only one I will ever want."

She swallowed hard, cleared her throat, and lifted her chin at just the right angle. "Then we better get it right the first time."

Under his thumb, her pulse rate fluttered, and nervousness buffeted against him. She worried and he knew her well enough to recognize it wasn't her mistrust of him, but apprehension over her own abilities. He vowed that before this night was done, Gen would recognize her own innate sensuality. "Take off your dress, my sweet. I love to watch you disrobe. Seeing glimpses of your smooth, creamy skin and imagining where I should touch you first makes me ache with need."

Her aura was crimson, flushed with desire and heat for him. Despite his weakened state, his body responded to her desire, his cock hardening at the thought of completing their mating.

But never again would he ask for more than she could give. "Be sure this is what you want, Gen. I refuse to undo a bond."

In answer, she slid one strap of her dress off her shoulders, holding his gaze the entire time. His mouth watered as she shrugged out of the dress, the soft fabric clinging to the tips of her breasts. Heart pounding in his ears, he reached for her, unable to wait another second to touch soft skin. The soft mounds overflowed his hands, and she threw her head back as he rolled one puckered bud between his thumb and forefinger.

"So lovely . . ." He bent his head for a taste.

"Rhys," she gasped, arching toward him, fingers tunneling in his hair, holding him to her. As if he would ever let her go. "I want to feel you inside me again."

He groaned, flicking his tongue over the stiffened peak, wanting to do exactly as she said. Easing her back onto the bed so he could remove her dress, he vowed, "Soon, my sweet."

Lifting her hips, she helped him bare her body, shamelessly spreading her legs to show him her state of readiness. He almost lost his seed when one of her elegant fingers slid down to her sex, toying with the pink folds. Her heavy-lidded gaze locked on his. "Now."

"Temptress," he rasped as she strummed her clitoris, using her lube to ease her way. She glistened, wet with desire, her colors growing brighter as she climbed the peak. Gripping her wrist, he pulled her finger to his mouth and sucked the digit between his lips. His taste buds exploded with the remembered glory of her essence. "You want to fight dirty? I planned for this."

He dangled the rope he'd pilfered from their bag earlier, trailing it between his fingers.

Her lips parted and her passion strengthened. "What are you going to do with that?"

Taking her wrists in one hand, he tied a secure knot, to bind them together. "Everything, anything you want me to."

Her heart raced as Rhys secured her bound hands to the headboard. He threaded the rope between her heaving breasts, sliding it teasingly across her nipples.

She should stop this. It was wrong to submit to bonding with him when she had every intention of leaving him. But the little voice in her mind, the troublemaker, the rebel, whispered, *Just this once. You've earned it.*

The rope slithered over her belly, and she could feel Rhys's touch as it moved over her skin. His gaze reflected pure emerald fire that threatened to engulf her. How could he still want her after the last time?

Because he was Rhys, because he could forgive her humanity, the same way she'd accepted his.

Urging her to lift her hips, he wove the silky cord around her belly and the small of her back. There was enough tension in the lead to restrict her movements but enough give so she could squirm under the sensual onslaught. He didn't dally with her exposed nether bits, and she bit her lip to keep from begging him to touch her there, to tease her folds with his hands and lips, with the rope holding her in its power.

"This is part of the ceremony?" she asked as he tied a knot in the corded length.

His deft fingers tied another knot, and he moved the length up between her splayed legs. "It's whatever we need it to be. I've been practicing my knot tying specifically because I knew how much you craved this."

Sweat gathered on her forehead and between her breasts. She licked her dry lips and watched as he tugged the rope up between the apex of her legs. One knot pressed against her rear entrance and the other just inside her slick feminine channel.

He wove it up and through the loops on her waist again, before meeting her gaze. "How does that feel?"

The way he'd fastened the cord gave her just the slightest play. Tugging on her bound arms moved the rope between her legs, forcing the knots deeper inside her passages. Arching her spine caused them to slide forward, and when she relaxed, they slid back into place. Her eyes fixed on his as she purred, "Delicious."

Shucking his shirt, Rhys moved over her to tongue one of her stiff nipples. The hand holding the other end of the rope hovered above her pelvis. He let the end brush against her throbbing clit, just a light, teasing kiss. The small fleeting sensation made her ache for more.

Spreading her legs wider forced the knots at her openings to press harder against the sensitive tissues. The smooth line running between her lips was a shade off of perfect, the pressure there unbelievably arousing.

Rhys switched his attention to the other breast, tugging the bud with his teeth. "I want to be inside you in the worst way, to feel what you're feeling, what produces this glorious rainbow of your aura. I want to shove my cock so far inside you as you come and then ride your beautiful body all night. But do you know what I want more than anything else?"

Gen shook her head, half delirious from the sensual torment. "What?"

His gaze burned into hers. "The promise of forever with you. To know that tomorrow night you will let me worship you again, and every night. "

The honest sincerity in his eyes, her own fears and hopes all bound inside her like her flesh was held by the rope, it was too much. "I can't think, not like this."

"There's nothing to think about, love. Just say yes, that you'll be with me forever. It's what we both want." He rained a series of hot, sucking kisses over her abdomen.

"It's not smart," she panted as he settled between her legs.

"But it's right." Yanking the rope from the belt at her waist, he moved the cord from between her legs.

28

"Rhys." She arched off the bed as he bent and thrust his tongue deep inside her core. His hands gripped the undersides of her knees and pushed her legs back so she was fully open to him, her glistening pussy invading every sense. Never had paradise been so close. He licked her savagely, and she grew wetter, her honey dripping down his chin, down her crease. Pushing harder, he licked and sucked the puffy pink lips, using his tongue and teeth until she bucked wildly, needing release. Rhys laved her cream, seeking her every secret. Her moans filled his ears—along with whispered pleas he had no intention of heeding. She was his, and he would brand her in every way, make her recognize that he was master of her body and she owned his soul.

With the lightest touch, he flicked the very tip of his tongue over her clit once before seeking her gaze. "Do you still plan to leave me?"

Her chest heaved as she struggled for breath. "I can't stay with you, Rhys."

A finger surged into her sheath at the same time he asked, "Why not?"

Her inner muscles fluttered, and he withdrew, tracing his finger down the seam of her body in a caress designed to tempt more than satiate. Pleasure and agony emanated from her. He recognized the feeling because his cock swelled to bursting. Bending down, he sucked her hardened clit between his lips, reveling in her gasp but releasing before she could find any real satisfaction. "Give me a good reason."

Something akin to a sob escaped her throat. Sweat trickled between her breasts, her entire body straining for release. Sucking in a shaky breath, she said, "You have things to do . . . important things—"

This time he used two fingers to delve inside her, pumping her hot little passage until her lube dripped down. So soft, so slick. "The only thing I want to do is pleasure you." Again he withdrew, this time circling her anus with his wet fingers.

Her whole body trembled with the need for release, her aura so bright he could barely see. Or perhaps it was lust that fogged his mind, jealousy because she could even *consider* living without him. He no longer had that option. "Tell me you'll stay with me always, and I'll let you come."

Though tears of frustration welled in her eyes, she held his gaze. "That's coercion."

"You bet your sweet ass it is." Pinning her legs with his forearm so she didn't hurt herself with her wild undulations, his teeth dragged over her throbbing clitoris, tugging the sensitive bud lightly.

"Anything else," she sobbed. "You can have anything else."

"I want you. Forever." He let his breath fall on her overly sensitized flesh, allowed her to see the need burning in his gaze. "How long do you think I can keep you like this? Poised on the razor's edge, throbbing with need? If that's how I'm to get my forever out of you, I'll do it. So much for my important things."

"This is insanity," she whispered, but he saw the flush of pleasure his words stirred in her. "You can't keep me like this—" A wordless cry interrupted her statement when he tongued her folds in a rapid tremolo. Again he fingered her slick passage in a quick move and then dragged a finger down her seam. She gasped as he breached her anus with his wet finger. The bud resisted at first, but he applied steady pressure, insisting he be the first to take her like this. First and last, for always.

Rising up, still penetrating her lightly, he stared into her wide eyes. "You're in no position to tell me what I can and can't do. Either say no and walk away or give me everything. You got my body back, Gen, and it wants you, all of you. Deal with it."

Flushed and trembling, she nodded once. "Okay."

He moved his thumb to circle over her throbbing bud. "Okay, what? Say it all, Genevieve. So there will be no more misunderstandings between us."

"I will stay with you. Always." She held his gaze and spoke clearly. "There will never be another for me." Pure white coated her aura as she spoke the unrepentant truth.

Emotions washed over him in a torrent. Relief, anxiety, but love and need burned it all away. Working the knots of rope at her wrists, he freed her arms. His cock rubbed against her wetness through the fabric of his pants. He looked down, honestly shocked he hadn't ripped through the thin material. Letting her go took enormous amounts of willpower, but with a fortifying breath, he stepped back and released her, yanking his pants off until his shaft sprang free.

"Come inside me now." She held her arms out to him, and he did, stepping back out of the fabric pooled around his ankles, aligning his sex with hers and thrusting hard. The time for games was over and she'd agreed. He would hold her to her word.

Her hot little body clung to him greedily, and he angled her hips so he could stroke deeply. Sensations licked at him, flames ready and willing to consume him. He'd experienced her before, but this was the first time his flesh melded with hers while the promise of a future together floated within his grasp.

"Every night, Gen, I'm going to do this to you. Every. Single. Night." He punctuated each word with a hard thrust. "We'll burn through your entire cache of toys and props. I'll take you in every way. You are mine."

Sweat trickled between her breasts, and he bent to lap it up, his motion forcing her legs over her head. His cock swelled within and he swiveled his hips, stirring her hot little passage. She was so wet, her lube coating his shaft in a river of liquid lust. It spilled out of her, running down her crease, coating his balls, and still he thrust, wanting more, wanting all she had to give.

"Do you want me to take you in all ways?" Again he probed her anus with his finger so she understood his meaning.

Her eyes glowed in the dim lighting, color high on her cheekbones. "Only if I can do the same to you." He felt her hand slide down his back, nails following the seam of his body until she toyed with his own hole. His cock surged within her, the tiny sensation of her finger at that forbidden entrance driving him close to madness. He came in a hot rush, his seed filling her up, but his shaft remained erect. Craving more.

"One thing at a time," he rasped, pulling out of her and rolling her over.

"Rhys," Gen gasped as he slithered between her spread thighs, again licking and sucking her sex. Her lube coated his face, and she shook, the need to come again bearing down on her like a comet caught in a planet's atmosphere. Their loveplay had been kinky before, but this felt different. Rhys wasn't just bringing her pleasure—he was branding himself on her.

His tongue delved into her sheath and that finger returned to her anus. Circling the sensitive bundle of nerves and making her squirm atop him. His finger, slick with her own juices, breached the opening, impaling her. She'd never believed she'd enjoy such attention to that particular area, but the thought of his thick cock stretching her there made her come in a rush.

He pulled away long enough to mutter, "Again," and set back in with renewed determination, alternating his tongue between teasing her clit and filling her channel. A second finger surged inside her, stretching her on a rack between pleasure and pain. *This is the way sex was meant to be,* she thought hazily as he pushed her higher, further, past boundaries she never knew her mind had set. Hot and wet, achingly earthy with no walls between lovers.

Her hips bucked into his face as she climaxed yet again. Falling to her hands, she panted, scrambling to reassemble her scattered wits. With a final lick, Rhys moved out from under her and sank his cock into her saturated pussy.

"I want to be good and wet so I can glide right in here." He scissored his fingers in her rear, preparing her to accommodate his girth. Withdrawing his shaft and fingers, he gripped her hips. "Are you ready for me, sweetness?"

All she could do was nod.

He went slowly, pushing that thick shaft up inside her channel. Her lube did ease his way, as she felt the head of his shaft scrape along nerve endings she had never been aware of before. He only made it a few inches before her body tightened up. *He'll never fit.*

The pad of his thumb found her clit, dabbled in a soothing, coaxing manner. "You feel so good, Gen. All of you. Can I come inside you?"

She scowled, not understanding what he meant until a

trickle of his consciousness eased into her mind. Sighing, she opened to him, both body and mind, wanting him. The words whispered through her awareness, not hers or his, but theirs. *In all ways, in every way. Without boundaries or limitations.*

Ah, gods, Gen. Rhys spoke on that level, on their level of shared consciousness. Losing herself with him, she pushed back, stretched and bent herself to accommodate him, as he did her.

When the ache started inside her sex, he moved his hand to caress her there. Thumb rotating over her throbbing clitoris, he played with her body in the way only he knew how to do.

She surrendered to him, coming in a rush, letting herself merge with him even more deeply.

Of its own volition, the rope rose up, circling around them until it bound them both. She gasped, awed by the thrum of magic coursing through it, the power that had slept until their love awakened it. Silken cords caressed his skin, and she felt it just as when it had touched her own flesh. Winding its way through arms and legs, exploring, inviting every part of her to join with every part of him. Her already overwhelmed senses grew even more alert, taking in the way his crisp pubic hairs felt against her ass cheeks, the sweat that ran between her breasts, the glide of the rope as it wove around them, lifting them up. Locking them together in this sensual embrace.

"This is your doing," Rhys gasped as the knot he had formed for her nestled at his own rear passage, giving him another taste of what she was feeling. "I can feel your mind in the rope. It tastes of your emotions, your passion and strength."

Following the rope's lead, Gen wrapped her essence around him and he went over, too, bodies linked in mating, minds connected, and hearts beating as one.

"Get off my ship," Zan growled at Gen, pointing a laser pistol at her. She turned from where she was watching the crates of candles being unloaded to stare at him.

Her gaze went from his face to the weapon and back. "You can't be serious." Though she'd been about to tell him she was ready to go, having the option taken from her rankled.

"There isn't enough reward in the universe to make me keep you on board for another second. What's to stop you from stealing my ship again?"

"Z-Zan," she sputtered, but he waved her down the gang-plank.

Rhys waited down below, a small smile playing across his lips. In one hand he held her bag.

Her jaw dropped and she studied the two men. "You planned this!"

Nana, Gramps, and Tanny stood off to the side with Gia. All were smiling, but none more than Rhys.

"I know what a devious creature you are. I had to protect my investment." He tugged lightly at the emotional bond that now linked them together.

She looked up at Zan. "Thank you."

He grinned wickedly. "I'll be sure to ask the favor be returned one day."

Held securely in Rhys's arms, Gen watched as the living ship took off. "What did you bribe him with?"

Rhys slid his gaze to Gia. "A happily-ever-after. Later."

Gen nodded and surveyed her new home. "I'm glad you're so wicked."

He stroked her cheek. "Sweetness, you have no idea the depths of my depravity."

Warmth bloomed deep inside her chest. "I plan to find out."

Turn the page for a special excerpt from
Kate Douglas's novella "Dream Catcher," in

NIGHTSHIFT

A sizzling collection of
erotic, paranormal stories by
Kate Douglas,
Crystal Jordan, and
Lynn LaFleur.
An Aphrodisia trade paperback on sale now!

1

In orbit behind Earth's moon—present day

Zianne? Is he the one? Is he strong enough? Smart enough?

I think so. He's very strong—I heard his voice over such a great distance, but I don't know. We've waited so long. How can I be certain?

We're dying, Zianne. All of us. There's no time to hesitate. There are hardly enough of us left to matter.

No. Don't say that. We matter. We must.

Then go. Even I sense this one. His world will nurture us for now, but this man . . . this one man will be our salvation.

Silicon Valley—April 1992

"Fucking chicken scratch." Mac Dugan wadded up yet another lined yellow page covered in pointless doodles, equations, and code. He reached overhead, aiming for the Sloan's Bar and Grill sign over the trash can.

Powerful fingers closed around his wrist.

Jerking his arm free, he spun around, prepared to take a swing at whatever idiot had interrupted his mini-tirade. When he saw who it was, he laughed. "Christ, Dink. Haven't seen you in ages. You trying to get yourself killed?"

"Nope. Just trying to save your stupid ass."

Mac grabbed the beer Dink handed to him. "Who says my ass needs saving?"

Dink grinned. His wide smile, along with the collar-length blond hair and thick dark lashes framing light blue eyes, made him almost too pretty for a man. "I do," he said. "That redhead, Jen? The one who was with you last month? She's all cozied up to the bar with your nemesis."

"You mean Bennett? Crap." Mac took a sip of his beer and fought the compulsion to glance over his shoulder. "I didn't know he was here. With her? Shit. Why'd I ever go out with her?"

"Because you were horny?" Dink snorted. "She keeps looking this way. Maybe she wants to get laid again."

Mac shook his head. "Not by me. What about Bennett? Is he watching us?"

Dink chuckled. "Nah. He's too busy staring at her cleavage."

"Fucking jerk. Weird she'd be here with him after . . . well, shit. Maybe I'm just paranoid." He avoided turning in his seat to stare at Phil Bennett. Even if the guy was responsible for totally fucking over his life, Bennett was more than welcome to the redhead. Except . . . It was like that stupid cartoon lightbulb flashed on in his mind. What if Jen and Phil had been an item before she came on to Mac? What if she'd been using him to get stuff—like his project notes?

"Of course you're paranoid." Dink was obviously reading his mind. He took a swallow of his beer and cocked one eyebrow. "You have a right to be, after what happened." He glanced once again at the couple. "On the other hand, you sure you don't want to get laid? She looks interested, and she's hot."

Mac laughed. "How do you know? You like guys."

Dink flipped him off, but he didn't deny it. At least his sexual preferences had never gotten in the way of their friendship. "I know gorgeous when I see it, male or female. She definitely fits the description."

Mac shrugged. "I know the red hair's not natural."

"It didn't seem to matter at the time."

It hadn't. He'd met her just a couple of days before the shit hit the fan. She'd come on to him, made it patently obvious she wanted to get laid, and it had been too damned long since he'd gotten a piece of anything but his right hand. "What can I say? She caught me in a weak moment." He waved his hand at the pile of discarded notes in the trash. "That's what counts. I know what I want, how it should look and what it needs to do, but I can't get the damned program to work."

Dink held up both hands and shook his head. "Hell, don't look at me. Starving grad student, future TV news guy here, not developer of weird software. You're so far past me on all this computer shit I wouldn't know where to start. What about the guys in the lab? I hear they're doing amazing stuff."

"I'm barred from the lab after what happened." He practically snarled. "Bennett's lies got me booted out of the program, cost me the grant and the rest of my scholarship. I'm just about out of cash." He held up the beer Dink had bought him. "Thanks for this, by the way."

"Well, fuck." Dink glared at him. "They were wrong, Mac. You know he stole your work. I still think you should fight it."

Mac forced a quick smile. "Thanks, man. Unfortunately, Phil had the notes, not me. In his handwriting. My originals are missing. Even the floppy disks are gone, so there's no reason to believe me. Besides, his uncle's the dean of the department."

"And Bennett's a lying turd."

"I agree, but it earned him a clean shot at the grant we were competing for." Mac shrugged, but he couldn't let it go. When he lost his access to the campus computer lab, he'd lost his only link to the new World Wide Web and contact with other software developers. His scrapped-together computer was too limited to test the programs he hoped to design, the ones he knew could bust him out of obscurity.

Right now, his future was totally fucked.

Keeping his back to Bennett and the redhead, Mac finished off the rest of his beer and shoved away from the table. Then he carefully stuffed his notepad in his backpack and looped the pack over his shoulder.

Dink tossed back his beer and rose as well. "Not so fast, brain-boy. You're coming with me."

"Where?" Mac folded his arms across his chest and gave Dink the kind of stare that generally intimidated most guys.

Except Dink, who just laughed. "Don't try that 'death to evildoers' look on me, big guy. My computer crashed. That's why I was looking for you. I want you to retrieve a paper I just finished. Gotta have it for tomorrow, man, or I'm screwed."

"That I can probably do." What threw Dink for a loop was usually a simple fix for Mac. He loved computers, and with the way technology was improving, it was obvious the twentieth century was going out with a bang.

Mac intended to be part of the explosion. He'd built his own system—and Dink's, for that matter—from scratch, but Mac's wasn't anywhere near as fast as the computers in the lab on campus. He needed faster, more complex equipment to accomplish his goals. It was so damned frustrating, living in Silicon Valley where everything was happening at warp speed, aware of so many new innovations, and yet stuck on the fringes without the equipment he needed to handle his ideas.

Shit. Just one more thing totally out of his control.

He glanced at the bell tower marking the center of the campus he'd thought of as home for the past seven years, and fought back a surge of anger. The dean had accepted the project Phil Bennett turned in, decided Mac was lying when he accused the bastard of theft, and then had the balls to say they'd let him drop out of the postgraduate program rather than formally charge and expel him.

He'd lost his scholarship and access to the lab. Lost any chance of qualifying for the grant he needed to continue his work. Lost everything because that little weasel had somehow stolen his project, lied about it, and gotten away with it.

Even worse, the incident was going on Mac's record. A black mark against his name, against the honor and integrity he'd always valued so much. No matter how bad it got, he'd never compromised. Never. Now this.

Why the fuck was it always an uphill battle? He was so damned tired of fighting life on his own, but other than Dink, he'd been alone since the foster care system booted his ass out at eighteen. The academic scholarship to the university had saved him. Until Bennett screwed him over.

If he could just get his life in order, maybe things wouldn't look so damned bleak, but now—right now—it all sucked.

Big time.

"Dinkemann, you are such a horse's ass." Mac kept his voice down as he stopped to throw a blanket over Dink's prone form on the couch. He stood over his sleeping buddy, remembering. They'd been through so much together. Growing up with a guy in the same crappy foster home created a link like nothing else. Even though they were complete opposites, Mac loved Dink in a way he couldn't explain. There was nothing he wouldn't do for him.

Well, almost nothing, though Mac couldn't deny he'd thought about it. Dink was gay and loved Mac, and while the thought of sex with his buddy had crossed his mind, Mac himself hadn't crossed the line. Yet.

Maybe it was all the beer he'd had tonight, but for some reason the thought of loving Dink that way didn't bother him as much as it had. *You've had way too much to drink, Dugan.*

It was definitely time to go home. Quietly, Mac closed the door to Dink's tiny apartment. Fueled by more beer than he'd needed, he hoped he'd be able to make it back to his apartment without getting arrested for public intoxication.

He rarely drank this much, but seeing Jen and Phil together tonight had thrown him. The more he thought about it, the more he was sure she'd stolen those pages of notes the night they'd fucked like bunnies until he finally fell asleep. She'd been gone when he finally dragged himself out of her bed and went back to his own place. Maybe she hadn't slept as soundly. Was she the one who'd ripped out the pages that had turned up in Phil Bennett's precise handwriting?

Had Phil used those hours to break into his apartment and steal the floppy disks with the research and all his notes?

There was no way to prove it. The pages were gone, along with the disks, something he hadn't noticed until it was time to prepare the grant application. And then it was too late.

Only Dink believed him, but their bond went deeper than mere friendship, sometimes so intensely visceral it was barely a step away from sexual attraction. Sort of how he'd felt tonight.

Except Mac knew he was straight. He'd never questioned his own sexuality, never doubted how much he loved women. In fact, tonight he'd gone off on a riff, rhapsodizing over the ultimate fantasy female. He could still see her—tall and athletic with long black hair and violet eyes. Dink had thrown in a computer nerd personality. What had he called her?

"A nerdette." Mac laughed, his voice echoing in the quiet night. "Just what I need."

Mac figured he was nerdy enough for two.

Dink, of course, had fantasized over the ideal guy—a guy who sounded suspiciously like MacArthur Dugan—tall, lean build, thick waves of caramel hair, a killer smile, and sapphire blue eyes—Dink's terms, not Mac's.

Dink had never hidden his feelings from Mac. So why did Mac feel as if he were keeping secrets from Dink? He loved Dink. Just not *that* way. Or did he? Damn. Mac stopped, grabbed the front of his jeans, and adjusted the crotch. Why the hell was he getting hard? Thoughts of Dink, or of his fantasy woman? Shit.

He focused on Bennett and the stolen project, and fury spurred him on. With his gait not quite steady, Mac made it up the stairs to his fourth-floor apartment in a matter of minutes.

Still pissed.

He and Dink had discussed how absurd it was. Why would Mac lie? If he didn't know the material, his ignorance would prove him wrong, but the dean refused to allow Mac to defend himself.

He'd never cared much for the dean, and the feeling had obviously been mutual, but the man's response to Mac's claims went beyond mere dislike. He'd been absolutely irate with Mac and had immediately taken Phil's side. What could Dean Johnson gain from his nephew winning the grant instead of Mac? Family unity or something stupid like that? Was that worth risking his tenure? Possibly, but probably not. But what else? Shit . . . Mac knew the program inside and out, with or without the notes and floppies. Did Bennett? No. No way.

Yet Mac still hadn't been allowed to defend himself.

Which left him guilty with no recourse. Cursing, Mac dug through his pants pocket for the key, fumbled with the damned thing, and promptly dropped it.

He leaned over to pick it up and almost fell on his face when the world spun a little too fast. "Oh . . . shit." He grabbed the key, stuck it in the lock, and after a couple of fumbles, got the door open. Moving very carefully, he managed to get inside his apartment without falling on his ass.

He leaned against the closed door a minute and let the world right itself once more. Then he tossed his backpack on the floor and slipped out of his jacket, but when he turned to dump his coat on the chair, something sweet tickled his senses.

He sniffed the air.

"What the hell?" Mac inhaled again, drawing the rich scent into his lungs. Vanilla? Honey? It was vaguely familiar, but he couldn't quite place it. Flipping on the light in the kitchen area, he glanced around to see if he'd left anything out.

The counters were clean, the sink empty except for a coffee cup and a cereal bowl. He sniffed the air again, but the scent that had seemed so pervasive eluded him now.

Yawning, seriously regretting those last few beers, Mac headed to the bathroom for a shower. If he relaxed enough and went to sleep thinking about the new graphics program, maybe he'd dream a solution. With any luck, his subconscious—what Dink called his lizard brain—would figure it out.

Except once he'd stripped and stood beneath the hot spray, his damned lizard brain focused on his dick instead of the program. Mac glanced ruefully at the tip of his cock.

The broad head with its dark slit stared up at him as if begging for attention. "Shit. You're supposed to be ready for bed." Grinning like an idiot, he wrapped his right fist around his shaft and cupped his testicles in his left hand. "Wonder what it means when a guy has conversations with his cock?"

He refused to answer himself. Instead, Mac leaned against the tile wall with the hot water beating down on his chest and shoulders and stroked himself with a firm grip, stretching soft, pliable skin over hard meat with one hand, rolling his balls between the fingers of the other.

His mind wandered as the pressure grew. He wanted a visual, but the redhead just pissed him off and her image quickly faded. He thought of Dink, but that was more than a little unsettling. Then his fantasy morphed into a woman with long black hair and intelligent violet eyes.

She smiled at him, and he knew her. The one he'd described earlier to Dink—the perfect woman. Mac's ultimate fantasy.

His cock actually jerked within his grasp. He was leaking pre-cum now, almost faster than the shower could rinse it away. He tugged harder on his balls, rolling the solid orbs between his fingers, squeezing his fist tighter around the base of his dick, finding a rhythm he knew couldn't last.

His balls sucked up close between his legs. He tightened his grasp and squeezed them almost painfully as his fantasy woman floated just inside his field of vision. He concentrated on her face, on the deep, violet eyes and cascade of coal black hair curling around her shoulders.

She was too real, too perfect for him to have invented her, but Mac had no idea where he'd seen her. She was beyond gorgeous, miles beyond any woman he could recall. The scent of honey and vanilla filled his senses and raised his temperature. She gazed up at him with the water cascading over her shoulders, across the fullness of her perfect breasts. Her nipples were a deep rose against porcelain skin, their tips drawn tight.

She smiled and then slowly dropped to her knees and nuzzled his groin as the spray slicked long, dark hair back from her face and steam filled the shower stall. The tip of her tongue slipped between full lips and she licked the side of his shaft, nipping daintily just at the juncture where his cock rooted to his groin. His entire body tensed.

The room spun. Too much beer, too much sensation, but her mouth on his dick anchored him. Deep crimson lips encircled the broad head. He groaned, thrust his hips forward, and she took him deep. His hands dropped to his sides as she worked more of his cock into her sweet mouth.

"Fuck." The curse slipped out on a whisper. He slapped his

palms flat against the wet tile to stop the walls from spinning when the muscles of her throat tightened around his sensitive glans.

"Shit. Holy, holy shit." Mac squeezed his eyes shut. His knees went weak, his head spun. Cursing steadily, he leaned his head against the tile as his hips rocked forward into the hot, wet clasp of her mouth. Her teeth scraped the sides of his shaft and the muscles in his buttocks clenched. He struggled for control, but she hummed deep in her throat and the vibration was a shock of pure fire running the full length of his shaft.

"Fuck. Oh . . . fuck." His hips jerked and his climax boiled up and out. He tried to open his eyes, to watch her, to prove she truly existed, but it was impossible to fight the pulsing throb of orgasm. Just as the woman was impossible. There was no one kneeling at his feet. That wasn't the flick of her tongue licking away the last drops of his seed. No, it was merely the most vivid sexual fantasy he'd ever had in his life.

What else could it be?

Legs trembling, breath heaving in and out of his lungs, Mac opened his eyes. He was alone. His cock lay soft and flaccid over his throbbing balls. He'd come without touching himself. Shot his load into an imaginary mouth and felt every lick of her tongue, every deep, sucking draw of her lips and cheeks.

Still too damned drunk, definitely spaced, Mac stared at the empty shower in front of him. At the spot where the woman had knelt. Slowly shaking his head and seriously doubting his sanity, he scrubbed the stink of the long day off his body. Then he turned off the water and toweled dry with trembling hands.

The scent of vanilla and honey teased his nostrils, but he refused to consider the connection. Half-asleep, physically drained, he crawled into bed and turned out the light. He'd barely pulled the covers over his bare shoulders before sleep claimed him.

2

There it was again, that sweet scent that made him think of warm vanilla wafers. Crawling out of a sublimely sexual dream featuring his latest fantasy female—a dream that faded away as consciousness returned—Mac sniffed the air. Had the smell of cookies awakened him?

He really wanted to get back to that dream.

The room was still dark, but the same tantalizing sweetness he'd noticed earlier filled his nostrils. Stronger now. Closer.

He reached for the lamp on the bedside table. A soft hand stroked his chest. Mac sucked in a gasp of air.

Scrabbling for the switch, he flicked on the light and shoved himself back against the headboard.

Blinking beneath the bright light, he stared into the face of a woman too perfect to be real—eyes so purple they sparkled like amethysts beneath thick, sooty lashes, and hair as black as night. Her skin was fair, her lips full and lush. If he'd dreamed her into existence, she couldn't have been more perfect, and that was the only way she could have gotten here, because he sure as hell hadn't invited anyone in tonight.

"Who the hell are you?"

She frowned. Her dark brows knotted, and two tiny lines appeared between them. "I'm Zianne," she said, as if he should know. "Don't you remember? And you are Mac."

She spoke with a soft accent he didn't recognize, in a voice that was low and sort of raspy. Hinting of sex and secrets, it raised shivers along his spine.

He shook his head. He'd been so damned drunk when he left Dinkemann's place—had he met her somewhere tonight? He'd never had an alcoholic blackout in his life, but if this was the result, he'd definitely been wasting his time.

He flashed on the fantasy he'd had in the shower. The same woman beside him in bed? No. That wasn't real. She wasn't real. He'd imagined that. Hadn't he? Was he imagining her here, now?

Impossible to imagine her scent, the weight of her warm body against his. Her touch. He inhaled a deep, shuddering breath. "Where'd you come from?"

She shrugged as if he were a complete fool for asking, and for a minute he thought he must be, because there was no way in hell he'd ever forget bringing someone like Zianne home to his apartment. There wasn't enough alcohol in the world to make him forget a woman like her.

A memory flashed through his mind, of Zianne kneeling before him in the shower, her mouth . . . *Dear God. Her mouth!*

She smiled with those perfect, lush lips and stroked his cheek with her fingertips. Her touch was soft and warm. Perfect.

"You brought me here." Her scent enveloped him, stealing his thoughts from the question.

Fresh-baked cookies. Vanilla and honey . . . why does she smell so familiar? And then it came to him, the memory so subtle it held a dreamlike quality. Comforting smells from a childhood he'd long forgotten. A time when his parents still lived, when he'd had a real home, a real family.

A time before he was four years old and the world as he knew it ended. No matter. He couldn't go back, couldn't change the car accident that took his mom and dad's lives, the accident that left him unharmed and alone. Quickly Mac blocked the actual pain he experienced whenever that time intruded.

He couldn't change what was, though he could enjoy the spark of memory from before. Could enjoy the warm scent of Zianne in his arms. Mac took a deep breath and stared into those unbelievable violet eyes. Who in the hell was she?

Zianne smiled, leaned close, and kissed him, enveloping Mac in more of that subtle, sweet perfume. Her lips moved slowly, warm and soft, over his mouth. Sex personified.

Need blossomed. Need on so many levels, so many different wants and desires. Love. Sex. Companionship. Friendship. Other than Dink, he'd been alone for so long he'd forgotten what it felt like to have someone close, someone who mattered. Zianne's kiss promised to fill needs Mac had forgotten he ever had.

Her taste was even sweeter than her scent. Zianne's mouth moved over his, tasting, nipping, licking. She slid closer until she lay atop him, until her lips covered his and her tongue probed the sensitive flesh above his teeth, inside his mouth. Her hands were in his hair, her fingers separating the strands and sending shivers of pure fire along his spine. She held him and kissed him deep; explored his mouth with her mobile tongue.

He remembered the way her lips had felt around his cock. It had to have been her, but how? He couldn't have imagined something as real as her mouth on him then. On him now. She'd sucked him deep, taken his seed and swallowed every drop. Now she made love to his mouth, the intensity of her kiss pulling all he was, all he had to give—just as she'd done before.

Mac's body grew hard beneath her long, supple length. His cock rose between her thighs, his muscles rippled beneath his skin. The weight of her breasts on his chest made him strangely angry. He wanted to see them. Wanted to nuzzle his lips and face against their softness, but she'd taken control and he didn't fight her for dominance. He had no will of his own. None.

He couldn't fight her. Could only lie here beneath her perfect body as she made love to him. As she took him, raising up on her knees, grabbing his turgid length in her fist, placing the broad head between her thighs.

There was the briefest awareness of soft, damp curls, of even softer, wetter lips. Then she arched her back and came down on him, all in one smooth, flowing motion that drove him deep inside. He felt heat and the ripple of flexing muscles, then a smooth, wet channel gripping him in an unforgivable vise, pure sensual pleasure personified in this perfect woman.

He raised his hips and thrust hard against her, reaching now for those breasts she so proudly displayed. His palms cupped their weight, his fingers found the taut nipples and he pinched them. She moaned and he twisted the sensitive tips, waiting for Zianne to beg him to stop. Instead, she moaned her pleasure and her hips moved over him until he and she caught the same rhythm.

He stopped pinching and lightly stroked and teased the rosy tips, then cupped her breasts fully in his hands as their bodies danced to an unseen orchestra, to the beat of the heavy drum of thundering hearts, to the song of blood rushing through veins and the discordant harmony of straining lungs.

Caught in a maelstrom of unimaginable lust, he thrust into her, grabbing her by the waist, lifting her up, pulling her close. The slap of flesh against flesh echoed, of lungs gasping for air as they raced each other to the finish. Zianne's body was hot and alive, quivering beneath his hands, her eyes hooded beneath their dark fringe of lashes, her full lips parted. She watched him. Watched him with an intensity that might have frightened him at another time.

Not now.

Now Mac was trapped in a delirium of need, his body connected at a visceral level he'd never experienced, his heart and soul held by too many emotions he couldn't identify. Emotions he didn't try to name, because they couldn't be. They couldn't exist in his world. Hadn't existed in MacArthur Dugan's life since that long-ago time before his parents died.

He'd not known true happiness since then. Nor had he felt real love, and he couldn't feel it now. This could not possibly be love, not this amazing sexual experience with a woman he didn't know, a woman he might never see again.

The thought left him bereft as it flitted through what little bit of his mind still functioned on a conscious level. Then everything fled, wiped out by the full-on experience of orgasm. By the overwhelming sensation of everything he was, everything he had to give—all of it flying out of him, leaving him entirely. Leaving Mac, and entering Zianne.

She arched her back and pressed close. Took his heart, took his soul, took his seed. She cried out as her long nails dug into his ribs, leaving red furrows behind. He welcomed the pain. Added it to the sensations ripping him in two as he practically came apart, pumping his seed deep into her welcoming body.

Mac's heart thundered in his ears. He felt its counterpart in Zianne's racing heart when she collapsed against him. Her tangled hair covered his mouth, her lips were pursed against his sweat-slick chest, blowing tiny puffs with each escaping breath.

It took everything he had to raise his right hand and stroke her smooth shoulder. Enervated, he was weak as a kitten, yet his mind seemed unnaturally clear. Impossible, considering how much he'd had to drink tonight, but he was more aware of this woman, more aware of his body and the way it connected to hers, than he'd ever felt with anyone before.

Her inner muscles still pulsed in a slow, rhythmic clench and release around him, and he wanted nothing more than to make love to her again. To repeat what had been a singular experience, something he'd never once felt in his twenty-six years. They'd shared more than mere sex. There'd been something else, a connection he couldn't explain. A feeling of *knowing,* as if Zianne knew and understood him in ways no one else ever had.

Or ever could. As if he knew Zianne the same way. Except Mac knew nothing at all. Who she was. Where she came from. How he'd met her. How she'd come to be in his apartment.

In his shower?

So many questions. So much he wanted to talk to her about, but his eyelids grew heavy and his heart rate slowed. His breath no longer huffed in and out of his lungs as if he'd run a mile.

Zianne lay across him, apparently asleep with his softening penis still buried deep inside her. He knew there were things he should wonder, but her body was soft and warm over his and her perfume took him back to that childhood he barely recalled.

With the scent of honey and vanilla, and Zianne's thick, black hair tickling his nose, Mac tightened his arms around her waist and drifted closer to sleep. They'd talk in the morning. For now, though, his world felt right. As if the problems bedeviling him for so long weren't problems at all. Not with Zianne in his arms. As long as he had her beside him, Mac imagined he could do anything. Anything at all.